Silver

HAVE
OF 79 GREAT NOVELS
OF
EROTIC DOMINATION

If you like one you will probably like the rest

A NEW TITLE EVERY MONTH

Silver Moon Readers Service
109 A Roundhay Road
Leeds
LS8 5AJ
United Kingdom

http://www.adultbookshops.com

Silver Moon Books of Leeds and New York are in no way connected with
Silver Moon Books of London

If you like one of our books you will probably like them all!

Write for our free 20 page booklet of extracts from early books
- surely the most erotic feebie yet - and, if you wish to be on
our confidential mailing list, from forthcoming monthly titles
as they are published:-

Silver Moon Reader Services

109A Roundhay Road

Leeds

LS8 5AJ

United Kingdom

http://www.adultbookshops.com

or leave details on our 24hr UK answerphone
08700 10 90 60
International acces code then +44 08700 10 90 60

New authors welcome
Please send submissions to
Silver Moon Books Ltd.
PO Box 5663
Nottingham
NG3 6PJ
or
editor@electronicbookshops.com

THE STONEHURST LETTERS first published 2001,copyright J.L. JONES
The right of J.L. JONES to be identified as the author of this book has been asserted in accordance with Section 77
and 78 of the Copyrights and Patents Act 1988

THE STONHURST LETTERS
by
J.L Jones

Preface: PRIVATE

The letters in this volume were written in 1832, but they were suppressed until just recently as they contain detailed information concerning one of those periods of history that many of us would rather forget, a time when falsehood and hysteria overrode reason.

An educator by the name of Derek Hunter authored these letters while he was on sabbatical from Rosewood Academy for Girls, an institution where corporal punishment was approved of and used in liberal doses, and the letters are addressed to one of his fellow teachers at the academy. Both men enjoyed birching the bare buttocks of errant students.

Hunter's sabbatical took him to the home of a friend and former Rosewood colleague, Neville Olford. Olford lived in a remote section of the country and had become the Chief Magistrate of his village. In this area, young girls were being persecuted, legally being put to the whip and even sex-tortured because much of the populace believed that these girls had become infected with some sort of evil spirit, an evil that had caused the crops to fail for several years and thus causing a blight on the entire vicinity.

Olford had taken delight in thrashing the Rosewood students when he was headmaster at the academy, and, in his position as magistrate, he was in a position to mete out much more severe punishments to the girls brought into his courtroom, sentencing them to naked public floggings and having them put into the village stocks nude. The man took pleasure in this even though it was his duty to do it. He would go so far as to take some of these girls under his roof as wards of the court, acting as their sole guardian and disciplinarian.

The clergy of the area were also involved in this persecution, and most of them took great delight in putting these unfortunate young girls through strange penance rituals. These rituals included enforced nudity, flagellation, bondage, and purification by ordeals of sexual abuse.

It is hoped that the reader of these letters will see them as a warning as to what can happen when ignorance and superstition are allowed to run their full course.

Letter 1 PRIVATE

Dear Bertrand,

After a long and most arduous journey, I've finally arrived safely at Olford's manor. Three days travel by horse and carriage is not my idea of a pleasant time. Our accommodations at the roadside inns were less than comfortable, and the patrons were often boisterous. This is an agricultural area, where the crops have failed several years running, and many people have taken to drink as solace.

As often occurs when general misfortune arises, a scapegoat will be sought, and the citizens here have found theirs. In general, they are an ignorant and superstitious lot, placing great stock in their religion, but I fail to understand what that might be as it resembles nothing I've ever encountered. They speak constantly but vaguely of the concepts of good and evil, and, through this muddled thinking, they've become convinced that the young women of the vicinity are to blame for the blight on their lands. This belief holds that some sort of evil is lurking within these girls, manifesting itself in a contagious nymphomania. They further believe that these infected girls are so highly desirous of lustful encounters that the men sense it and thus neglect their fields and herds.

Because of this widespread hysteria, these young girls are persecuted mercilessly and can be brought to trial for the slightest flirtatious behavior or even for their manner of walk. The public pillory and whipping post are both still in use here in these hinterlands, and the magistrates hereabouts sentence girls to them often and without hesitation.

"It's well that the little sluts should be punished," an older gentleman said to me one night in the tavern where I was having a drink. "They're the cause of all that's wrong in these parts, and

7

things won't be right again until we've whipped the evil out of every one of them."

He was quite serious, so I didn't press the matter further.

The priests—I use the term lightly here—of their so-called religion have become almost as powerful as the law of the land, sometimes issuing their own edicts and decrees. They too persecute these young women and force them into penance rituals of a most unusual nature. I've overheard talk and have learned that the girls unfortunate enough to go through these rites almost always do so without clothing and are usually flagellated severely in the process.

Our coachman stopped to feed and water his horses in the last village before we reached Olford's domain of Stonehurst. I'd just gotten out of the carriage to stretch myself when I heard shouting coming from the center of town. A fellow in tattered clothing came dashing by, and I inquired of him as to what might be going on.

"They've sentenced another of the little whores," he called out over his shoulder, not breaking his stride. "She's about to take her flogging."

Yes, Bertrand, I enjoy the chastisement of feminine buttocks, as do you my old friend. Admittedly, we're both delighted when it becomes our duty to use the birch rod on a student, but this was something different. I'd never witnessed a public flogging, so I followed the crowd through the earthen muck of the wet street, dodging a horse and rider here and there, until I was in a place where I could see just what was going on.

Two burly men, both of them in the uniform of constables, were hauling a girl toward a tall post in the middle of the square, the post being outfitted with iron rings high up, leather straps affixed to each ring.

The fair girl being dragged along had bright, ginger-colored hair and what appeared to be a fine body under her long skirts and billowy blouse.

8

Once they'd gotten her as far as the post, they halted, each man holding one of her wrists, she trying vainly to wrest herself free of their strong hands.

Out of a building, which was apparently the courthouse, a tall man emerged, still in his court robes and wig and carrying a piece of parchment. He, too, halted near the post.

"Good people," he read out once he'd unfurled the parchment, "the accused before you, Sarah Browning, has been duly convicted of lewd and seductive behavior in public, and she has been sentenced to be put to the flogging post, naked, and given 7 stripes of the leather quirt 3 times, a total of 21. Following her flogging, she will remain on the post for one hour, still naked, as an exhibit of warning to any of her like. This sentence, issued by Chief Magistrate, the honorable Franklin Hale, is to be carried out immediately. So be it, and take heed all would-be offenders."

As he rolled up the parchment, he nodded to the constables, and they began divesting the captive girl of her clothing, no easy task as she was still putting up a glorious struggle.

"You'd best cooperate, young lady," one of them snarled at her. "If you don't, I'll make certain that your punishment goes all the worse."

While one of them pinioned her arms to her sides, the other yanked off her high-button work shoes, stockings, and the undergarments beneath her skirts, she kicking all the while.

"They'll get her clothing from her, no fear," one woman near me muttered under her breath. "She's fortunate she's not living in Neville Olford's village. He'd sentence her to more than 21 licks of the quirt for sure."

It took me a moment to realize that she was speaking of our old friend and colleague. Of course, we both know that he too used to enjoy the birching of girlish rumps when he was with us at Rosewood Academy, but I wouldn't have thought that his new post as Chief Magistrate of Stonehurst would have turned him genuinely cruel.

9

But I quickly dismissed what I'd heard when I looked back to see that the constables were now tearing off their victim's skirts and blouse. She wore nothing under the blouse, and within another half minute, they had her fully naked.

Being without clothing before such a large gathering seemed to subdue the girl, and they were able to secure her into the leather straps of the post with a minimum of struggle.

"Now she'll get what she deserves, and we'll be that much closer to ridding our lands of this curse," I heard someone saying while they were tying the girl.

"I suppose I do take pity on her," his companion said, "but we've no choice. It's the only way to purge these unfortunates of the evil within them."

Facing the post with her hands well above her head and fastened into the straps, toes barely touching the ground, Sarah Browning's physique was charmingly displayed. And while I thought that the treatment she was receiving was on the harsh side, I couldn't help but relish the sight that her nude body made in such a fetching pose. Her breasts were adequate enough for a girl her age, taut and forming well, her hips slender, the buttocks shapely.

Craning her head around, she saw that one of the constables was taking a leather quirt from his belt, readying it to use on her exposed posterior, and this caused her to begin her fruitless struggles yet again.

"No, you can't use that horrid thing on my bare skin!" I could hear her cry out. "It will burn me throughout."

This protest merely brought a pleased smile to the man's face, and I couldn't help but notice that many others in the crowd were also watching the proceedings with a great deal of enjoyment.

I heard the quirt as it whistled through the air, and when it landed on the naked girl's bottom, she shrieked and gave a mighty pull at her fastenings as her body slammed into the rough wood of the post. Seven times she was struck, and her wrenching about

10

grew more frantic with each blow. The girlish buttocks wagged themselves back and forth while her breasts drove at the flogging post. The little feet danced in the wet earth, tossing bits of mud upward onto her legs as reddish stripes rose on the buttock-flesh.

A groan of relief came from her open lips when the leather instrument ceased to strike, her body relaxing itself.

Someone in the throng gave a low chuckle and said. "Perhaps the whore's forgotten that she's to take 7 stripes 3 times, not just once. She has to take what she just received twice more."

Those around me found this comment amusing, and general laughter went up, everyone apparently delighted with the poor girl's plight.

The constable gave her the second set of strokes slowly but with more force, pausing between licks to watch the girl struggle. And I had to admit to myself that it was a most arousing sight to behold. She was straining at her bindings, her body becoming more strictured. Her fingers were splayed open, the prancing toes stretching, the ginger hair flying about while she kicked her legs this way and that, making the bare pubis visible to all.

Some of the fight seemed to have gone from her when she was given the last 7 strokes. Her young body seemed resigned to its fate, but then I sensed something altogether new and different happening to the girl. She seemed to have become accepting of her flogging, her buttocks almost welcoming the quirt, rising slightly to meet it when it flew toward her crimson rump.

"Ohhh!" she moaned out as the ordeal was nearing an end. "My poor bottom is on fire."

But her body grew slack for a moment as her sex-mound rubbed itself at the wooden surface of the post. And then she glanced over her shoulder with just the faintest of weak smiles on her face as she suddenly grew rigid and pressed her sex directly at the post.

At that point, all but the smallest portion of the pubis was hidden from my view, but fascinated I moved round slightly to

11

obtain a better view and I'm certain I detected a few glistening drops of sex juice forming on it, a most incredible sight. Had the girl spent herself while being flogged in public? I've seen our girls at school blush and become a bit giddy after a birching, but is it possible for a girl to actually orgasm while being punished?

Our coachman was ready to leave when I returned, and as I clambered aboard with my fellow passengers, I was still wondering about what I'd just witnessed. As we rode from the village, I was able to get one last look at the unfortunate Miss Sarah Browning. She was still hanging naked on the flogging post, her wrists occasionally pulling at the straps that held her fast while passersby smirked at her predicament. These people seem to take a great deal of pride and even enjoyment in the conviction and punishment of those they perceive as transgressors.

Another half day's journey brought us to Stonehurst, and from there all I had to do was hire a wagon and driver to transport myself and my belongings to Neville's house. It was about an hour by the slow way of wagon, but that gave me the opportunity to see that this vicinity is truly one of the most bleak of the entire countryside. The village itself is large, and apparently was at one time prosperous. The streets are cobbled with stone, but the shops are in disrepair. and the slightly ragged citizens rush about with seemingly no particular purpose. It's as if they are searching desperately for some means of livelihood.

Once we were out into the countryside, I saw that some of the farms had been deserted, many others lying fallow.

"It's hard times we're having," my driver said to me at one point, "but it will all be over once we've caught each and every one of these strumpets and beaten the evil from them."

I arrived quite late, finding that Neville had already retired for the night, but his houseman showed me to my quarters where a cozy fire was burning. And there was a lovely young girl there who was fixing up the bed and turning down the covers. She was quick and efficient, but she hurried from the room when I thanked her for a job well done.

I slept soundly and rose early to write this letter, Bertrand. The sun is up now, and the housekeeper has been in to tell me that Olford's free to spend the day showing me around his library and the grounds. I suppose I'll be able to get down to work after that.

I'm certain that you will want to know how our friend is faring, so I won't seal and post this letter just yet. Instead, I'll wait so I'll be able to send you my further comments. Until then...

Dear Bertrand,

Well, you might say I've had both a remarkable day and evening, and I must take this opportunity to tell you of the astonishing things I've witnessed.

At breakfast, I found Neville to be in fine spirits, feasting on eggs, meats, and coffee, a glass of port at the side. Well into his fifties now—he's 15 years our senior, you know—and still a handsome devil, no fat on him, his hair dark, and he's grown a long and pointed goatee, making him look every bit the official magistrate.

His greeting was a hearty one. "Ah, my good friend and trusted colleague Derek, Derek Hunter," he said as we shook hands. "Sit and nourish yourself. You must be famished after your journey."

Indeed I was, and we used the long repast to get reacquainted. Neville was very curious about how we're getting by at Rosewood Academy for Girls, and he finally asked if our students are still just as pretty as when he was our headmaster. He even wanted to know how many rumps we'd birched last term.

"I miss the ones who used to misbehave on purpose," he said with a fond smile of remembrance. "They enjoyed baring their buttocks for the switch, I'm certain. Oh, they had a hard time of taking their punishment, but they seemed to feel it was worth it for the peculiar afterglow it gave them. Believe me, as chief mag-

13

istrate, I sentence my share of young ladies to the whipping post, and I know what I say is true."

That gave me the opportunity to ask him about the persecution of the young girls in this part of the country, but he was vague, telling me I'd understand after I'd been there awhile and seen his manner of meting out justice.

"For now, just remember that these people are desperate and need something to focus on," he said as he rose. "You'll see this afternoon when I take you by one of their churches. Perhaps I can explain once you've seen their thinking in action. But I know you're anxious to see my library. Come along, professor."

As he led me toward the library, I was able to look about my new surroundings in the full light of day. Neville's house is a large and comfortable structure of wood, the furnishings of fine craftsmanship but quite sparse, very little decoration, much in the fashion of the Puritans.

As you might imagine, the largest room of his dwelling is the library, and I was thrilled to be in it. Never have I seen such an array of volumes dealing with ancient history! This room, located on the second floor, is richly appointed. There is a huge fireplace, a mahogany desk, leather chairs and a matching davenport. There's even a priceless Oriental carpet on the floor.

We spent a long morning in this academic treasure trove, exploring the vast amount of knowledge that Neville has accumulated in a single room.

During our second hour there, a girl entered the room, the same one who'd been in my bed chamber the night before, and now, not being road-weary, I was able to take a better look at her. She had a delicately-molded shape, a small but well-formed bosom, and a mane of light-brown hair that hung about her shoulders and partially over her chest. She was clad in a long gownlike dress that had worn thin and was tattered at the sleeves and hem. The dark garment adhered closely to her body when she moved, and it appeared that she might be nude beneath it. Her bare toes peeking from under the frayed hem tended to confirm this suspicion.

She'd come in to give Olford a message from the kitchen cook, and he spoke to her in a terse, businesslike manner, making it hard to tell if she was his concubine, mistress, or simply one of his servants, and I suppose he detected my curiosity.

"Amanda's a ward of the court, one of the accused girls you've been hearing of," he told me after she'd departed the room. "It's my responsibility to help her mend her ways."

His way of speaking seemed to invite questioning, so I asked him just what he meant.

"She was brought into my courtroom, accused and convicted of brazen conduct," he said to me while he was placing a weighty volume back up onto a high shelf. "I sentenced her to a naked birching in the public stocks and a heavy fine. She took her birching, of course, but her parents were unable to pay the fine. As a favor, I offered them the opportunity to give me guardianship over her until such time as she can learn to behave herself, this in lieu of the fine. They really had no choice but to turn her over to my care, and you can trust that I will indeed purge that girl of her whorish behavior."

I didn't know what to make of this. As Neville spoke, his eyes had a strange glint of pleasure in them, much like the look he used to take on when he was punishing a Rosewood student, but now this look was much magnified.

"Of course if the girl should disobey me in any way, her fine becomes due immediately, and that would mean her parents would have to turn their farm over to the court," Olford was saying. "I can tell you that this very fact insures her obedience to me."

At any rate, I was all set to get down to work there in the library, but he reminded of our visit to a nearby church. "We'll have to go by horseback," he told me. "This church, if you can call it that, is on the grounds of my estate, but it's a fair distance away."

15

The church building came into my view after we'd crossed a small bridge of stone. We'd come some several miles through a dark forest, and I'd been surprised during this trip when we'd come upon two men in uniform, also on horseback. Out of my earshot, Olford exchanged a few words with them, and they went on their way.

"Guards," he said to me simply once they'd departed. "I keep seven of them in my employ. These are unusual times we live in, Derek, and I choose to protect my holdings. They also help me in bringing errant girls back to the grace of obedience. You'll see what I mean soon enough."

The church was made of the same stone as the bridge we'd crossed and set in a grove of tall and dying trees that were made to appear all the more gloomy by a fog that was setting in. We went through the gate of a rusted iron fence, and then our horses had to pick their way carefully through weeds grown thick.

"We'll find Vicar Dowling in the rectory up ahead," Neville said to me while we were passing by a small graveyard where the headstones were sinking into the unkempt earth. He was pointing to a small house at one side of the church building.

As we drew close, a tall and emaciated man in a black suit and shirt emerged from the rectory building.

"Hello, Olford," he said with a crooked smile. "You've come to see the girl at penance, I trust."

"Indeed we have," Neville was saying as we dismounted. "Just lead the way and we'll have a look at her."

Vicar Dowling seemed anxious to be about the business, and he led our way down the path to the church, keeping several paces ahead of us.

"My family donated this land to the people of this faith generations ago," Neville whispered to me.

The church was without windows and dismal, although it had fine wooden pews to seat at least 100 people. Several candelabra burned near the altar, and the air was thick with incense.

16

And then, to my amazement, I saw a girl who appeared to be entirely naked kneeling before the altar. As we walked up to one side of her, I saw that she actually was naked save for a small piece of white linen draped over her sex. This then was the girl at penance!

She was a comely creature with a trim figure and an ample bosom. Auburn hair trailed down over her shoulders. Her bare buttocks rested on the cold stone of the floor, the feet curled up beside. Her head was bowed as if in prayer, and when I looked at her clasped hands, I saw yet another amazing sight. Right before her, there was a heavy ring of iron embedded in the floor with a short chain of 3 links run through it. Sturdy manacles were welded onto each end of the chain, and the nude's wrists had been shackled into them. This was apparently what she'd been assigned as penance, and a cruel penance it is, I thought, to chain a girl naked and kneeling. But I soon learned that she was being subjected to still worse!

"What are you using as a flogging instrument?" Neville asked Vicar Dowling, a thin smile of amusement at the corners of his lips.

"The birch switch only since she sought penance on her own," Dowling replied. "Her family brought her to me after she volunteered that she'd had certain thoughts concerning men. After she confessed to me, I brought her in here to do her penance." He turned to me. "Pretty thing, isn't she?" he asked in a way that told me he relished this aspect of his duties.

"Yes, she is," I said, "but isn't this terribly harsh treatment?"

"Better this than for her to act on her thoughts and come before our good magistrate, right Olford?"

"Well, certainly," Neville answered with a firm conviction. "This is far better than a public pillory and lashing."

Then it seemed to be time for Dowling to get to the business at hand. He strode away from us, walking over to the altar area, which amounted to a dais raised a few inches above floor level, a carved pulpit, and a stone table with a few thick and battered books lying on it along with some sort of utensils.

The kneeling girl looked up at him as he lifted a birch switch from the table. Her face seemed somehow serene even though she was obviously frightened.

Dowling dipped the fingers of one hand into an earthenware bowl filled with oil and rubbed it over the rod. Then, after dipping his fingers again, he smeared oil onto the girl's buttocks.

"The oil aids in flogging," Neville said to me. We were at a distance where Dowling couldn't hear us. "It causes the sting of the rod to penetrate deeper."

Standing to one side of the girl, Dowling held the rod out in front of her. "Pay homage," he said.

She knew just what was required of her. Leaning forward as far as she could, she placed her lips on the birch and held them there until the vicar pulled it away.

"Thank you," she said, addressing the rod and then put her forehead down on the floor to leave her buttocks raised for thrashing.

"Emily West, you have had lewd thoughts and confessed as much," Dowling was saying as he took up a stance behind her. "For this your naked flesh must endure the penance of being flogged."

"Yes, Vicar Dowling," she replied dutifully, "and I thank you for allowing me to do penance at the altar."

Dowling began bringing the birch down on the girl's behind, the strokes swift and sure but spaced far apart. Sometimes he'd wait as long as 10 seconds between the cruel licks, but the sound of the thin and flexible wooden switch on nude skin resounded through the church each time.

The unfortunate girl was trembling and biting her lip in an effort to take her penance in a thankful and brave manner, but that didn't last long, and she was soon shrieking each time the rod struck at her buttocks.

"Yes, my child," Dowling said as he gave the flesh an especially hard stroke. "Cry out and let your sin escape from you."

"Thank you, Vicar," Emily murmured through her gasps.

"Perhaps now you'll understand why I must govern these simple folk with an iron hand," Neville said to me. "The young lady before us truly wishes to repent. The belief in this plague of evil has grown so strong that the girls themselves take it seriously. Many of them think they've become irresistible, and they like it, even act on it at times. Thus, what took root in superstition is now becoming reality."

What he said made sense, but it seemed to me that the way these girls were being treated was highly cruel, and I couldn't resist mentioning this.

"You must remember that we're not dealing with naughty schoolgirls who need their bottoms warmed to improve their study habits," he replied, sounding a little exasperated. "These are young ladies who could ruin their lives through whoredom and possibly even bring destruction to the economy of this entire region."

By this time, Dowling had given the girl a dozen licks, and I could see that her buttocks were turning a pinkish and inflamed color. She'd begun to pull at the chain that held her to the floor, making her breasts jiggle about. Peering closer, I saw that the breast buds had grown stiff, but I couldn't be sure if it was from the chill of the room, the heat of the switch, or perhaps even some odd satisfaction she might be experiencing.

Neville walked closer, motioning for me to come with him, and when we were near the girl, Dowling ceased the birching.

Emily peered up over her shoulder at us, a look of shame on her face. And that look didn't surprise me allowing that she was almost naked in front of three adult men, her bottom freshly-birched.

"Care for a go at her?" Dowling said and held the rod out to Neville.

"Yes, I do," he replied. "Perhaps I can teach this charming

19

young lady a lesson that will keep her out of my courtroom."

As the vicar and I stepped back to watch, Neville readied the instrument of pain. He had that same amused smile on his face and looked quite imposing standing there in his high riding boots and cape.

Neville brushed the hair from the girl's shoulders. "This penance is a mere trifle compared to the sentence you'd receive if found guilty in my courtroom, Emily," he said as he gave her back a quick three strokes of the rod. "First off, you'd be flogged with something more effective than this switch. I'd have you punished with the lash, the quirt, or even the whip. And you'd take your flogging in the town square before anyone who might care to watch."

He was stroking his goatee now as he appraised her buttocks. "I'd have you strung up between the pillory posts by your wrists, and your ankles would be fastened near the bottoms of the posts so that not even your toes could touch the platform," he was saying as he gave the orbs of her bottom three stripes. "I don't think you'd care much for that, would you, dear girl?"

"No, sir," she said, her voice timorous with fright.

Neville went on, warming to his subject. "And I don't think I need mention that you wouldn't have a stitch of clothing on," he chuckled. "You'd be stark naked. And before your flogging even began, your sex would be shaved, giving everyone a clear view of your cunt."

Thrice more he burned the birch across the defenseless skin of Emily's behind before he walked over and returned the rod to Dowling.

"I think you've taught her a good lesson," Dowling said as he took the switch. "I'm almost done with her for now. I'll see you gentlemen out in just a moment."

He went to the girl and pulled the piece of linen from between her legs. "You'll spend the rest of your time in penance fully nude," he said to her. "I'll be back later to administer the next of your floggings."

"Thank you, Vicar," she murmured, keeping her gaze fixed to the floor.

Just as we turned to leave the church building, I took one last glance at the kneeling girl, impossible to resist as she made for a most erotic sight, and I was almost certain that I detected a hint of moisture about her pubic region just as I had with the girl I'd seen publicly whipped! This I considered most unusual and made a mental note to question Olford on the matter.

Well, Bertrand, I'm happy to report that I was able to spend the rest of this day and much of the evening in the library, organizing my notes and the materials at hand. In the morning, I'll be able to begin the research I've come here for. It's comfortable at Olford's, and his dining table certainly doesn't reflect the want of the rest of the region.

Neville and I had cognac before retiring, and I was able to seek an answer to my question concerning the moisture formed on the girls I'd seen punished. Right off, he reminded me of how the girls of Rosewood Academy often become flushed with excitement after we've given them a dose of the birch, a flush, he pointed out that reflects sexual arousal.

"Once again, we're dealing with something much stronger than a schoolgirl spanking," he said by way of explanation. "The extreme punishments that the girls hereabouts are undergoing seem to almost transport them into quite another world. And, yes, I've seen many a girl actually orgasm while she was being whipped."

He then went on to tell me that Vicar Dowling would probably keep Emily in the rectory with him overnight, ostensibly to pray with her, but in truth he'd use her for sexual purposes until dawn.

"Oh, yes," he said with a hearty laugh when he saw my shock, "after the old codger's done with beating her to his wicked heart's content, he'll probably tie her to his bed and fuck her all night,

21

and she'll be so delirious she'll barely know what's happening to her."

"But surely she'll tell someone," I said.

"Perhaps," he said with a wave of his hand, "but if she should, Dowling will just say that it's more of the evil coming out of her or that she's simply lying. She might even be punished again for telling an untruth."

That's how this most unusual day ended. I'll post this letter with the next mail rider who comes by, and I'll do my best to write often even though I'll be engaged in much research. I'm sure you'll want to hear of the strange goings-on in this bleak region of the country.

　　　　Sincerely,
　　Derek H.

———

Letter 2

Dear Bertrand,

Well I've settled into a regular and productive schedule of work here at Olford's. His magnificent library is so complete that I could possibly be done sooner than I'd expected and be back at Rosewood before the next term begins.

Olford's home runs with a precise regularity. His housekeeper, a stout and stern woman with a thick Eastern European accent who goes by the name of Ruth, oversees the daily schedule, doling out the more menial work to young Amanda Smith. Hector, the houseman, keeps a low profile, but I often see him from the library window.

The weather is often dreary, each morning dawning in a fog that often lingers for the day, but within the house, there are always cozy fires burning.

One of my more pleasant diversions has been the lovely Amanda popping into the library, checking to see if I'm in need of anything. She's a saucy little thing, and when she stands in the light of my lamp, I can see clearly the outline of her lithe body beneath the long dress that Olford keeps her in.

I must tell you here, as you are a man who's interested in the birching of feminine buttocks, what occurred two days ago. Amanda came into the library while I was working at the desk. She was walking with a jaunty swish and had a flirtatious smile on her pale lips that I don't think would have been there if she'd known that Olford had entered the room just a few paces behind her.

As she curtsied and asked if I was ready for tea, Neville spoke, surprising her.

"That sort of misbehavior is the very reason that you've been placed under my guardianship and confined to this house, Amanda," he said.

"I wasn't misbehaving, sir," she said when she whirled about, fear in her wide eyes.

"You're fibbing to me girl," he said to her flatly, "and I think a bit of punishment would do you some good. Now stand out in the center of the room and remove your dress."

"But, sir, Mr. Hunter is right here and..."

"And you'll be birched right in front of him," he said, his voice becoming angry. "Now you'd best bare yourself if you don't want a few extra licks of the rod."

With eyes downcast, Amanda walked slowly to the center of the room, unbuttoned the dress and let it fall. And then I learned that I'd been right about her going about nude beneath the garment. She had nothing else on; a sight to behold!

Her fair skin was flawless, her body trim and taut. She had

girlish breasts, tipped with pink nipples, and her buttocks were a gentle arc. Oddly, her pubis was entirely smooth-shaven.

Neville came over to stand near her, grasping her shoulders and turning the girl so that her back was to him, giving me a full frontal view of her.

Amanda's hands went to her pubic mound, covering it as if trying to hide from my gaze, a feeble attempt at modesty.

Our old friend seemed to no longer be angry with the now-naked girl. Rather, he began massaging her shoulders and speaking to her in a most gentle manner.

"You know why you have to accept regular birchings, don't you, dear girl?" he said kneading her flesh.

"I suppose so, sir," she murmured.

"I have the responsibility of turning you into a proper young lady," he said to her. "If I don't cure you of your ways I'll have to collect your fine from your parents, and that would mean they'd lose their land. You don't want that, do you?"

The girl stiffened in his grip. "Oh, no, sir!" she gasped.

"Then you'll take your corrective thrashing with a good will, won't you?"

"Yes, sir," Amanda was quick to say. "Thrash me good, Mr. Olford. I don't wish to bring misfortune to my family."

Well, Bertrand, I don't think it really necessary to tell you how much I was enjoying, and, yes, admiring, the way Olford was handling this girl. Ever so persuasively, he was lulling her into her punishment, explaining how beneficial the rod could be for a girl like herself.

He gave me a knowing glance as he guided Amanda to face the wide sofa with the upholstery of deep maroon velvet. Here, he had her get down onto her knees, her upper body resting over the velvet, breasts pressed to the fabric.

"Hands behind your back in the usual posture, Amanda," he said as he produced a short leather belt from a pocket of his jacket.

She knew the routine and placed her hands behind herself, wrists crossed.

With a few quick and practiced flourishes, Olford strapped her hands together, and then she was ready for punishment—bound and nude, kneeling with her bare rump proffered and ready for the chastening of the birch. And I must say that the sight caused a most pleasant stirring in my trousers.

And then, pleasing me even more, Neville asked if I'd be willing to administer the girl's flogging. "I haven't had the opportunity to observe your technique since our days together at Rosewood," he said with a chuckle. "I remember that you used to be quite adept at freshening a naughty bottom."

As he spoke, he was taking a long birch rod from behind the door and handing it to me. He keeps a supply of these switches, as well as bondage equipment and other flogging devices, all about the house.

Gladly, I took the rod from him. The sight of Amanda's fair behind was irresistible, and I longed to make it ache with the stripes of the birch.

"I usually handle it the way I did at Rosewood," Neville replied when I asked how many strokes she might need. "A girl is flogged until she's learned her lesson."

Wonderful! I had free rein to give that bare nymph an unlimited birching!

Standing to one side of her, I paused before beginning the punishment, savoring the little naked posterior. Oh, how it trembled and blushed as it awaited the first searing stroke of the rod.

Amanda's face was turned to one side, and I could see that she was nervously biting her lower lip in anticipation of the pain that she'd soon be undergoing. And when I raised the rod to begin, her buttocks clenched tightly.

In rapid succession, I gave her three sharp strokes, quick and efficient, causing an equal number of pinkish stripes to rise on the tender girl-flesh.

Amanda lurched forward with each stroke, ëohí sounds coming from her mouth as her wrists yanked at their leather bonds.

Then I began flogging that adorable rump in earnest, drawing an X pattern of stripes across the pale skin and making the poor girl wrench about at the velvet of the sofa. Her little feet were kicking, the toes curling in toward the soles to form an arch.

After a dozen strokes, I had her whimpering for mercy while she wagged her buttocks back and forth in a vain attempt to avoid her switching.

"Bravo, Hunter," Olford said to me as he signalled for me to give the girl a brief respite. "I see that you're still a master of bottom-warming."

He was taking a seat on the sofa, close enough to put a hand on Amanda's shoulders and hair but not so close as to interfere with the further flogging of her buttocks. Then he began massaging her and running a hand through her brown tresses.

"You're behaving so well," he said to her, "but I haven't heard you thank Mr. Hunter for being kind enough to give you this flogging. You know how badly you need it."

"Thank you, Mr. Hunter," she murmured. "Perhaps I need more."

Neville gave me a knowing look and pointed through her thighs to show me that her smooth pubis was showing signs of becoming moist. When he went back to massaging the girl, I began flogging her afresh, and it was most interesting. I always give a Rosewood student a good talking-to as I'm finishing her punishment, and that's what was happening now except that she had two men working on her, Neville stroking her hair and speaking to her of improving her behavior while I flogged her naked buttocks. She was promising him that she'd be the best of girls and squealing in pain at the same time!

By the time I was done with her, Amanda's behind was red and quivering.

Neville helped her to her feet and then let her stand there, shame-faced while he rang for Hector. "I'm going to have her put into some strict restraint for a couple of hours," he said to me. "Hector will attend to her from this point on."

"Please, Mr. Olford," Amanda cried when she realized what was going on, "don't turn me over to Mr. Hector while I'm bound and without clothing. Please don't let him see me like this. Allow me to cover myself!"

But it was too late. Hector was already entering the room, and his eyes caught fire when he saw the state Amanda was in, taking an obvious delight in her bound nudity.

Indeed her appearance was enchanting. She was flushed from being switched, breasts swollen, and her smooth pubis palpitated slightly with the hint of a glow about it. And, of course, her little bottom was a throbbing-red color, fresh from being under the rod.

As I admired the sight of the trussed lovely, Neville was telling Hector what was to be done with her. He wanted her taken to a special room and put on something that he referred to as "the platform."

"Give her at least a couple of hours there, Hector," he was saying, "more if she should give you any trouble. Check in on her regularly and give her buttocks a few swats each time you do. That should take some of the liveliness out of her."

Hector seemed quite pleased with this assignment, and he was quick to take Amanda by the elbow and lead her from the library. She looked back over her shoulder, a pleading look in her eyes, hoping, I suppose, that Olford might change his mind, but that was clearly out of the question.

After they'd departed, Neville and I spoke for a few minutes, he inquiring as to how my research was coming along, but even as I answered his questions, my mind was elsewhere. I was becoming very curious as to what this platform might be, and I finally had to voice this curiosity.

Olford laughed and became apologetic. "I seem to have forgotten that you're not yet familiar with how I have to handle these wards of the court when I take them under my wing," he said. "Come along and I'll show you. Hector will have her rigged up by now."

We had to go down a long hallway, finally coming to a tall, oaken door. Here, Neville took a heavy iron key from a pocket and unlocked the portal.

The door opened into a large, spacious room that was almost empty. The windows were curtainless, and a slight chill prevailed as there was no fire burning. There, in the middle of the wooden flooring, standing about two feet high, was an odd platform, and Amanda was strapped out to it. The platform was constructed of heavy wooden planks that had been polished smooth. Tall and sturdy posts were mounted at the corners.

Amanda barely touched the apparatus. Long straps of leather were fixed to her wrists and ankles, the opposite ends of the straps attached to the tops of the posts. Thus, she was spread upward, her body pulled into the shape of an X, only the slightest portion of her stomach on the platform, the hands and feet pulled painfully back up in the air.

As we walked in, Hector was just finishing with tying the nude girl. Her eyes were wide with confusion, lips parted.

For a few moments, the three of us stood there and simply stared at her. And, squirm as she might, there was no way that she could hide her open and exposed sex from our prying gazes. The poor girl had been spread for viewing, and there was nothing she could do to conceal herself.

"I see that Hector has you trussed up snugly," Neville said to her with a leering grin. "Are you comfortable enough?"

"No, sir," she said. "Why do you do this to me? I took my birching well enough, didn't I?"

"Yes, and I'm pleased with you, Amanda," he replied. "In fact, I'm pleased with all the progress you've made since coming

28

to live here, but it's been slow going. You're still much too frisky and flirty for your own good. If I should send you back to our fair village at this moment, I'm afraid that the citizenry wouldn't be too happy with you, and they might even banish you from their midst or insist that I collect your fine from your parents. Your parents wouldn't like that, would they?"

"No, sir," she said softly, looking off to one side.

"Then I'm sure you'll be happy to spend a few hours here on the platform," he said. "It's to your benefit, and I hope you realize that I'm trying to be of help to you."

The bare Amanda sighed. "Yes, sir, and I thank you," she said.

Neville picked up a fresh birch switch that was propped against the platform and began lecturing the girl, telling her how he wished for her to develop into a well-behaved young lady, and as he spoke, he emphasized his words with the birch, snapping it at the buttocks, teasing her with it, tickling the more sensitive areas of her nudity. This, as you can well guess, made for an engaging show. Each time the birch touched her flesh, the girl couldn't help but writhe in her bindings and make an all the more fetching display of her physical charms.

Yes, Bertrand, I know that we've had many a Rosewood girl under our control, but I'm finding that there is something entirely different about having a girl bound up, helpless to resist any advance, fully available for torment. Watching a girl as she twists about in inescapable restraint is something that seems to awaken the most ancient of lusts.

Olford turned the switch over to his houseman just before we departed the room. "See to her, Hector," he said to him. "Do with her as you see fit."

The full enormity of being left alone with the massive Hector overwhelmed Amanda all at once. "Please, Mr. Olford," she whined, "don't leave me like this. I'll be ever so well behaved."

But it was done with, and Neville closed the door behind us, leaving Amanda trussed and naked, alone with Hector.

_____

An hour or so later, I had occasion to pass by the vicinity of the room where Amanda was being held captive, and when I heard her voice from within, I couldn't help but to pause and listen.

"You can't do this, sir," she was saying. "I must learn to be good."

Then I heard the muffled laugh of a man. "You'll do as I say," the male voice said. It was Hector. "You're naked, and I've got you bound up good. You don't want me to give you a tit-whipping, do you?"

She answered in garbled tones, and then I heard the sound of a man taking his pleasure in female flesh. This was followed by the sound of Amanda gasping and groaning.

"Please, sir," I managed to discern. "Don't!"

There was no way to tell for certain, but I'd be willing to wager that Hector was using the helpless Amanda for sexual gratification.

I must close now, but I'll be in touch soon. In a few days, Neville and I are going over to Vicar Dowling's church to watch Emily West, the same girl I saw at penance on my first day here, being put through some sort of purification ritual. And on the last day of this week, I'm going into the village with Olford to watch the court system in action. He tells me that we'll probably be returning with another ward of the court, and he seems quite enthused about this prospect.

Until then,
The Best to You,
Derek H.

Dear Bertrand,

I hope you are well at this writing and that all is clear sailing at Rosewood.

As I've told you, Neville spends much of his time in Stonehurst, and he's informed Amanda, in my presence, that I have full authority to discipline her at will, a most pleasant duty by my standards.

Over an evening cognac, Olford explained why he keeps Amanda's pubis shaved. "I do the same with all of the girls that I take in here as wards of the court," he told me, sipping the cognac and warming to his subject. "I also have it done to the girls that I sentence to public flogging. Think of it. A girl with a shaved pubis is truly and fully nude. She has nothing to conceal even her most intimate portion. In total nakedness, her submission is complete, and she becomes just that much more obedient."

It made perfect sense, but I also felt as though it increased her sexual vulnerability.

"Exactly right," he said to me when I voiced this opinion, "and that does still more to enhance her subservience."

During this same conservation he let me know that I could certainly count on the aid of both Ruth and Hector should I need help in Amanda's punishments.

"Ruth's quite creative when it comes to restraint," he told me. "If you should wish to have our sweet Amanda bound, call on the woman. She's strong, and she'll bind that girl up securely for you."

At first, Amanda seemed somewhat subdued whenever we were alone in the library, but then she took up her flirtatious manners anew. Of course I rather enjoy her coquettery—you know how enticing it is to have a barefoot nymph at your beck and call—but I've promised Neville that I'll see to her deportment during his frequent absences.

Then again, I'd thoroughly relished birching her luscious hind end, and I suppose I've been looking for a legitimate reason to repeat the process. But I don't wish to take unfair advantage of my authority over her and warned the girl several times about her behavior.

"And are you going to switch my bottom, sir?" she asked when I cautioned her.

"That's exactly what I'll do if you don't conduct yourself in a more ladylike manner," I told her.

"Goodness," she said as she set a coffee service down on the library desk, just the hint of a secret smile at the corners of her lips, "I hope you won't make me remove what little clothing I have on."

Then and there, I decided that she was due for chastisement.

"Very well, Amanda, you know how your Mr. Olford feels about that sort of talk," I said, putting my work aside, "and you know I've been given the responsibility of keeping you disciplined. So now you may strip yourself, and you'll be quick about it if you know what's good for your buttocks."

She'd almost been daring me to do just what I was doing, but now she seemed surprised that she'd gotten herself into yet another sticky situation.

I pulled at the bell rope twice, the signal to Ruth that she was needed, and when I turned back, Amanda was standing there in the full nude, her left arm crossed over her breasts, her right hand covering her shaven pubis.

After picking up the ever-handy rod, I took up a stance behind the girl, admiring the perfect flesh of that pink young creature. She seemed even prettier than I'd remembered, and I found that I was anxious to crisp her buttocks.

"Well, it seems as though you're going to receive the flogging you were hinting at," I said to her.

She was beginning to tremble a bit, becoming frightened now as she realized that she might have gotten in over her head. "I don't wish to be flogged, Mr. Hunter," she said softly. "I don't know what gave you that idea, but please take pity on me. I'll do whatever you say."

Ruth was entering the room, looking quite stern in a starched dress and thick, functional shoes, and, just as Hector had done, she became aglow when she saw that Amanda was nude and about to be punished.

"You rang?" she asked.

"Yes, Ruth, I need this girl bound up so she'll stay in one place while having her backside switched. I'll trust your judgement as to a suitable posture and means of restraint for her."

Ruth took the girl by one elbow and began leading her from the library, telling me to come down to the second bedroom on the right in a few minutes. "I'll have this scamp into the leathers by then," she said.

Olford had been right about Ruth's ability in matters of bondage. By the time I entered the room, still carrying the switch, she'd trussed Amanda up neatly and most securely. This being a guest room, there was a huge four-posted bed against one wall, its sturdy, wooden posts reaching toward the high ceiling.

Amanda was facing one of the posts at the foot of the bed, tied to it and looking quite out of place in such comfortable surroundings. The room, like most of the house, was sparsely furnished with a few rich and well-appointed pieces, much mahogany, some brass, little decoration. Ruth had just struck a match to a laid fire, and the room was beginning to glow with a cozy warmth.

Amanda had been strung up by the wrists, her hands high above her head, the wrists were crossed and fastened tightly with a leather belt, the belt secured to the ornate scrollwork of the bedpost. The legs had been left free, but Amanda had been pulled up so far that only the very tips of her bare toes touched the polished wood of the floor, leaving her off-balance and swaying slightly against the heavy post.

"I trust you'll find that she's well in place for a decent tanning," Ruth said to me after I'd surveyed the bound girl, but as she spoke I was noting that the middle finger of her right hand was slick with moisture. "Shall I bind the feet up?"

I said it wasn't necessary and told her I'd ring if I needed anything more.

"Yes, she can do some dancing as she is now," Ruth was saying with a laugh as she departed, but I barely heard her. I was too busy noticing the pinch marks on Amanda's buttocks.

Without speaking, I put the rod aside and went to stand directly behind the girl. Then I placed my hands about her waist and let them slip round her to feel her sex, finding it wet, pulsing, and in an obvious state of arousal.

"Ruth's been pinching your bottom and toying with your puss, hasn't she?" I asked her.

The girl squirmed in my grip but remained silent, apparently afraid to speak up.

"Tell me, dear girl," I said to her. "I want to know, and it's no blame on you what someone does to you while you're trussed."

"Yes, sir" the girl whispered, "she pinched my behind terribly and stuck her finger up inside of me. Mr. Olford allows it. Please don't punish me for what she did with me."

I stepped back and retrieved the rod. "Of course not, Amanda," I said, "but you will have to be punished for the somewhat forward behavior you exhibited earlier."

She glanced over her shoulder, and when she saw me readying the switch, she seemed to brace herself, knowing that it would soon be searing over her bare flesh.

I suppose I gave the girl more punishment than she actually deserved, but the sight of her bound up to that pole and prancing beneath a flogging was a sight much too enticing to give up quickly. The reddish stripes appeared immediately on the fine skin, and

34

by the time I'd given her a mere three licks, she was squealing and yanking at the leather that held her fast to the post.

"You don't have to flog me, Mr. Hunter," she said as her breath came quicker. "I'll do anything you say, anything, sir!"

"Yes, you will," I told her in no uncertain terms, "and a healthy dose of the rod is going to ensure just that."

By this time, she was pulling at the straps hard enough to make the leather chafe at her wrists, and, just as Ruth had predicted, the girl was dancing about, the little toes skittering at the floor as the precious buttocks flung themselves back and forth, the lustrous hair swinging across her shoulders.

Yet I continued, entranced with having a trussed and naked girl so fully at my disposal. I had her in a position where I could do as I chose with her, and just the very idea of it gave me a huge surge of excitement.

And then the sweet girl increased my pleasure by begging me to cease flogging her.

"Please, sir," she was saying as she twisted in her fastenings, "it's making my bottom so very hot and sore. Take pity on me."

Even as she spoke, I became aware of what was happening within her. Her body was becoming flushed as she endured the rod, and she'd begun grinding her vulva at the post each time the birch crossed her buttocks, her movements so animated that her thighs were driven apart, the delicate feet tossing up into the air. This, of course, gave me a better view of her nude sex, and I saw that it had grown even wetter, the moisture now dripping from it in small rivulets.

The girl's loins were becoming aroused as she was flogged, the fire of the birch burning through to her pubis!

After giving her a few finishing licks, I put the rod aside and went to stand behind her, and there I did something that I've always wanted to do with a punished Rosewood girl. I reached between her thighs and tested her for sexual excitement, finding that the smooth mound was quite warm to the touch, fairly vibrating and sopping with sex fluids.

I caressed the silken flesh gently, my longest finger sliding up and down the opening to her crevice.

Amanda let out a sigh of relief. "That feels so much more pleasant than being beaten, sir," she murmured as my caress went deeper.

"I would imagine so," I said to her. "And I see that your puss has become aroused again. You ache within, don't you? Tell me the truth or you'll be flogged a second time."

"Yes, sir, I do," she said, closing her eyes as if hiding a secret from me. "There's a great itching inside of me, and I wish I could scratch at it. Can you help me?"

The implication of what she was saying was quite clear, and already I was loosing my trousers and removing my stiff penis. Once I had it out, I poked it around between the firmness of her upper thighs, slipping it through.

"Suppose I stick this up inside of you?" I said into her ear. "Would that help with your itch?"

"Yes, sir," she replied, "but I don't want to be accused of whorish behavior."

"You're not at fault, dear," I told her. "I caused you to be in this condition by taking the birch to you. Now I'm going to give you some relief."

Amanda gave a sigh of gratitude but said nothing as I further invaded her thighs, my member aimed at her pubis. She merely parted her legs a bit, opening herself. After all, she was bound and powerless to resist.

How fresh she was, so very responsive to my touch, the youthful flesh quivering in anticipation of being penetrated.

At eighteen summers she was no virgin, but I had to prod at her with all my might to work my penis into that taut slit, and even once I'd gotten in an inch or so, it was still rough going. Her vaginal walls were small and compact, almost too tight to enter, but, with a lustful zeal, I managed, finally cramming her little vulva to the top.

To my amazement, that bare girl went into full and unbridled orgasm the second I'd rammed fully into her. "It's wonderful sir," she shrieked out. "Please don't ever stop."

I took my time, fully enjoying her as she went through a long and apparently intense series of orgasms. Her pubis clutched at me, the juices flowing in warm trickles.

Then, when I'd taken full advantage of the position I had her in, I spent myself within her loins, taking full satisfaction in her tender and willing body.

Even as I was unstrapping her a few minutes later, I was thinking of just how much gratification I might use this whipping girl for.

It was just the next evening that Neville and I went to witness the purification of the lovely Miss Emily West. The night was a dark one, and we drove to Dowling's church in a one-horse carriage that was well decked with lanterns, Neville at the reins.

"I think you'll appreciate this exhibition," Olford said as we were drawing into the churchyard. "If nothing else, it will demonstrate to you the sort of ignorance that I deal with as magistrate."

In the gloom of night, the crumbling old church building seemed even more foreboding, and, as we alighted from the carriage, I heard the far off howl of some sort of wild animal.

The scene inside was indeed a strange one. Three men, whom I learned were the church Elders, plus Vicar Dowling, were gathered near the front of the pews, all of them in formal black attire and talking in hushed tones. A few tall candles burned in sconces mounted at the wall, and several more flickered in a candelabra near the stone table of the altar.

But it was Emily who captured my full interest. The girl was lying face down on the table, which had a velvet covering of a deep purple color draped over it. She was nude, save for a piece of white cloth lying across a very small portion of her buttocks. Her body shone with a coating of oil, and her arms were flung out in front of her, the hands lying near the corners of the table. Her feet, too, were near the corners at the opposite end of the table. She was breathing softly and evenly, her creamy bosom nestled into the thick velvet.

"It seems as though the pretty Miss West was caught masturbating and now must pay the price," Neville said to me in a low tone as we approached the front of the church where the elders stood with Dowling. "More than likely the good vicar sent her home from doing penance with her loins still afire, and she had to do something to relieve herself. But, still, she was caught, and she must submit to the penalty that her congregation demands or they'll bring her into my court where things could go much worse for her."

Dowling introduced me to the elders, somewhat grayish gentlemen, and they shook hands solemnly, thanking Neville and me for coming as witnesses, although I felt certain that they would have proceeded with their plans for the girl whether we'd come or not.

Acting as if it were some sort of sacrament, Vicar Dowling served wine all around, and as we touched glasses, a very old woman in a dark cloak and cowl entered from a side door, carrying an earthenware jug and walking toward the naked girl on the altar.

"That's Bella," Neville said in an aside to me. "She lives somewhere in these forests and possesses the secret knowledge of concocting potions from roots and herbs, potions that can induce ecstasy and altered mental states. Dowling employs her services regularly for this sort of ceremony."

Reaching the stone table with slow and halting steps, Bella touched the girl lightly on the forearm, beckoning for her to turn herself over. Once Emily was turned, the piece of cloth falling off,

38

the woman bade her sit up and then offered her the jug to drink from.

Tilting her head and letting her hair fall back over her shoulders, Emily was able to drink only sparingly before the woman took the jug away from her. A few drops of the liquid were still on her lips, and I saw the girl lick hungrily at them, her eyes bright as if she'd discovered a magical elixir.

With a few soft words, Bella had the girl lie down on her back and open her trim thighs to fully expose her sex, which I now saw had been shaven clean. Then, from a deep pocket in her cloak, the old woman took out a swabbing brush and dipped it into the jug. When the brush came out it was coated with the potion, an emerald-green substance, and Bella began brushing the liquid onto the sex of the prone nude, first coating the outside of the little hillock and then slipping it into the open crevice.

As her insides were painted with the mysterious liquid, Emily's fingers began clutching at the velvet, and her buttocks rotated themselves slowly in a small circle. The potion was having some sort of effect on her.

"Once Bella has her prepared, the girl will be receptive to the purification treatment," Dowling was saying to me. "She'll be more than willing to undergo the rigors necessary to purge her of the menace that's invaded our lands."

But as he spoke, I glanced over at him and saw a glow of cruelty about his features, lust for the naked girl on the stone table.

After giving Emily's nipples a few dabs of the potion, Bella had her resume the facedown position and then swabbed the greenish liquid between the girl's buttocks, sliding the brush briefly into the anus.

When she was finished, Bella placed the tiny piece of cloth back over Emily's buttocks, giving the girl at least some hint of modesty. Then, after the elders had thanked her, the woman left by the same door she'd first come through.

Neville and I took a seat in the second row of pews while Dowling and the other three men went into what seemed to be a well-rehearsed ceremony. Two of the elders went to the ends of the table and held Emily down by her wrists and ankles, the naked girl appearing quite helpless in their strong, gnarled hands. At the same time, the third elder was picking up a thick and battered book from the pulpit and then going to stand to one side of the altar, opening the volume.

"We're almost in readiness, gentlemen," Vicar Dowling was saying as he took a leather strap from an ornate wooden box. The strap was outfitted with an intricately-carved handle and had several white ribbons dangling from it.

Then he stood behind the table, facing the pews, Emily lying lengthwise before him. Ever so slowly, he removed the girl's one and only covering and tossed it to the floor.

"Emily West, you engaged in the act of masturbation and confessed to your crime when apprehended," he said as if by recitation. "In my right hand is the lash of purification, and it will now be used on the flesh of your body until you are thoroughly cleansed."

I'd purposely sat at an angle where I could see Emily's face; curious about the trancelike look that had come over her while the old woman had been applying the potion. And I saw now that the expression had deepened. There was an obvious fright written on her face, but her eyes had become glazed over as if she were staring toward a most divine and faraway sight.

"Your flesh will now suffer for its sins," the vicar said as he raised the lash high. "May you be purified."

As the ominous-looking instrument came toward Emily's buttocks, the man standing with the open book began reading, his words coming out in a monotone. It was some sort of chant, mostly unintelligible for me, but it sounded somewhat Gregorian, and I thought I recognized a few words of ancient Celtic.

The crackling sound of leather on naked flesh filled the room as Dowling began flogging the girl, and I saw her body jerk as soon as the lash seared across her buttocks. He whipped her with methodical, well-spaced strokes, each stroke landing squarely on the vulnerable flesh of poor Emily's behind.

It's become quite apparent to me that the rigors of the lash are much greater than that of the rod, and Emily was unable to contain herself. She was supposed to be accepting of this treatment, but she began struggling at the hands that held her, shrieking each time the leather burned into her tender skin.

"You'll pay the price for your vile act," Dowling said to her above the words of the chant. "Your cleansing will be complete only when you've suffered."

As he was speaking, the ecstatic expression on Emily's face became still more intense, and even though her cries continued to ring throughout the room, a look of strange pleasure filled her eyes. Her buttocks now began humping themselves up and down to the cadence of the lash, her pubis squirming itself into the luxurious softness of the velvet.

"I'm certain that, among other things, Bella's potions are aphrodisiacs of the most powerful variety," Neville said to me. "They seem to induce both physical and mental rapture."

Judging by the way that Emily was now bucking at the stone table, I couldn't help but see Olford's point. The girl was still shrieking, and her pleas for mercy seemed genuine as if she truly wished to escape the whipping that she was undergoing, but there was an element of pure sexual energy radiating from her.

As the elder holding the book continued the monotonous chanting, Vicar Dowling whipped the girl with a vigor that was obviously born of a basic cruel streak within his being. He was smiling as he blazed the lash at his captive, licking his lips at the sight of the struggling nude.

Emily's pleas for mercy seemed to be more heartfelt when the lash began strapping over other parts of her body. Dowling was now using the leather on her upper thighs and her back, caus-

41

ing these areas of nudity to throb with the same red color as the buttocks.

"I know this must be difficult for you, my child," Dowling intoned as the girl begged for the ritual to be ended, "but you must endure this ordeal through to its end if you want be truly cleansed. Your desire is to be purified, isn't it?"

"Oh, yes, Vicar Dowling," the girl moaned. "You must whip me thoroughly."

And in the dancing light of the candles, I could see that all of these churchmen were happy at the state they'd driven their victim to.

When Dowling seemed satisfied that he'd flogged the girl quite enough, he set the lash aside, and at the same time, the chanting ceased.

Emily was left lying there, whipped yet still animated, her body still writhing about.

Dowling was taking long straps of leather from the wooden box, handing them out to the other three men at the altar. Then all of them grabbed at the girl's wrists and ankles and began tying the ends of the straps to them.

They didn't have much trouble with the restraint of her hands. After they'd attached the straps around the wrists, they fixed the opposite ends to the legs of the heavy table. But the feet presented a problem. Emily seemed to realize suddenly that she was being fastened down hand and foot, and her body began its own involuntary struggle at being rendered still more helpless.

"Get hold of this whore," Dowling said, his voice filled with anger. "She's going to learn the folly of her ways and learn well."

Two of them had a sure grip at her twisting ankles, and the other two fixed the straps around them. Then they drew her feet out to the corners of the table, stretching her punished body, and tied the other strap ends to the supports at that end of the table.

Now the bare and quaking girl was truly helpless, and even though she was pulling at her fastenings and breathing heavily,

42

she seemed resigned to whatever fate might be about to befall her.

"You've resisted your cleansing, Emily West," Dowling snarled at her. "For this you will observe an all night vigil of prayer while you are without the slightest scrap of protective clothing and chained to the ring before the altar. You will also be subjected to yet another flogging, which will be administered to your rebellious flesh at dawn."

"Don't force me through that, sir," Emily murmured as if knowing that it was useless to protest. "I truly couldn't help myself. I didn't know what I was doing."

Dowling ran a greedy over her buttocks, feeling them with a look of ownership, then tweaking the sore flesh until the girl squealed in pain.

"I'd be quiet if I were you," he said to her, continuing to squeeze the reddish skin. "You are a masturbatrix who'll be punished until clean. Your lies and complaints simply make your situation all the worse."

The elders had seated themselves, and now all of us watched as the vicar sprinkled the girl with water and mumbled some sort of vague incantation. Finished, he lit an incense burner, and as the air became perfumed with a sickly-sweet odor, he moved the candelabra to one side of the altar, causing the nude figure of young Emily to be bathed in a circle of lighting.

"All is ready for this girl to pay the final penalty of purification," he said in a voice so loud that it reverberated from the high ceiling, and, as he spoke, he picked up a heavy bell and rang it once.

I couldn't imagine what further tortures Emily would be subjected to, but I was soon to learn. Dowling sat alongside the elders. Then a small door just behind the pulpit opened and in walked a tall figure wearing a black robe and hood, the hood with only slits cut out for the eyes and mouth, a most unnerving sight.

Neville leaned to my direction, speaking in a whisper. "The

hooded man is known as Brother M.," he said to me. "No one but the vicar knows his true identity."

The robed man walked to the altar with slow and solemn steps, stopping near the end of the table where Emily's feet were tethered. How forbidding he appeared, how powerful he seemed in contrast to the naked girl so helpless in her leather fastenings. And when she looked over her shoulder to look at her new tormentor, her dazed eyes filled with horror, her mouth opening with a silent plea for leniency.

"You were found masturbating yourself," Brother M.'s voice said from within the hood. "Now you will be given what you were seeking. May you learn your lesson from this experience."

He was mounting Emily from behind, the front of the dark robe opening and flapping out to either side of her prone body. With a start, I realized that he was invading the defenseless girl with his manhood!

With the robe draped about her body, it was impossible to ascertain whether Emily was being penetrated in her vulva or her anus, but as the hooded man drove himself into her flesh, she screamed in astonishment and shame both.

"Please don't allow this, Vicar Dowling!" she cried out. "Please don't let the elders see this."

"You've brought this upon yourself, my girl," he said in the silence, "and now you'll take your correction."

As I looked from face to face, I could see that all of these churchmen were delighting in Emily's plight, each of them wearing a look of deep satisfaction as the naked girl's pleas echoed through the dark recesses of the old stone structure.

There was nothing to be said about the way the girl was being treated, so I simply sat with others as the hooded Brother M. took his pleasure with the girl. He gave his victim a fierce pounding, thrusting himself at her forcefully again and again, causing Emily to begin an incessant moaning that grew continually louder.

Looking into her eyes, I could see that she'd lost touch with

44

reality, and it was impossible to tell if this was due to the flogging she'd endured, the fucking she was now being given, or the potion that Bella had administered. It seemed likely that her condition had been brought about by a combination of all three of these factors.

"No!" she cried without warning. "My insides are on fire. What are you doing to me?"

And then it was clear for all to see that she'd gone deep into orgasms, an apparent torrent of them that slammed through her and make her struggles still more frantic.

She began babbling, talking of being in a dream, of being caught at masturbation, even of the second flogging that she'd take at dawn.

"You must flog me severely, Vicar Dowling," she was saying. "You must flog me until I can bear it no longer and then flog me still more."

The expression on the vicar's face told me that he planned on doing just that.

When Brother M. had finished with the girl, he departed, and then Dowling escorted Olford and me to the door. I took a look backward to see the elders gathering about the bound and naked beauty on the table, and they seemed in no hurry to release her. The sight made me shake my head and wonder what they would now do with her.

On the drive home, all I could think was that if Emily had been an innocent sort of girl to begin with, she'd no longer be so after the way she'd been treated.

"That's correct," Olford said when I voiced this sentiment. "As I've told you, this entire situation is growing from within and nurturing itself. All I can do as the magistrate of these people is to keep the peace in any way I can."

Let me close this letter, Bertrand. Please stay in touch. I'll be curious about the new students arriving for the coming term at Rosewood. Will we, perhaps, have fresh bottoms in need of birch discipline?

    I wish you well.

    Sincerely yours,

    Derek H.

Letter 4 PRIVATE

Dear Bertrand,

Your letter arrived yesterday, and I was glad to hear that everything is going well at Rosewood. The new student you mentioned sounds like a live and pretty one, and, from everything you say of her, it appears that we'll be taking the birch to her hind end some time during the coming term.

I've become aware of certain facts that I dare not speak of with anyone in this vicinity, so please bear with me if I seem to be unburdening myself on you.

It is quite true that these unfortunate folk have fallen on some very hard times, and, just by looking at their overgrown fields and tumbledown buildings, one can easily see how they feel as if some sort of curse has befallen them. At times, I can even understand how their superstitious way of thinking might lead them to believe that the young women of the region are the keepers of this evil as the girls themselves have taken to sometimes acting out the part. Just yesterday, for instance, I went out horseback riding and found myself at the border of a nearby farm. Catching a glimpse of something pinkish in color moving about behind a thick growth of trees, I went closer to investigate.

I could hear the twittering giggle of a young female voice, and when I rode into the clearing where the sound was coming from, I was more than a little surprised at what I saw. There, leaning against the trunk of an oak tree, was a blondish girl clad in naught but a few field flowers tied together and girdled round her hips.

"If you'd give me some coins, sir, you can do whatever you like with me right here in the grass," she said with a bold smile on her lips.

As she spoke, she stepped away from the tree and twirled herself around in a circle, giving me a still better view of her rather delectable body.

I won't deny that the idea of giving that impudent little thing a few coins and having my way with her didn't have its appeal, but I thought better of it and told her how dangerous her behavior was.

"Don't you know what's going on hereabouts?" I said to her as she exhibited herself. "If the wrong person heard what you've said to me and reported you to the authorities, you'd be in for a public flogging at the very least."

"Yes, but they'd have to catch me," she said, "and they can't do that since I'm a slut filled with evil. I'm the whore of the woodlands."

I cautioned her again, but she wouldn't listen, and once she saw that I entertained no ideas of making use of her "services," she scampered off into the forest with a laugh that was almost hysterical.

I mention this incident, Bertrand, as an illustration of how these girls are fulfilling the ignorant beliefs of the older generation and causing them to take shape in reality.

Also, I'm finding that the longer I'm here, the more clear it becomes to me that there are certain people who are glad of the situation concerning these young nymphs. You and I both know that we take a certain enjoyment in disciplining our Rosewood students, sometimes even being glad when it becomes necessary to take switch to buttocks. Well, some of these people seem to be taking an equal, if not greater, delight in seeing the girls of the village publicly flogged or undergoing strange penance rituals.

47

And it's all too easy for anyone to accuse a girl, no matter how innocent she may be, of this so-called evil behavior just as an opportunity to see her divested of her clothing and put to the lash. Sometimes, I even have the idea that our own Neville Olford falls into this category.

At any rate, the real news I have for you is that Olford has taken in another ward of the court, an incredibly lovely young creature by the name of Tarin Blake. He took guardianship of her two days ago on the day I went into the village to see his courtroom in action.

On the night before this journey, Neville had a guest to dinner, the mayor of Stonehurst, a white-haired gentleman with a decided and strong penchant for the female form.

Ostensibly, the mayor had come to talk of some sort of upcoming elections, but the dinner conversation centered mostly on Tarin Blake, who would come before Neville and his tribunal the next day. The girl had been accused of working on the Sabbath and, of all things, flaunting herself naked whilst in the fields, exposing her nude body to two hunters and enticing them.

"The girl's a problem, Olford," was Mayor Blythe's opinion. "It's imperative that you make an example of her and then remove her from the public eye."

"I agree," Neville said to him, "however, these charges against Tarin have been raised by a drunken stepmother who's jealous of her."

"I understand that," the mayor agreed, "but the girl's proud, and it's not only her stepmother who's jealous of her youth and beauty. The women of our district dislike her, and the men are tired of being said to lust after her."

The mayor's bent of mind was that the populace would settle for nothing less than seeing Tarin sentenced to a naked and public flogging. His plan was for Neville to then take the girl under his guardianship, simply to let people forget her.

"There are many who feel that she's the primary source of all the misfortune that's befallen our lands," he said, "the repository and fount of all the evil that's about, and I shudder to think what might happen to the poor girl should the villagers become even more outraged with the whole situation."

Both of them nodded, apparently in assent to this plan.

Pretty Amanda had been in and out of the dining room several times, serving, swishing her sassy bottom as she flitted about barefoot.

"And now to the matter of the girl who's currently under your roof, Neville," the mayor said while she was out of the room. "Is she in need of a fanny-warming? If so, I'd be more than glad to lend a hand."

The three of us laughed over this, and Neville said that he'd have the girl prepared for a birching. "That's her primary business in being here, after all," he said, "to learn the joys of disciplined living."

He left the room, returning a few minutes later to tell us that Amanda would be ready soon. "My housekeeper is getting her out of her clothing and into something more comfortable," was the way he put it.

"Something more comfortable such as the bondage of leather straps?" the mayor asked.

Again we laughed just as Ruth entered the room.

"Amanda's been put on the platform and readied for the birch," she said to Olford.

I begged off going along with them as I had some paperwork to put into order even though the thought of sweet Amanda, nude and fastened up to the platform, was an arousing mental picture. But I felt that the mayor would probably want free access to her and felt as if my presence might only complicate matters.

I went off to the library, and only minutes after lighting the lamp and settling down to my notes, I heard the sound of the rod on bare flesh and girlish cries of distress. Amanda was indeed being put to the birching that the mayor had spoken of.

The sounds died out after a few minutes, and then Neville came walking into the library, asking me how my research was progressing.

I gave him a brief idea and then asked about Amanda.

"Oh, Mayor Blythe wanted to spend some time alone with her," he answered. "He sometimes feels that it's his duty to lecture these accused girls."

"I take it he does more than that with them," I said.

"Yes, of course," Neville replied, "but you must understand that these girls have lost all rights once they've been taken into the custody of our judicial system. They no longer have any say over who does what with them. If the mayor's feeling in need of a feminine body, it's his privilege to use Amanda to gratify himself."

I saw what he meant but didn't comment.

And it was very late when I heard the mayor leaving the room where Amanda was trussed up.

As Neville and I rode into Stonehurst the next morning, I was surprised at seeing so much activity. The village had a carnival atmosphere about it, the people seemingly in fine spirits, the taverns doing a brisk trade.

"It's often like this on days when the people are fairly certain that a public flogging is in the offing," Olford said when he saw my expression. "I've another girl accused of evil behavior coming before me in addition to Tarin Blake. The people feel that they can count on at least one flogging for sure, and they're especially excited about the possible sentencing of Tarin."

As we came near the village square, I could see the outlines of the grim pillory posts against the gray sky, a raven perched atop one of them, and drawing still closer, the wooden stocks became visible, and, there, a naked girl was being held, her neck and wrists confined in the stocksí cutout holes, head and hands poking out the other side.

"That young lady came before me just a few days ago," Neville was saying as I stared at her. "Her crime was small, and I was lenient with her. She has only to spend one hour each morning for a week there in the stocks and take a mere 3 strokes of a single-thonged lash at the end of each of those hours."

With our horses picking their way slowly through the milling crowd, I was able to get a good look at the captive nude. She was bent slightly at the waist, her bare feet occasionally shifting, and she was of a fine rump and bosom. As we rounded the square, I saw that she'd been gagged and blindfolded with leather beltings. But even with these devices strapped onto her, a look of shame could still be seen on her face.

Passersby jeered and made lewd comments as they strolled by the hapless girl, and I couldn't help thinking that she might be just as glad to be wearing the blindfold so as not to have to look directly at her tormentors.

After leaving our horses with a livery stable, Neville and I parted ways, he going to his chambers and I to sit in the court-room. Here, I found the atmosphere almost as raucous as that of the streets. Even before the court came to session, a bailiff had to twice call the room to order.

All around me people were muttering about the infamous Miss Tarin Blake, apparently bent on seeing the girl either punished severely or banished from their midst. And there was a certain amount of lewd interest in the mode of punishment itself.

"I wouldn't mind seeing that delicious little girl strung up nude in the pillory," I heard one man saying to another.

"Neither would I," his companion agreed. "Say what you might of her, she's a joy to behold, and I'd certainly love to take a gaze at her while she was without clothing."

The women near me seemed still more vehement in their desire to see this girl punished. All they spoke about was a fond hope of seeing her whipped.

Then Neville and his two court clerks entered, all of them

looking quite imposing in their black robes and curled wigs, and the people grew quiet. Neville appeared every bit the Chief Magistrate with his long goatee, book and gavel in hand.

The first two cases were simple civil matters, easily disposed of.

Then came one of the young girls accused of evildoing, a Miss Polly Taylor, a fair creature in long pigtails. She was employed as a maid servant, and her mistress had charged her with theft.

"I took only some soup that was offered to me," the frightened girl told Neville.

"I offered her only enough to tide her over until the dinner hour, and the ungrateful snip slurps up an entire bowl," her mistress sneered. "And what's worse, your honor, this girl has taken to sashaying herself before my husband in a most provocative manner. It's as if she's trying to lure him to her bed chamber. She's one of the evil ones, I tell you."

It was clear what was really going on, but Neville seemed almost bored with the duty before him. The townspeople wanted their idea of justice, and, in order to keep the peace, he was obligated to give them what they wanted.

He shuffled through some papers, then looked up and spoke. "Miss Polly Taylor, your mistress has an unblemished reputation here in Stonehurst," he said in a level tone, "so I can hardly take the word of a serving girl over hers. Therefore, I find you guilty. The bailiffs will take you immediately to court chambers where you will be divested of every stitch of your clothing and shaved of any and all bodily hair. You will then be taken to the square, fastened into the stocks and given one dozen strokes of the birch rod and one half dozen of the leather lash. So be it."

His gavel landed on the high desk with a thump of finality and two bailiffs appeared at Polly's side.

The girl kept plaintively insisting on her innocence, almost sobbing, as she was dragged from the room, but it was of no use to her. Looking at the girl's mistress, I could see that she was suppressing a smile at Polly's discomfort.

Then Tarin Blake was brought in to stand before Neville and his tribunal.

Instantly I was struck by the innocent yet sensual beauty of the girl. She was quite young, nubile, and moved with the lithe, supple grace of a wild animal, cat-like. Her body was clad simply clad in a frayed skirt of a dark brown color and a faded white blouse, the blouse falling from one of her shoulders, the skirt very short and displaying much of her slender legs. This very display of flesh is enough to get a girl in trouble hereabouts, but Tarin Blake seemed unaware, or perhaps uncaring, of how she presented herself to the world.

When she drew close enough to stop before Neville's desk, I noticed that her skin was of the olive hue that one usually associates with Mediterranean peoples. Her black and lustrous hair was extremely long, falling in disarray well down her back and into her eyes, the strands tousled not from a lack of grooming but simply because of the way they grew.

As she stood with her hands behind her back, appearing to be placing herself at the mercy of the court, Neville looked her up and down, openly drinking in her youthful beauty. But even as she was appraised by the man seated high above her, she remained defiant behind her large and innocent eyes.

"Tarin Blake, you have been witnessed working on the Sabbath and doing so while naked," Neville said to her, his tone stern. "Tell this court what you have to say for yourself."

"I am innocent, your honor," she said, staring directly into his eyes. "It's true that I did those things, but I did so only because I was ordered to by my stepmother. My only crime is that of being obedient to her wishes."

Neville called the stepmother forward, a sneering, rough woman, and then Tarin told what occurred on the day in question.

One of the Blakesí prize sheep had become stranded in the

deep part of a stream, the waters were rising and Tarin's step-mother had commanded her to wade out and fetch it. When she started into the stream, Mrs. Blake told her to remove all her clothing so as not to soil it. Tarin, knowing that two hunters were nearby since her stepmother had pointed them out to her, was reluctant to strip herself, but the woman had insisted, and she'd obeyed. The two hunters, seeing this from a distance thought that Tarin had merely decided to do some frolicking on the Sabbath and had reported her to the authorities.

"She's lying," your honor," Mrs. Blake said. "I caught her flaunting herself before two strange men as if she wanted them to take her right there in the woods. She's filled with more evil than any ten of these young whores."

Neville questioned both thoroughly, but it was obvious that he'd find Tarin guilty. The audience was murmuring, all of them anxious to see this particular girl punished for her crimes, and, in the back of the courtroom, the mayor was standing with a look of apprehension on his face. The people of Stonehurst were becoming angry.

"Tarin Blake, by your own admission, you have committed the acts that you're accused of," Neville said to her, "and this leaves me with no choice but to have you punished."

Tarin listened almost impassively, tossing her hair back and revealing a portion of her small but budding bosom, her full lips parting as her large eyes silently said that she saw the hypocrisy of this courtroom charade.

Neville then pronounced the girl's fate. "You will receive 21 strokes of the six-thonged lash while fastened between the pillory posts of the public square," he said to her. "Before you are brought to the pillory, you will be taken to court chambers, and there you will be stripped naked by the bailiffs, then shaved of any and all bodily hair."

Tarin remained unmoved, seemingly without fear.

Then Olford called the girl's father forward and told the man that his daughter's crimes were severe enough to warrant far more than a flogging. After consulting his book of ordinances, he levied an enormous fine, telling Mr. Blake that he would be held immediately responsible for the entire sum.

"I haven't that sort of money, your honor," Tarin's father told him. "I'd have to sell all of my lands, leaving my family with nowhere to go, and I doubt I'd even find a buyer in these times."

"I will offer you another choice then," Olford said. "In lieu of the fine, Tarin will be remanded to my custody and legal guardianship until such time that I think that she's mended her ways. During that time, she will live under my roof, obey my rules, and submit herself to my methods of correction. Should she fail, your fine will become immediately due."

Suddenly, Tarin turned to her father. "Turn me over to the magistrate," she said to him. "I promise that I'll obey him and you won't lose your holdings."

With a look of dismay about him, Mr. Blake agreed to Neville's terms, and a buzz of approval went through the audience while the stepmother smiled with a twisted sort of glee.

Neville banged the gavel. "This court stands adjourned," he intoned. "Tarin Blake's flogging will take place within the next ten minutes."

As the courtroom emptied, Olford motioned for me to join him in his private chambers, and when I walked in he offered me glass of whisky. "Let's relax for a minute before we go out there to witness the punishment," he said. "It seems I gave the people what they wanted, though the prospect of having that young lovely as my ward is not altogether unpleasant."

As we toasted, he wore a secretive sort of smile, relishing the idea of having Tarin Blake under his control, no doubt.

"It shouldn't take long for them to prepare her for the lash," he was saying as we drank up. "The girl didn't have many clothes on, so it won't be much of a job to strip her down, and I doubt if there's much, if any, pubic or body hair to be shaved off."

By the time we got outside, the square was fairly mobbed, the mood of crowd even more festive than before, men coming from the taverns with glasses still in hand. The town's businessmen were well represented, but most of the audience were farm folk, using this as entertainment, macabre as it might be. Some of them, fresh from the fields, were still carrying pitchforks and other such implements.

With the townspeople deferring to Neville's authority, we managed to draw quite close to the pillory, and there I was able to get a good look at the dreaded apparatus. Simple in construction, it was a platform of roughhewn wooden planks perhaps six feet square, with two very tall posts, thick timbers, mounted at each side of it. Near the top of each post was an iron ring with a long strap of leather attached to it. Similar rings and straps were fixed a few inches from the bottoms of the timbers.

"I think she'll keep herself still once she's been attached to those posts," Neville said to me. "And everyone will certainly have a good view of her."

I couldn't help but agree.

As I continued gazing at this arena of flagellation, a sudden hush came over the crowd. Then a cheer went up, and I saw that Tarin, her body nude and shaven, was being led to the platform, two bailiffs holding her tightly by the wrists as she stumbled along, trying to keep up with them.

Once they'd half-dragged the girl up onto the platform, standing her in the middle of it, the two burly men began fixing her into a most degrading position of restraint, first tying her wrists into the upper straps and hoisting her simultaneously. By the time they'd secured the knots, only the tips of her naked toes touched the wood of the platform.

The feet came next. The bailiffs pulled them over to the strappings fixed low on the posts, lashing the ankles securely into the ends of the leather straps, her toes lifted off of the rough planks. When they were done with her, the girl was suspended in the configuration of an X, her body fully exhibited, no part of her able to touch the platform.

"You must admit that her nudity couldn't be more complete," Neville was saying as they finished trussing the girl. "In that position, even the bottoms of her feet are exposed to view, and, with her sex shaved, she doesn't even have her little patch of wisp to hide behind."

He spoke in the tone of a man proud of his creativity.

If I'd thought Tarin Blake to be of singular beauty before, the memory paled in comparison to the sight she now presented. Her body was sculpted; the lines clean and chiseled, the flesh ever so firm and lean. The pubis was small, a tiny triangle tucked between her thighs, and her breasts were perfectly-molded, standing high and tipped with tan nipples that seemed to be in a state of erection, possibly from exposure to the elements.

One of the bailiffs was removing a six-thonged whip from a hook mounted on one of the posts while the other applied oil to Tarin's buttocks, obviously enjoying the opportunity of fondling the girl. His hand was causing her body to twist itself slightly within the restrictions of the bindings, making her appearance all the more lovely.

"Her preparation consisted of more than just having her clothes taken from her and her pubis shaved," Neville said, leaning close to me. "You may see this girl orgasm before her audience."

"Whatever do you mean?" I asked, my curiosity high.

"While being stripped and shaved, she was also stimulated with an artificial penis," he told me, "and this will create some very unusual sensations in her flesh once the lash touches it. By being already in a state of arousal, she'll feel far more than simple pain while being flogged. The heat of the whip will be conducted through the buttocks and into the loins, further stimulating the pleasure triggers there and easily causing her to orgasm no matter how she might try to control herself."

What he said made perfect sense when I thought of the way

Amanda had behaved whilst I'd had her tied up to the bedpost.

All was in readiness, Tarin nude and tethered hand and foot to the heavy posts, buttocks oiled for flagellation, her smooth body stretched out so very tightly in the strappings.

And her torturer was standing behind her, the whip poised and ready.

Tarin's body surged forward when the first stroke of the oiled thongs hissed across her naked buttocks, the smooth vulva pressing upward and out. She remained rigid for a fraction of a second and then relaxed, but already the second stroke of the whip was befalling the exposed flesh, causing her to lurch forward once again.

The whipping of Tarin Blake was one of the most erotic and astounding sights I've ever witnessed. The flagellator striped his victim's buttocks with a cruel zeal, leaning enthusiastically into the job in hand while being spurred on by the cheers of the crowd, but never once did Tarin lose her dignity. Each time the leather crossed her buttocks, her mouth and eyes would open wide in fresh surprise, and after about five strokes, she would scream when the whip seared into her flesh, but never did she cry out for mercy.

She writhed about in her bonds, her fingers clenching and opening. The bare feet twisted and sought the platform while her nude body threw itself from side to side, her long tresses tossing about her face and breasts. Even so, not once did she plead for the flogging to be ended.

"Lively thing, isn't she?" I heard one of the onlookers saying.

"Indeed," a man's voice replied, "and her wagging about makes for a fine show of her cunt."

Then, after she'd endured perhaps fifteen strokes of the six-thonged instrument, I saw what Neville had been speaking of. With her pubis fully uncovered, I could see that it was beginning to quiver with an excitement that seemed clearly sexual in nature, and tiny drops of wetness were appearing on the shaven skin, quickly becoming thin and glistening streams that trickled over her upper thighs.

Then it happened. Tarin gave out a strange shriek that was clearly born of an abject suffering, but a suffering that had blended with some dark and unnameable pleasure.

Just as Olford had predicted, the whipped and naked girl had gone into orgasm!

I suppose that one would have to have some inside knowledge to fully realize what Tarin was now undergoing. The villagers all seemed to think that they were simply having the good fortune to witness an especially animated flogging victim, but, after what Neville had told me, I could easily see that Tarin was going through orgasm even as her punishment continued.

As the last stroke fell, Tarin's nude flesh quaked with one final spasm of climactic rapture. Then she went almost limp in her bindings. The bailiffs had to hold her in their arms as they loosed her, as it was easy to see that she'd collapse to the platform without aid.

"Amazing, wouldn't you say?" Neville said to me with a wry chuckle. "It should be an interesting time taming this one."

I nodded in agreement.

—————

As I said at the beginning of this letter, Tarin's been living here at Olford's home for two days now, but I've seen little of her. He tells me that, after her public flogging, she needs rest before beginning a program of discipline designed to purge her of the dangerous pride she carries.

I've seen her twice, and I'll admit that she's most appealing to me. Already, I find myself looking forward to seeing her receive the same sort of birchings that the naughty Amanda so often endures.

The whole situation here is most interesting in a rather macabre fashion, and even though I'm quite busy in the library lately, I'll do my best to keep you posted as I feel I'm learning things that might come in handy for both of us in the punishment of our Rosewood girls.

Take care of yourself,

In All Sincerity,

Derek H.

Letter 5 PRIVATE

Dear Bertrand,

Please forgive the long interval since my last communication. As I've mentioned, my research is going well but, with Olford's library being such a veritable gold mine of information, it's keeping me quite busy. In fact, he wishes to lend you one of his books, and I'm shipping it under separate cover. If you'll remember, I told you that he's made the more esoteric section of his library available to me—the volumes dealing with the somewhat forbidden topics of bondage, flagellation, and even question by torture. Recently, I came across a treatise concerning flogging in the schools entitled "Flagellation of the Female Student, a Means to Better Learning." This is the one I'm sending you as I feel we can both make use of it as a guide to handling the Rosewood students guilty of misbehavior.

Speaking of the girls at our academy, I've begun to wonder about their reactions to the birch since witnessing what happened to both Amanda Smith and Tarin Blake while they were forced through punishment. We've both seen our students become flighty as their bottoms blush beneath the rod, and almost always their faces glow once we're done with them. It makes me wonder if perhaps our students, some of them anyway, might be looking for something more intense. It's certainly a subject we might think on.

And now to the enjoyable subject of Olford's new ward of court, the lovely Miss Tarin Blake. As I mentioned in my last letter, I didn't see much of her when she first arrived, but she crossed my path on a few occasions. When we passed, she'd open her wide lips in the hint of a smile, her bright and alert eyes looking directly into mine, but she didn't speak.

Neville keeps her dressed in a more sparse fashion than he does Amanda. He's given the girl a dress of a deep but faded forest-green color that has sleeves but is so short that the ragged hem scarcely covers her rounded behind. She must go about with no undergarments and, like Amanda, without benefit of shoes or stockings, her feet nude at all times. With her legs so charmingly displayed, she makes for an arousing sight. Her hair is so long that it hangs to her elbows and lower back, drooping across her eyes and giving her a waifish appearance that's a bit out of place for a girl so fiery.

On Tarin's fourth day here, Neville came into the library early and announced that he was about to give her the first taste of the sort of discipline that she'd be subject to while under his care.

"Ruth and two of the guards are preparing her now," he told me, "and I'd appreciate your presence. I'll explain fully later, but it appears that I'm going to have to ask for your help in getting these young ladies into proper modes of behavior. Neither of them can be safely sent to live among the villagers with the way they conduct themselves at present. And it looks as if I'll be taking on new duties that will make me even busier than I am now."

Of course, I told him that I'd be glad to lend my assistance.

"I much appreciate it," he said. "I hope you'll come along then and see how these girls need to be handled.

As is usually the case in this part of the world, the morning was a bleak and dreary one, a chill in the air and fog banks scudding through the trees and around the corners of the house.

Olford led me to a large outbuilding located about fifty yards from the main house, a gloomy structure of stone that he told me had once been used as an animal stable back in the days when this estate was still being farmed.

"That was a very long time ago," he was saying as we entered it through a small wooden door at the side. "It's been gutted since then, and I now use it for other purposes."

It was just as gloomy inside as out, the floors of solid stone, no windows save for slats high on the walls. Just a few of the stalls were still intact, and there was no ceiling, only high rafters and beams supporting the peaked and darkened roof.

After lighting a lantern, Neville led the way to an area some distance away where tall candles were burning. I couldn't tell what was contained within the ancient and decaying old building as most of it was cast in shadows.

When we stepped into the circle of candlelight, I saw Tarin, nude and bound up to a thick and heavy timber. The timber, severely angled, was propped against a wall, and Tarin was lying face up on it, her tender skin pressed directly to the wood.

The girl looked quite helpless. Her hands were drawn well up above her head with the wrists strapped together at a solid wooden peg embedded in the timber itself, and the guards, under the supervision of Ruth, were just finishing with restraining her feet. They'd pulled her legs up and behind the timber, making her bend at the knee, and now they were crossing her ankles X-wise to strap them together. Once tied, they used a longer piece of leather to fasten them up to another peg mounted up in back of the timber. Thus, she was hanging by her wrists, her feet up and off of the floor, her toes pointing upward.

When they were finished with strapping the girl into place, the two men stepped away from her, affording me a clear view of her. How desirable she appeared as she tested the fastenings, her flesh straining as she scraped herself against the rough wood, the buttocks worming about as she fought the stringency of the position they'd placed her in.

Neville was looking over some flagellation tools lying on a table, various whips, paddles, and rods, and he spoke to me in a confidential tone when I took myself away from the sight of Tarin and joined him.

"This girl is going to have be treated differently than Amanda," he said to me. "Amanda's really nothing more than a mischievous imp who's developed a dangerous ache between her legs. The one on that timber has become strong and proud as a result of being mistreated by her drunkard of a stepmother. It's admirable, but I'm going to have to induce obedience in her. I shudder to think what the people of Stonehurst might do with her should they convince themselves that she's the primary source of their troubles. You saw how they loved seeing her flogged in the pillory. Imagine what they might do if provoked to take justice into their own hands."

After selecting a rod of braided leather that had about a dozen slender and short thongs at the very end of it, he went to stand before the captive nude while the rest of us stepped back into the shadows.

Tarin looked so vulnerable. After all, the girl was nude and powerless before five fully clothed people, her pubis on forced display. She didn't turn her eyes from us, but she couldn't keep herself from a slight writhing of shame.

Olford ran the tips of the rod over the side of the girl's body, causing her to shiver with apprehension. Then he held the tool at his side and used his free hand to caress the inside of her thighs, letting his fingers trickle their way upward until he was cupping the shaven V of her sex, grinning as he began fondling her in earnest.

"You are now legally under my custody Tarin," he said to her, his tone businesslike. ¡This means that you are subject to my authority. During your stay here, you are to be fully obedient to the wishes of others. Is this clear to you?"

Tarin took a deep breath before speaking, reluctant to surrender. "Yes sir," she finally said, "I'm afraid it is."

"The way you answer doesn't imply your full cooperation," Neville said as one of his fingers caressed the inner folds of the nude pubis. "So it appears as though I'll have to illustrate what I'm trying to convey to you. Perhaps that will inspire you to a more enthusiastic embracing of your new way of life."

He stepped back a few feet and readied the whipping tool, and he must have made a frightening sight to the bound girl as he stood there in his high boots and long coat, the candlelight playing across his smiling face.

The tips of the rod went slashing over Tarin's breasts, not with terrific force but hard enough to cause very faint stripes to rise on the fragile skin. Five more times he burned the instrument across the perfect flesh, and each time the girl wrenched at her fastenings, her pubis thrusting itself upward.

As Neville stepped back another few inches, I saw that Tarin's sex had just the faintest glistening of moisture about it.

"Allow me to continue my demonstration of your new lot in life," he was saying, taking aim with the braided rod.

With an expert flick of the wrist, he snapped the thongs upwards over the girl's naked pubic mound, forcing a shriek from her full lips. "Why do you do this to me?" she wailed. "You know I'm innocent of any crime."

"You worked on the Sabbath and ran about naked in the outdoors while strangers watched," Neville replied while giving her several more licks. "That's why you find yourself in your present situation."

"I was ordered by my stepmother," she gasped as she endured the cruel leather discipline.

The girl was struggling now, and I could see that her punished breasts had become swollen even as her delicate pubis endured being punished. And I'll confess that the picture she made was one of an odd beauty. Her young flesh was aglow from the struggle it was engaged in, strained to its limit by the brutal posture of her bondage.

Neville ceased the whipping of her vulva and began walking away. "It seems that I'm not getting my message across to you, Tarin," he was saying, "so I'm forced to advance your indoctrination yet another step, and I'll warn you now that I won't be satisfied until I receive nothing but polite and agreeable answers from you, not this back talk of yours."

He nodded to Ruth, and, as if on cue, she began directing the two guards in the placing of Tarin into a fresh manner of restraint.

The two men, after releasing the girl from the leather straps and lifting her down from the timber, took her by the wrists and led her to stand in a place where a heavy iron chain hung out of from somewhere in the shadowy ceiling. The chain had a thick hook attached to its end.

"This girl will be placed into a hoisting," I heard Ruth saying to the guards. "I doubt she'll be quite so arrogant then."

How frail the nude Tarin appeared in the hands of two large, muscular men. With a short belt of supple leather, they buckled her wrists together out in front of her, then lifted her hands and ran the iron hook of the chain through a ring woven into the belt.

While Tarin was being fastened up, Ruth had gone over to a support post where a tremendous pulley-wheel was mounted. Chain was wound around the wheel, one end of it disappearing up into the beams of the roof, and once the girl's wrist bindings had been fixed to the hook, Ruth began turning the crank-handle of the pulley-wheel.

"I think that chain apparatus was once used to bring bales of hay up into a loft area that's no longer there," Neville said as I watched in fascination, realizing that the chain of the pulley-wheel and the one hooked up to Tarin's wrists were one and the same.

"And what happens to her next?" I asked.

"She'll be flogged again and remain in the bondage that they're placing her in now until I get some semblance of cooperation from her," was his reply. "I can't really expect abject compliance from a girl such as Tarin during her first week with me, but I at least expect to see that she's willing to make the effort."

The chain had now tightened to the point of raising the naked girl's hands well above her head, and still Ruth continued to turn the crank, pulling the chain up ever higher until Tarin's bare feet began to rise from the stone flooring.

"How do you like that, Miss Pretty," Ruth said when Tarin looked up toward her hands as if wondering what was going on.

Once the feet had been raised about two inches into the air, Ruth ceased to pull the girl up and further and notched the crank-handle into place.

Even though I felt sympathy for her, I couldn't help but view the girl as a living work of bondage art, an erotic painting with a nude as its subject come to life. Hanging as she was, her youthful contours stood out high relief to her surroundings, her tender flesh in sharp contrast to the stone and the heavy wooden beams of the old building, the drops of wetness on her vulva shining in the ghostly light of the tall candles.

Armed now with a short lash of oiled leather, Neville stood to one side of the victim while the rest of us stood back to view the proceedings. Even at his approach, the defenseless girl began to writhe yet again, causing her suspended body to sway in a small circle of rotation.

This time Tarin received a thorough and no-nonsense flog-ging. Neville used the lash on her buttocks only, not speaking to her at first, simply beating the vulnerable orbs until Tarin took up a frantic wrenching at her bindings. Her legs flailed, kicking at nothing and causing her sex to be still more exposed to view. One leg at a time would bend upward occasionally, the toes of the foot pulled out tight.

"Ahhhhh," came at last from her open mouth after she'd taken perhaps twenty strokes of the burning leather. And finally the girl broke down, pleading with Neville to take pity. "I've done noth-ing to deserve being treated in this way," she cried. "My bottom can endure no more of this horrid flogging. I beg you to stop."

This was apparently exactly what Olford had been waiting to hear. He stopped thrashing the girl and came to stand in front of her.

"That's more like it Tarin," he said to her with a pleased smile. "Why you worked on the Sabbath or ran about naked makes no difference to me. The fact remains that you did exactly those things, and I want you to admit it right now and with no qualifications. If you choose not to, there are five of us here to flog you, so we can easily keep this up all day. Do what you think best."

She looked briefly at the lash in Olford's hand and then admitted to her crimes, this time saying nothing of her stepmother's commands.

But Neville wanted still more from his captive nude. He told the girl that he was prepared to leave her hanging where she was for the rest of the day if she didn't obey his next command.

"And I'll be leaving you in the custody of the two gentlemen who've been kind enough to assist with putting you into restraint," he told her.

Tarin, already under a great deal of strain from dangling at the end of a chain, now looked over at the guards to see that both had great bulges in their trousers that betrayed what they were sure to do with her should they have her all to themselves. And it was easy to see that she knew she had no choice but to comply with Olford's wishes.

"I'll do as you say, sir," she murmured.

"Very well," he said, "you'll be released now but only so you can carry out my next command."

As Ruth and the guards began loosing the girl, Neville told her that if she didn't want to be placed right back into the same position, she would masturbate while lying on the floor.

A look of shock passed over Tarin's face, but she said nothing, the knowledge that she was now under Olford's control dawning on her fully.

Once she was free, Tarin lay herself slowly down onto the floor, shrinking back when the cold stones touched the tender skin that had been warmed with the lash. But she managed to do as she'd been told.

Thereafter followed the most abandoned display of sexual release one might ever see. I think I can safely say that Tarin was truly reluctant to masturbate before an audience, yet I think I'm equally safe in saying that her loins had been ignited during both of her floggings, the first in particular, and that the opportunity to satisfy herself by any means available came as a relief to her.

"She wants it," Ruth was saying, making her penchant for the feminine physique obvious. "All of these sluts do."

Tarin eased herself onto her back, her long tresses forming a blanket beneath her as she opened her slender thighs and slid the longest finger of her left hand up and down on the outside of her crevice.

Within moments, she seemed to drift off into a world of her own. Juice began to flow from her punished mound, and she slipped the finger into herself, slowly screwing it in and out. Then her lips parted, and a low groan of primitive satisfaction came from her mouth.

When she lifted her buttocks off of the floor, supporting her body with her feet and shoulders, pumping up and down to the rhythm of the finger, Neville walked over to stand next to her.

"Open your eyes and look at me Tarin," he said to her. "I want you to thank me for permitting you to masturbate yourself."

She did as he'd said, staring up at him, but her eyes had a faraway look about them.

"Thank you, Mr. Olford," she moaned. "This is so much better than being beaten."

"Have you learned that you're to obey me?"

"Yes sir, I have."

"Very well, then you may have your climax now," he told her and walked away.

His words triggered something in that naked girl, and she went into an immediate flurry of orgasms that tossed her about on the harsh flooring. But hard stone didn't seem to bother her at all. She squirmed herself about with no regard for comfort, abandoning her body to the pleasure flowing through it.

And at a nod from Olford, Ruth went to Tarin's side, a birch rod in her hand, and began flogging at the bare girl. The rod striped all over Tarin's body as she writhed about, but she didn't seem to care. Orgasm had become paramount to her.

Late that night, Olford and I had a most entertaining conversation with our customary evening drink, he telling me that he was going to have to be traveling to other districts to advise his fellow magistrates on the unusual cases they were now having to deal with.

"This hysteria is reaching epidemic proportions," he told me, "and some officials are simply at a loss as to how to handle the problem. Apparently, the way I've gone about it is admired and they want my help in handling the more delicate aspects of some of these matters."

He went on to say that he, in turn, would have to rely on me to administer the discipline so much needed by both Amanda and Tarin.

"As I mentioned this morning, Amanda's no real problem," he said. "Most of her mischief doesn't amount to much more than high jinks, but she doesn't understand what dangerous times we're in the midst of. The essential reason she's here is because of her habit of flirting with our village's more respectable citizens, and I'm speaking of the most flagrant sort of coquettery. She has a way of placing herself in danger. I suppose you've noticed that she'll sometimes almost invite a birching and then find herself in over her head."

At that point, I couldn't help but relate my recent encounter with the girl, telling him of what had transpired while I'd had her hitched up to the bedpost.

Olford thought it amusing. "That makes my point exactly, and that's just what the lively young Amanda needs," he laughed. "You'd be doing me a favor if you'd flog some sense into her and fuck the harlotry out of her at every opportunity. Better you and I doing it than some vicious band of villagers."

He then went into the subject of Tarin. He thought her situation to be far more dangerous than Amanda's.

"The women of Stonehurst are jealous of her because of the proud way the girl has of carrying herself," he said. "I can't help but admire her spirit, but for her own safety we'll have to humble her, and this, of course, can only be accomplished through flogging and sex-torture as you saw clearly this morning."

At this point, knowing how he used to savor birching the naughtier bottoms of the Rosewood girls, I simply had to ask if the prospect of taming his newest ward was an altogether unpleasant one.

Before he spoke, he smiled for a moment and stroked his goatee. " I see no harm in enjoying one's duties," was his reply.

_____

In closing, let me say, that I'm learning much concerning the value of punishing a girl into a better way of life, and I think we should review the policies now in effect at Rosewood. Only occasionally do we have a student remove all of her clothing for punishment, and, of course, we never make use of bondage. But I've discovered that a girl's birching is far more effective when she's forced to take it fully nude rather simply baring her buttocks. Also, it seems that rendering a girl helpless through bondage also aids in giving her a sense of humility. Perhaps if we make it a policy to have our students strip for their floggings and bind them up as well, we could do them far more good without increasing the number of strokes they're obligated to endure. Please give these matters your consideration

I'll now be able to write more often as Neville has used his authority to have the post rider come by this way daily.

I hope the book arrives to you safely and soon.

Please wish me good fortune in my new role as disciplinarian to Amanda Smith and Tarin Blake, and I'll certainly let you know how I do with each of them.

My best to you.

Derek H.

Letter 6 PRIVATE

Dear Bertrand,

I'm at my desk in the library as I write to you, my work still progressing at a much faster clip than I'd imagined. For a change, there's a warm sun shining in clear skies today, and I've just returned from the window where I've been watching Amanda and Tarin frolic about in the grass. They appeared quite carefree, scampering about barefoot in a game of catch-the-kitty, and their youthful laughter gave me a sense of invigoration.

Neville is has gone off to the village, presiding over one of his many administrative duties.

Tarin's presence has thus far been most stimulating. She's a very polite young lady, bright and very knowledgeable for a girl of her age though I've learned that she's had little formal schooling.

Several fascinating events have occurred since I last wrote to you, and I'll relate herein what happened in the hope that you can make use of the information the next time you're called upon to discipline one of our students. With all of the firsthand experience I've been garnering, I think I should probably begin keeping notes on the subjects of flagellation and its related practices for use upon my return to the academy.

At any rate, it was only two days after Tarin's first session of discipline that I was called upon to take Amanda to task. It was early in the afternoon, but I hadn't yet seen her that day as it had been Tarin serving me. I'd heard a commotion at one time, but, as you well know, I easily lose touch with my surroundings when engrossed in work, so I was a little surprised when I looked to up find Ruth standing there with a scowl on her face. According to her, there'd been a problem with Amanda. The girl had been rattling about the house, playing with Neville's big Russian Wolfhound and making a general disturbance.

I wasn't really interested in all of the trifling details. Rather, I knew that this was a chance to give Amanda a legitimate dose of the sort of discipline that might well keep her out of danger whenever Neville decides to set her free.

"It will be a pleasure," Ruth said, brightening, when I told her that I'd leave it up to her as to how Amanda should be restrained for her punishment. "She'll be ready within ten minutes. Just come out to that building where the new girl was whipped."

After entering the old stone structure by the same door that Neville and I had come in by, lantern in hand, I did some exploring of the vast building, but I still couldn't quite make out exactly what might be contained within its walls. I saw a few strange-looking tables and benches, a huge wheel constructed of heavy planks with straps attached to it, and a tall ladder, all semi-hidden in the shadows.

Finally, I saw a flickering light coming from a far corner, the light of large candles mounted in wall sconces. That's where I found Ruth, and that's where Amanda had been fixed into a most rigid and unusual pose.

The first thing I noticed as I drew near was Amanda's dress lying in a heap on the floor. The girl herself was almost naked save for a scrap of soiled linen that been tied round her hips, covering scant portions of her buttocks and pubis.

72

She'd been seated atop a thick wooden post that was about a foot across and mounted into the floor, her legs straddling each side of it. Iron rings were set into the post—probably used for the tethering of animals at one time—and her ankles were tied to two of the rings at each side of it with leather straps, this position cocking her knees forward and holding her feet well off the floor. Additionally, her wrists were tied into a strap that hung from a high ceiling beam, holding her hands well above her.

"A most interesting feature has been added to this hitching post," Ruth told me as she beckoned for me to join her in front of Amanda. "Let me show you."

When she untied the scrap of cloth at Amanda's hips and snatched it away, I saw that a wooden phallus was stuck up inside of the helpless girl's sex, the phallus being nailed down to the top of the post and covered with an oiled sheath of leather.

"That little device makes for a most interesting flogging," Ruth was saying to me as I stared at the thing buried in Amanda's most tender spot.

I thanked the woman, asking if she'd come back in about a half hour to fetch the girl, and Ruth left, a little disappointed, I think. She'd probably been hoping to participate in Amanda's punishment or to at least watch while the girl was punished.

As soon as the woman left, I turned toward Amanda to see that she was looking at me with one of her mischievous smiles. It seemed that she didn't find the strict bondage to be all that bothersome, or perhaps the phallus up inside of her vulva was creating an effect that she found pleasant.

"And just what is that prankish smile all about, young lady?" I said, standing close to her and looking into her eyes. "You're here to be flogged, you know."

She giggled, not answering my question. "Do I look pretty perched up like this, Mr. Hunter?" she asked.

I placed my hands on her upper arms and rubbed them gently, and, looking downward, I saw that she was moving her pubis almost imperceptibly back and forth at the phallus, stimulating herself. "You're very pretty, dear girl, perched up or not," I told her, "but you've made a nuisance of yourself, so now your unruly bottom is going to have to take a thrashing."

Again, she didn't seem to really hear me. "Do I look pretty without clothing?" she asked.

"That's enough of that, Amanda," I said to her, my voice probably angry, as I went to a table where a few rods of birch and other flogging devices were laid out ready for use. "If you continue with this impudence, your behind will be birched all the more."

"I don't mind," she said, giggling now. "Horrid as the birch might be, it sometimes make me feel quite luscious inside."

As I walked back toward her, rod in hand, I saw that she'd begun pushing her sex at the leather-covered shaft in a most noticeable manner, and her smile had now become one of an undisguised arousal.

"You're just asking for a more severe punishment," I said as I took up a stance at one side of her. "It's just that sort of behavior that's keeping you captive here. If you acted that way down in the village, the ladies of Stonehurst would be sure to have you hauled right back into the courtroom, and who knows what might befall you there. Your family owes the court a huge fine, you know, and the people hereabouts don't like girls who act as you do."

"I don't care about them," she gasped, her smile disappearing and being replaced by an expression of need. "Birch my bottom sir. I want it. Birch me good."

"I'm afraid you've put me in the position of having to teach you a lesson, Amanda," I said to her. "Prepare yourself for a more than sound flogging."

"But that's what I want," she was bold enough to say. "Beat me hard. You know that this thing inside of me is making me want to move myself on it."

I made up my mind then and there to give Amanda something to remember. The idea of flogging the brazen nymph into

74

submission wasn't without its allure, but I also have concern for her. I've developed a certain affection for the girl, and I'd hate to see her in serious trouble simply because she behaves like a streetwalker at times.

When I began swinging the rod across her nude behind in strokes meant to burn, she actually arched herself out toward it as if she was anxious to meet the instrument. And when the birch connected with the bare flesh, she wagged her hips from side to side, licking her lips and squealing in delight.

"That burns so," she blurted out, "but I don't care because it's making my puss burn as well!"

The situation here was becoming both interesting and difficult at once. You know, Bertrand, that I don't mind a girl taking some pleasure from her punishment as long she's able to learn from the more painful aspects of it, but Amanda's behavior was making it necessary for me to flog her an extra measure.

With swift and forceful strokes, I turned the buttocks a healthy pinkish color, drawing a good dozen stripes over them, and this turned the nude girl's squeals to those more of suffering, but she was still managing to drive herself at the prong.

I told her that she might have gotten off with a light birching, but now she'd given me no choice but to take the lash to her. Even as I spoke, I was setting the rod aside and picking up a thin whipping lash of oiled leather, winding one end of around my hand in preparation to trounce her further.

Her eyes widened, and she suddenly grew very still. "Please, Mr. Hunter, not with that," she said, a tremor in her voice. "Please don't use the whipping lash on me."

Now I was getting the desired result. "You brought this on yourself with your brazen conduct, Amanda," I said to her. "Now you're going to take the consequences, and I'm hoping you'll learn from the experience."

Then I made the sound of leather on naked flesh crackle through the air and caused Amanda to fight against the bindings that held her so immobile. I first gave her six licks across her already-punished buttocks. Then I drew a red pattern of stripes over her back, searing the delicate skin and paying no attention to her shrieks.

She was heated through by the time I took up a stance in front of her, snapping the end of the lash dangerously close to her heaving breasts, getting ready to blaze it over the nipples.

"You're not going to use that thing on my breasts, are you?" the frightened girl asked. Oddly, her nipples were becoming tight and stiff in full erection.

"Why, yes, I am," I said to her. "In fact, I'm going to give your nipples some special treatment. But I thought you enjoyed punishment at times. Aren't you enjoying yourself now?"

"No, sir," she whimpered. "I was only being sassy when I said that. I didn't think you'd be so hard on me. Please don't use that awful lash on me any longer."

Somehow, I began taking pride in what I was accomplishing with this girl. Within a few short minutes, I'd brought her from acting like an impudent hussy to pleading with me for mercy. And then I knew, probably from long experience with disciplining the Rosewood students, that it was time to drive home a valuable lesson to the girl.

I flicked the end of the lash through the air, first letting it strike her left nipple, then the right, and Amanda cried out with anguish at the pain.

"How would you like to be breast-flogged in the public pillory?" I asked her.

Her breath was coming quickly. "I wouldn't, sir," she managed to say.

"Then you'll cease your unladylike behavior, won't you?"

"Oh, yes sir! I'll do whatever you say."

I then went on to lecture her further on the dangers of her actions, and I felt as if I was getting through to her. She'd stopped pushing her sex at the phallus and now listened to me carefully.

Once I saw that she was cooperating with the disciplinary procedure, I gave her the respite that she was in need of.

"You may now thrust yourself at the phallus again, Amanda," I told her as I laid the lash down and lifted the birch. "I'm going to use this rod lightly on your buttocks until you spend yourself all over the shaft."

She didn't have to speak. The gleam in her eyes and the way she smiled at me demonstrated how grateful she was for this privilege.

I suppose that the rump-thrashing I then administered couldn't really be called a light one, but it seemed to be just what the girl needed to achieve what she was seeking. As I birched the rounded globes, they were wagging back and forth, the fair skin pulsating as its color was heightened by the rod. Her toes twisted themselves in tiny circles as she tilted her breasts and face upward, her eyes half-closed.

And as she hammered herself at the phallus, a low moaning came from within her while liquid oozed freely from the fresh peach between her thighs.

I didn't have to flog her long at all. Within a minute, the girl had gone into orgasm, her movement at the shaft growing violent as she wrenched at her bindings.

"Is that what you wanted, Amanda?" I asked, not being able to resist chuckling at her antics.

"Yes sir," she groaned, "and I feel so blissful inside. Thank you!"

I flogged her straight through the experience, letting the birch punish right to the very end.

Amanda was just catching her breath when Ruth returned.

"This girl took her punishment well, and she can be released now" I said to her. "Let her have a bath and then she may rest in her bed chamber for the rest of the day."

As I strode from the circle of candlelight, I heard Amanda's voice. "I thank you, Mr. Hunter!" she called out, and that somehow gave me the feeling that I'd truly been of help to her.

———————

During the dinner hour that evening, Olford told me of a rather unsettling occurrence that had taken place in the province directly adjacent to this one. He'd heard of girls becoming runaways because they were under false accusations, escaping into the forests in an effort to escape harsh and unjust punishment.

"When captured, which they usually are, they find themselves in still deeper trouble," he said, "and yet these wayward girls are becoming more numerous each day, and they're a problem. Most of them keep themselves fed by stealing or, in some cases, even whoring."

"I believe I've met one of them," I told him and then went on to relate my encounter with the almost-naked girl who'd offered her body for a few spare coins.

He nodded as if already knowing of such vagrants and then went on to tell me of what had happened just over in the next province. It seemed that the constables had tracked down one of these runaways, finding her just in the nick of time. The girl had been held captive unlawfully by a group of three irate women for several days. These women, all of them spinsters, had discovered the girl hiding in a remote section of an estate belonging to one of them. They'd overpowered her and dragged her back to the main house, and there they'd taken her clothing and locked her in the attic, trussed and gagged.

"They took justice into their own hands, and I find it deplorable," was Neville's opinion of the incident. "We've enough problems without private citizens setting up their own courts."

When the constables located the girl, they'd found her in not the best condition. The three old maids had been purging her of evil with their own methods, subjecting her to constant flagellation and keeping her in strenuous bondage.

"When the constables arrived, these women had the poor girl fastened up to a tree," Neville told me. "She was hanging by her ankles, which is an excellent position for bringing a girl to humility, but I shudder to think what they were planning on doing with her next."

He went on to say that this was just the sort of thing that he was trying to keep girls like Amanda and Tarin away from, and what he said made sense.

In the late evening hours, I went to Amanda's room, finding her curled up next to some pillows that were propped at the head of the bed. She was nude, but as I walked toward her, she drew a dark blue robe modestly up in front herself even though it afforded little covering.

"Good evening, Amanda," I said to her as I sat near her on the wide bed. "I hope you're well after the rigors of a flogging."

She gave me the faintest of smiles. "I'm fine, Mr. Hunter," she said, her voice ever so soft. "I apologize for the way I behaved. It's no wonder you thrashed me as you did. I deserved it in the worst way."

"No, it's not what you deserved," I said to her, putting about an arm around her bare shoulders, "it's what you needed, and I'm sorry to say that you're probably going to need more of the same before Neville Olford releases you from his custody."

Then I told her the incident of the runaway girl, and Amanda's eyes grew wide with fear.

"Yes, that's the sort of times you're living in," I said to her, my tone quite flat. "You'll learn to behave or pay the penalty."

I was certain I'd made my point, and as I left the room, I glanced back to see that Amanda was staring after me, her face still wearing that same look of fright.

I'll close this letter now, Bertrand, in order to be at the gate when the post rider comes by, but I'll write very soon, tomorrow if time permits. I hope you're either destroying these letters or keeping them under lock and key. I write in the strictest confidence, knowing that you're interested in the sort of thing that's

79

going around here, but these letters in the wrong hands wouldn't do much for our reputations as educators.

Sincerely,

Derek H.

Letter 7 PRIVATE

Dear Bertrand,

You'll probably receive this letter shortly after my last as I'm writing again just the day after. Unlike yesterday, the weather has returned to what seems to be normal for this bleak region, damp, chilly air and constant fog.

I write so soon because there is yet another incident I feel you'll find interesting, this one involving Tarin Blake.

If you'll remember, Neville is an accomplished musician, and in his spacious drawing room there is a piano, a tall harp, and several smaller instruments. In addition, he has a vast collection of sheet music, some of it quite old and valuable.

I was passing by this room the other day when I heard the faint notes of a piece I recognized as being from the Renaissance, although I couldn't identify the composer. Looking toward the direction of the sound, I saw Tarin engaged in playing a small, silver flute, her eyes closed, fingers so artfully poised on the instrument, her full lips pursed.

I couldn't but help stop to admire the lovely picture the girl made. She was kneeling on the bright and polished wooden floor, the short velvet dress riding high and exposing a hint of her buttocks, her little toes peeking from out from under the rounded, girlish flesh.

As quietly as possible, I walked closer, listening to the beautiful music that she was bringing forth from the silver flute.

When she'd finished the piece, she opened her eyes, surprised when she looked upward and saw me. "I didn't know you were there," she said. "Mr. Olford gave me permission to make use of this flute. I play, you know."

"And you play quite well," I told her. "Where did you learn?"

"I had teachers before my father married his present wife," she said, looking away for a moment. "I'm trained in both music and dance, ballet."

As we were speaking, Ruth entered the room, her sturdy shoes destroying the quiet and the Renaissance notes that still seemed to be floating through the air.

"Come with me," she said to Tarin. "Mr. Olford wants to see you. It seems you're overdue for a birching, Missy."

"I've done nothing to deserve that sort of treatment," Tarin answered. "Why must I come along with you?"

It was a dangerous thing for a girl in her position to say.

"You'll come along with me because I say so," Ruth replied in a clipped tone, "and if you're not about it in one second, I'll report your insubordination to Mr. Olford, and we'll see where that lands you."

Tarin did as she'd been told, but she did it slowly, and she took the time to put the flute back in its case before following Ruth from the room.

"Mr. Olford asks if you'd come to his study and watch while this girl takes her discipline," Ruth said to me as they left.

She didn't elaborate as to why I was needed, but a few minutes later, I walked into Neville's study, a large room with no curtains or drapes and very little furniture. Neville was standing by the fire and motioned for me to join him.

As I crossed over to where he stood, my gaze was on Tarin. The girl stood in the middle of the room without a stitch on, her nudity looking especially splendid in the midst of so much clear space. Her hands were at her sides, feet together, as if at military attention. In fact, she presented a soldiers's bravery. The girl knew full well that she was in for a birching, yet she held herself rigid, showing no trace of apprehension. If anything, it seemed that she was taking a certain pride in her breasts and the most private area of her physique, the shaven triangle nestled in her crotch area.

Standing by the fireplace, Neville and I were just out of the bare girl's hearing range, and he spoke to me in a confidential tone.

"I'm going to use a special approach with this girl," he said. "She experienced a flogging with the lash the other day, so she knows what lies in store should she disobey. However, I plan to keep her discipline light, much the way the Rosewood girls are treated, whipping her only if necessary, a discipline based more on shame than suffering."

I nodded in agreement, seeing no reason to be harsh with this girl.

"Actually, she's quite a gem," Neville was saying. "I've learned she's an excellent pianist and flautist and dances the ballet as well. It's my belief that she can be brought to obedience without doing damage to her fine spirit."

I found I was glad to hear this.

Then it was time for Tarin to undergo the subtle lessons of the rod. After picking up a long, thin switch, Neville strode toward the bare girl, telling her that he wanted her down on her hands and knees.

Tarin obeyed quickly, and I was surprised at how gracefully she assumed this awkward posture, nary a wobble or misstep. Once she was on all fours, Neville stood just before her and told the girl to put her knees together.

"And then you'll place your elbows on the floor, pulling them up against your knees," he was saying while she complied. "I want the palms of your hands flat on the floor. Then you'll rest your forehead on the tops of your hands."

Tarin somehow managed to contort herself into this demeaning pose with just a few lithe movements, a display of how easily her supple body could respond to the most difficult of commands, her long hair floating down and splaying itself out on the floor.

Tarin's behind was now displayed in a manner that seemed to fairly invite the birch. The rounded orbs were propped high, proffered for punishment, and with her head bowed as it was, she looked as if she was paying homage to Neville's shining boot.

But he now went to stand behind her, the rod poised to strike. "My chief concern is for your well-being," he was saying to her in a tone of genuine benevolence, "and I don't want you to have to endure floggings of undue severity."

Then he gave the naked buttocks three quick stripes, not brutally but hard enough to cause the olive-hued flesh to glow.

"I demand obedience and modesty from you," he told her as he readied the rod to be used again. "Will you agree to behave in this way?"

"Yes sir," Tarin said, her voice clear and sure, "I will."

"I'm glad to hear that," Neville went on. "If you keep your word, the rod is the only instrument your buttocks will have to taste while you're living here. And they'll taste it regularly but only to enhance your obedience."

"Thank you, Mr. Olford," the girl answered.

"But should you fail to keep your word, I'll have you whipped severely with the lash," Olford told her, his tone now becoming stern.

"I understand, sir," Tarin answered.

"Very good. Now brace yourself to be switched."

I stood quietly by as Tarin took her disciplinary birching, and I'll admit that it was a most arousing sight. With slow, well-paced strokes, Neville turned the tawny flesh of the nude hindquarters to a light reddish color. He brought the rod back and forth across her in clean, expert stripes that seemed to cause just enough anguish to induce a sense of humility into the kneeling girl.

Tarin seemed to weather her birching fairly well. She managed to hold the taxing pose even though her buttocks were trembling under the smarting of the rod.

Eventually, after she'd endured about two dozen licks, I heard her breath coming out in gasps while her buttocks began a slight swaying as if trying to avoid the rod. Her fingers were clutching at the wood of the flooring while the little feet rubbed at each other, the toes curling in silent agony, yet still she remained in place.

I'm certain that Olford gave the girl at least three dozen stripes before he was done with her.

"Now you will thank me for giving you birch discipline only rather than having you leather-lashed," Neville said to her when he'd finished.

"Thank you, Mr. Olford," she managed to say between her rapid breaths.

"You've done well, Tarin," he told her. "You may stand."

Once the girl was up off of the floor, Neville told her to stand before his desk, again at almost military attention, still nude, hands at her sides, feet together. Then he sat down behind the desk and began telling her of his plans for her.

"I wish to thank you, sir," Tarin said to him at the end of a lengthy speech in which he told her that even while strict corporal discipline would continue, she could continue her music studies whilst under his guardianship. And it wasn't difficult to tell that she was truly grateful.

I'd taken a seat in a wingback chair, and as I watched Tarin being essentially lectured to, I marveled at her proud, youthful beauty. Even standing as she was, naked, her buttocks red from the flogging they'd been subjected to, her sex shaven to the bare skin and completely unconcealed from view, she was still somehow able to maintain a certain dignity.

When Olford told her that she could cover herself and go back to whatever she'd been doing, she gathered her dress from

84

the floor and left the room silently.

"Tarin's going to be somewhat of a challenge, isn't she?" I said to Olford once were alone.

He laughed, agreeing that she did indeed present a challenge, but he felt that the challenge was a pleasant one.

Even though things are highly interesting here at Olford's home, I find myself still thinking wistfully of the shady walkways and quiet study rooms of the academy, and, in some ways, I look forward to the end of my sabbatical leave and returning the hallowed halls of Rosewood.

My best regards to all

Most Sincerely,

Derek H.

Letter 8 PRIVATE

Dear Bertrand,

At this writing, Neville has been away for several days, giving aid and advice on legal affairs in other villages. Apparently our former colleague has quite a bit of finesse with the handling of the unusual situation here in these hinterlands. His absence has left me busier than usual, but I'm not complaining as the duties I'm performing are fascinating to say the least. My research is way ahead of schedule, so I've been well able to afford the time.

My chief daily duty has been the overseeing of both Tarin and Amanda, simply keeping watch on their deportment and administering whatever corrective measures might be called for.

Tarin's behavior has been exemplary. I've given her only two light birchings, but these were formal sessions of discipline already prescribed for her by Olford before his departure. Unfortunately, it seems that she's going to endure far more trying rigors at the hands of the church.

There have been times when I've had to smile at the way Amanda conducts herself. Try as she might, she simply can't seem to resist a pixie-like mischief, flirting and making a display of her girlish charms. She knows the consequences of such actions, but the girl can't seem to stop herself. Of course, I'm dealing with her firmly, and, again, I'll give the details below.

On the day of Neville's departure, I drove him to the village in the one-horse carriage. From there, he would proceed by coach.

When we were still about a half mile from Stonehurst, the forest at one side of the road ended abruptly, a church building of crumbling stone standing in the wide and weed-choked clearing. Then, to my astonishment, I saw that there was a partially naked girl being held there. She was seated on a solid block of granite that looked as if it had been the base pedestal for a statue at one time. The pedestal was round, perhaps a foot across, high enough to keep the girl's feet just off the ground.

Her only covering was a piece of white cloth wound round her hips and tied through her crotch, and her youthful body was a fine specimen of feminine comeliness, jutting breasts and firm of flesh, a mass of strawberry-tinted hair falling about the bare shoulders.

"Let's drive in there," Neville said when the girl caught his eye. "The church has become more public with its penance rituals lately, and I'd like to see just what's going on. In some ways, I feel like they're taking on too much authority, but I also feel as if they're saving the justice system a lot of trouble by putting a stop to the behavior of a least a few of these girls."

As we drew into the churchyard, I saw that the girl had been restrained in irons. Her wrists were behind her back, held together with a short length of chain that was fixed in place with a rusted and cumbersome padlock. Likewise, her ankles were shackled to one another but with a much longer piece of the heavy chain, the free end of it pounded into the dirt with a thick, wooden stake.

"They seem to have left her quite helpless for penance," Olford was remarking as we alighted from the carriage, "and that quirt must be what they're using to flog her."

He was pointing toward a short wooden post several yards away from the granite pedestal. Hanging on the post was a long, thin switch of woven leather, the quirt.

Neville was tilting the brim of his wide-brimmed hat back from his eyes and drawing his dark cape closer as we walked toward the chained girl. He seemed highly interested in this situation.

He was formal in introducing himself to the girl as Chief Magistrate of Stonehurst, then introducing me, acting just as if we were at a polite social function.

The girl gave her name as Molly Brandon, blushing and looking downward.

As Neville spoke with her, asking how severe a penance she was serving, I looked over toward the church building to see a man of the cloth approaching, dressed in black suit and white collar, introducing himself as Reverend Hornsley when he was close enough to be heard.

"Good afternoon, gentlemen," he said. "Ah, Magistrate Olford, how good of you to come by. Are you here to have a go at this girl to prevent her committing the vile acts harbored within her thoughts."

We had no knowledge of what he was talking about, but he seemed more than eager to explain. Just that morning, Molly had made a private confession to him as to the lewd sexual thoughts that had invaded her mind lately, and now she'd been sentenced to this penance. She was to remain chained and on the block for a period of five hours, and, during that time, anyone passing by who might want to use the quirt on her back and buttocks would be free to do so.

"And, believe me, gentlemen, she's had some quite extraordinary thoughts," he said, a note of excitement in his voice, "but once she's done here, I'll hold a private vigil with her, just her and me. After that, she should be cured."

It didn't take great deductive powers to tell that he was looking forward greatly to engaging in private vigil with a chained and almost naked girl.

"And if she's not cured?" Neville asked him.

"Then she knows where to come," he replied. "I'm always here to help these unfortunate girls."

A wagon with a farmer and his wife had drawn up while he was speaking. The woman, wearing a dour look about her, was the first to climb down.

"Mr. and Mrs. Still," Neville confided to me as Hornsley greeted them. "The woman's a religious fanatic and quite adamant when it comes to the severe punishment of any girl who's even remotely suspected of harboring evil within her."

"I heard the talk of this girl being held in penance and felt it my duty to come by and lend a hand," she said. "I've known Molly for years. The little wretch used to steal from my garden when she was only five so I'm not surprised one bit that she's become infected with this wickedness."

Neville and I stepped to one side as Hornsley handed her the quirt and explained the conditions and requirements of Molly's penance.

"This girl must accept the quirt over her back and buttocks from whoever might care to use it on her," he said to the woman. "You may give her as many strokes as you choose, bearing in mind that she came to penance voluntarily. I also implore you not to give her any permanent markings nor to flog her to a point where she should faint. She must remain conscious during her entire penance."

I suppose Mrs. Still was listening, but it was hard to tell with the way she was concentrating on Molly. She was licking her lower lip, obviously relishing the prospect of flogging the defenseless girl on the granite block.

"You may remove the cloth if you choose," Hornsley told her as she stared into Molly's eyes.

"And that I shall," she answered and ripped the white cloth away from her victim. "This whore is probably used to being nude before strangers, and I'll punish her as such."

Molly's blushing grew more colorful once she was sitting before us with absolutely nothing on, her little triangle of strawberry pubic down exposed, and she began trembling as the farmer's wife took up a stance behind her.

"Not so smart now are you, Miss Molly," she said with a laugh, running the quirt over the now-denuded buttocks. "You won't steal from me again, will you, you naked slut?"

"Please, ma'am," Molly replied, whining as her fear grew, "I was only a child. I hardly remember the incident you speak of."

With a sharp hissing sound, the angry woman brought the quirt over the naked flesh of the buttocks. "You deserve this penance for your other loathsome acts as well as that one," she laughed. "I know a whore when I see one."

Then she drew the quirt once again and began whipping at poor Molly with a pure vehemence, fire in her eyes, a thin smile of revenge on her lips, making it clear that she was carrying a grudge amounting to far more than a few stolen vegetables.

"Ahhh," came from the naked girl's lips each time the hot leather striped over her body.

She was twisting in the fetters that held her and causing the heavy chains to make clanking sounds. Her naked feet swung in the air as her ankles slammed at the chain around them, and as she fought the iron restraint, I saw her buttocks grinding at the stone block, the rough granite biting into her flesh.

"Does your bare skin sting?" Mrs. Still asked. She was smiling, taking delight in the girl's pain.

"Ever so much," the girl replied. "Please take pity. I'll never do it again."

"But I must help you in your penance," Mrs. Still told her. "You need this flogging. That's what you're here for."

"She's right, Molly," Reverend Hornsley was saying as he stepped in front of the girl, lifting her chin with the tips of his fingers and looking into her eyes. "Repent and confess, my dear."

There followed a twisted and depraved scene, Mrs. Still flogging Molly's back and buttocks with a cruel fervor while the good reverend made the girl repeat what she'd told him in private confession.

"I dreamed of men inserting themselves into me," Molly whimpered, "and I am so ashamed. Forgive me."

"She's nothing but a whore, for sure," Mr. Still said to Neville and me, "and we'll have no prosperity until each and every one of them has confessed and been scourged by the whip."

Olford nodded to the men but said nothing as he tapped my shoulder as a signal that we should be on our way.

As we drove from the churchyard, I could still hear the quirt singing over the naked flesh of a sobbing Molly.

Arriving in Stonehurst, we went to one of the less raucous taverns for some bread, cheese, and beer. While there, Neville went over a few things I should remember in his absence.

"You'll have some sport with Amanda," he said with a chuckle. "Keeping her in line usually isn't much more of a problem than what you deal with at Rosewood. Tarin's the one I worry about."

He then went on to tell me that I'd have to take Tarin to Vicar Dowling for absolution. "Sorry to put the burden on you," Olford said, "but her stepmother's a religious zealot of the worst sort, and she's been going about the village, probably while full of rum, and telling everyone that Tarin needs to do penance for her crimes. The townspeople seem to agree, so it's probably best that they're accommodated."

I must say, Bertrand, that the idea of putting Tarin into the hands of Vicar Dowling didn't sit exactly comfortably, but I'll also admit that the thought of her doing naked penance had an arousing effect on me, and I found that, in a roundabout way, I looked forward to escorting the girl to whatever ritual she might have to undergo.

After seeing Neville off, I spent some time knocking about Stonehurst, and I tell you that the mood of these people is an ugly one. Everywhere I heard muttered talk of the seeking out of the girls guilty of profane doings.

When I passed by the square, I couldn't resist stopping to gaze at the pillory posts where I'd seen Tarin so enticingly strung up for flogging, and the thought crossed my mind that she was even then back at Olford's place, and that I had full authority over her. I could do whatever I thought should be done with her, and, believe me, it was a heady realization.

_____

The next two days were quiet ones, and I plunged into my work, finishing up a segment of it and bringing a certain phase of the project to a close.

Feeling the need for a little reading outside my field, I picked up a volume that Neville had recommended entitled, "Disciplinary Rewards, a Guide to Bestowing Pleasure and Punishment." I suppose the pen-and-ink illustrations were titillating me somewhat when Amanda came into the library, asking if I was ready for my tea, and I couldn't help but pause to admire how her dress, however long it might be, clung so endearingly to her spritely figure.

Naturally, Amanda noticed my gaze and immediately began showing herself off by bending and putting another log onto the fire, swaying her slender hips while doing it. And as she stirred the coals, one of her little feet raised from under her dress and poised itself in the air, the bare toes stretched into a tight point.

Perhaps it was because of the drawings I'd been perusing— depictions of females in highly unusual positions of restraint—

that I found myself becoming caught up in the desire to take control of Amanda and possess her both. And she was certainly putting herself in the position of deserving the birch with her exhibitionism.

"Will there be anything else before I fetch your tea, Mr. Hunter?" she said when she put the poker down and turned from the fire. Her tone was innocence itself as if she hadn't been aware of the display she'd just made of her feminine charms.

I told her that tea could wait as I rose and went to sit down on a dark and comfortable wingback chair with an equally dark hassock before it. Once seated, I indicated that she was to approach me.

For once, Amanda was a bit slow in complying. She walked slowly across the room with a look of apprehension on her face as if she was wondering what she'd gotten herself into this time.

"Now then, Amanda," I said to her in the patient tone that I often use with the girls at our academy, "I want you to hike your dress up to just beneath your arms."

Silently, she obeyed, lifting her one garment by the hem and revealing her fair and creamy body an inch at a time. Somehow, she looked more appealing to me at that moment than ever before. She was just standing there without saying a word, her shaven vulva uncovered, the pert breasts so bare and pretty.

Then I told her to lie across the hassock, face down. Yes, Bertrand, I'd made up my to give her a good schoolgirl spanking!

Once she was in place, I reached into the drawer of the chairside table, already knowing that in there was a foot long ruler made of thick wood. And, of course, I showed it to Amanda, telling her that her buttocks were about to be thoroughly tanned. She gave a start, but I held her down firmly by the small of her back.

"You're not going anywhere," I told her, not being able to hold back a chuckle. "You're staying right where you are until I'm finished with you, and that won't be until your precious rump is the color of ripe cherries."

Before starting in on her, I set the ruler aside, and, while still holding the girl in place, I placed my free hand directly onto the rounded surface of her flawless bottom and began simply feeling it, delighting in the firm, warm flesh.

As I caressed the buttocks, teasing them with a few light pinches and tickles, Amanda wormed herself into my hand, arching herself upward.

"You must like having someone feel you," I said to her.

"I'm not sure, but you do it so nicely, Mr. Hunter," the almost-bare girl replied.

"Well, let's see if you like the way I paddle a naughty behind such as yours," I said. "It's time for your spanking."

With ruler in hand, I started in on the walloping of those bare globes of girl-flesh, systematically striking them with even, well-paced strokes that brought immediate squeals from my spanking subject.

"Oh, goodness," she cried out as the first red mark appeared, "that makes me feel as if someone is holding a flame to my bottom!"

She'd begun squirming about on the hassock, and I couldn't help but laugh at her antics. "That's the whole point of this procedure," I told her. "Hot bottoms are good for naughty girls."

As her squirming became more animated, her hands and feet flailing about, the dress began to fly around, getting in the way.

Putting the ruler down, I began unbuttoning the back of the dress. "If you want to twist around so, my girl, you can just take the rest of your spanking in the full nude," I told her.

Once I'd stripped her to nothing, Amanda seemed a little more subdued, but then, as girls her age will do, she began to revel in the freedom of complete nudity, squealing and bouncing at the hassock as I spanked her adorable little rump. And spank it I did! After I'd given her about two dozen stripes, I put the ruler down and used my hand instead. I wanted to feel the response of her flesh as it was being punished.

Amanda seemed to prefer my hand to the ruler. She wiggled each time I touched her, her squeals becoming mixed with a nervous giggling. And now her feet kicked more slowly, gently swishing through the air, and her fingers rested themselves on the floor, a sigh coming from her lips.

Stopping for a moment, I fondled the girl, learning just how warm the throbbing buttocks had become to the touch, and as I continued my physical exploration of her, I reached between her thighs, and she parted them, giving me easy access to her shaven sex. This intimate portion of her body was also warm, pulsating with the cadence of arousal, and it was moist as well, fresh juices coursing from within.

"Being spanked seems to agree with you, Amanda," I said to her as I groped at her sex. "Your puss is positively sopping."

"It's not the spanking, sir," she whimpered. "It's being so close with you. After all, I'm without a stitch of clothing, and I know full well that you can do as you please with me since I'm nothing more than a ward of the court. I have no rights in this house, and I can't help but wonder what you'll do with me next."

"And that excites your sex?" I asked.

She was hesitant in her reply. "Well," she answered slowly, "perhaps it does. It feels wet. Is it wet to your fingers?"

"Yes, it is, and I'll just wager that it's aching inside and that you'd just love to have something in there to take that ache away, wouldn't you?"

"You're correct, sir," she whispered. "Is that what happens to me now. Are you going to put something in there?"

I'd risen from the chair and loosened my trousers even as she was speaking, and as I prepared to enter her sex from behind, I asked, in a crude way, I'll admit, if she was ready to have me screw my cock into her.

Even though Amanda was no longer being spanked, she was still wiggling at the hassock. "Yes, sir, I am," she gasped. "I certainly am."

"How convenient because that's just what's going to happen to you next," I said as I got on top of her, my member going between her thighs on its way to her pubis.

The girl was eager, flagrantly spreading her sex and hunching her rump upward as I entered into the narrow crevice of her mound. Then, after getting a solid hold on her shoulders, I drove into her as far as possible, cramming her little container full.

As I began a steady stroking, Amanda's hands again started to wave about, and I could hear her feet hammering themselves at the floor as her hips wiggled beneath me.

"That seems to make you excited," I said to her.

"It makes me feel as if I'm pleasing someone," she moaned. "Am I pleasing to you?"

"Very much, my spanking girl."

Then she began thrashing at the hassock and babbling away, making me believe that she'd already gone deep into orgasm.

"A spanking agrees with me so much more than the lash," she shrieked. "Look how good I'm being."

I didn't answer, waiting to see what she was leading up to.

"Maybe I should never be punished with the lash or the whip," she was saying. "A spanking seems to suit me so much better."

Then I saw what the little scamp was trying to accomplish. "Don't try and strike a bargain with me," I said to her with an especially fierce stroke of my manhood. "You'll receive what you need, and you'll take it without question. Do you understand me? I should have you taken to the outbuilding for a thorough whipping with the leather lash just as soon as I'm finished with you."

"Please forgive me, Mr. Hunter," she said, her voice shaking. "I understand. I'll do as I'm told. Please don't have me whipped."

"'You'll learn obedience, Amanda," I told her firmly as I continued making use of her delicious body. "One way or another, you'll obey."

"Yes, I will," she cried out as she orgasmed. "Oh, I will, and

95

I'll love it."

Then I released my passion into her as I stroked her torso and remembered the shade of red that I'd turned her buttocks.

I'll close this letter now as I see the post rider cresting the hill a mile away. If I seal this now, I'll be able to send it with him.

Again, please keep these documents under lock and key as I fear there are many who wouldn't understand the subjects that I've dealt with herein.

Take care, and give my best wishes and greetings to my students.

Most Sincerely,

Derek H.

Letter 9 PRIVATE

Dear Bertrand,

I would think by now the book I sent has reached you, and I hope you're finding it helpful with new ideas for the discipline of our fair, young Rosewood students. If I've learned nothing else in this bleak region, I've learned that there are different approaches to chastisement, each of them having different results on the subject undergoing the treatment. I'm quite enthused at how we might be of help to our Rosewood girls by simply employing the correct discipline in each individual situation. Punishment is more than a certain quota of pain given for a certain amount of misbehavior.

Neville should be arriving back tomorrow, and I'm sure he'll be pleased that both Amanda and Tarin are toeing the line well.

I took Tarin to do her penance yesterday. It was especially

intriguing to witness as I've gotten to know her some during this last week, and I've found that she's a very special girl.

Our first conversation of any length took place out in the woods of all places. I'd decided to get away from my work by taking a walk, and I found Tarin off in a clearing near the path I'd chosen. She was kneeling in the grass, playing the flute and, in her tiny dress of deep green, the girl looked every bit the barefoot wood nymph.

"Hello, Mr. Hunter," she said politely as I entered the clearing. "I hope you're well today."

I greeted her, admiring her aplomb. After all, I've seen her in some very unseemly positions, watched her being flogged, even looked on while she masturbated herself, and yet she was able to address me just as if we were casual acquaintances.

"I suppose you're here to discipline my bottom," she was saying as she put the little flute into its case. "Shall I remove my dress?"

I had to chuckle at that. "No, Tarin, I'm just out for a stroll," I told her as I sat myself near her in the grass.

"I'm happy to hear that," she said, leaning toward me and resting on one hand. "I'm still sore from my last birching."

After a bit of small talk, I started asking the girl about herself, and she was surprisingly open with me, seemingly eager to confide in someone.

Through careful questioning, I learned that her father had only remarried less than a year ago, and that's when Tarin's life had become one of tribulation. Her new stepmother turned out to be a cruel and jealous woman, flogging the girl whenever the whim struck, especially when drunk on rum, and treating her like nothing more than a servant.

The abuse went still further, but Tarin couldn't say anything about it to her father. "He's in very bad health," she told me, "and he thinks that the woman actually loves him. I simply can't tell him what she really is. And things have gotten worse since the crop failures. She has everyone believing her when she tells them that I'm full of evil, and I've had to do horrid things to keep her appeased."

Horrid was a mild word for it. Mrs. Blake seemed to think that it was great sport to hang the girl up naked out in their barn, tying her wrists to a beam with harness straps. Once she had Tarin hitched up, she'd flog her without mercy and sometimes leave her dangling there for hours at a time.

"That's why it's probably easier for me to endure the floggings I take here than it would be for most girls my age," she said, looking directly at me. "It hurts me terribly, but, in a strange way, I've grown accustomed to it. There are even times when I'm proud of being able to withstand such pain."

Tarin was shifting her position in the grass, the tiny dress flitting around her bare buttocks, her breasts jiggling delightfully beneath the thin fabric, and as I gazed at her, I found I could barely wait until my next opportunity to take the birch, or even the whip, to the fine sculpture of her tawny and youthful buttocks.

My second conversation with Tarin came the day after our woodland encounter. The entire house was very quiet, and I was passing by the drawing room when I heard the faint sound of humming and someone shuffling about. Approaching the entrance to the room as unobtrusively as possible, I peered in to see Tarin in there alone. She was nude and engaged in an almost silent dance of the ballet, her only accompaniment being her humming.

It was a sight of true beauty, and I stood watching while the girl performed. Twice, she stopped and went to look at some sheet music lying on top of the piano. She'd study it and then return to her dance, apparently humming the music she'd just consulted.

Never have I seen a performance of such splendor. Without benefit of costume, Tarin brought the dance to life, her spirit soaring through the halls of magnificence. With her hands outflung, she would tilt her breasts skyward, her slender body in an arch, a thing of frozen beauty for a moment and then go flying through the air.

Such a dancer's body, so lean, not a wasted ounce of flesh. And her control was such that she was able to do a sustained pirouette without benefit of ballet slippers, balancing herself on the very tips of her bare toes.

When I made a slight sound, Tarin saw that I was standing there, and she halted for a moment in mid step. Then she grabbed up her dress and held it in front of herself.

"I'm sorry, sir," she said with a tone of apology and maybe even a bit of fright. "I didn't know anyone was near."

"Bravo, my girl," I said, clapping my hands lightly. "There's no need to apologize. I enjoyed your performance greatly. You're quite a dancer."

After fully entering the room, I locked the doors behind me and went over to sit down on a large davenport near the far wall, motioning to Tarin that she was to sit with me.

The girl has become more compliant it seems. She walked to the davenport instantly, not stopping to put her dress on, sitting near me in the spot I'd indicated. I'd given her no instructions as to putting the dress on, so she simply continued to hold the garment in front of herself. It did little to cover her nudity, just some of her bosom, a small portion of the cloth swaying over the shaven triangle of her sex.

Once again, I began asking her about herself, and as I spoke, Tarin curled her legs up onto the couch, tucking the feet up at the curve of her buttocks as if trying to be as modest as possible.

"I want to make dance my life," she told me after I'd questioned her about her training in the ballet. "My teacher has gone abroad, but I keep in touch with her by letter, and I plan to join her when things have gotten better for my father."

I'd rested my arm behind her, and I began running my fingers over her bare shoulders as she told me of her dreams. I could see her eyes lighting up as she spoke of dedicating herself to the rigors of a dancer's training. And when she became lost in what she was saying, she gestured with her hands, the dress falling into her lap.

"Leave it there," I said, taking hold on her wrist to keep her from retrieving the tiny garment.

When I released the delicate wrist from my grip, Tarin put her hands at her sides, and I began to run a hand over her breasts, kneading the flesh of those sweet and ripening fruits.

The almost-bare girl stared off into space. "I know that you can do whatever you like with me," she said. "If I should resist, Mr. Olford will give me a most severe punishment, and it will be all that much longer before I'm released from here."

"Yes, I can do as I like with you," I told her, "but that doesn't mean that you can't allow yourself to enjoy being caressed."

After I'd spoken, Tarin's body seemed to relax, and I again began to explore her nudity, fondling her breasts in a most comprehensive way, enjoying the sensation of the firm flesh in my hand, giving the peaked nipples the faintest of pinches until they rose up into rigid nubbins.

The girl was still telling me of her hopes as she closed her eyes, clearly appreciating my touch, and when my hand began grazing over her torso, going lower, she reached down and removed the dress from her pubis, setting it aside to bare herself entirely to my attentions.

"I've never seen anyone dance the ballet in the nude," I said to her as I began fondling the smooth V between her legs. "I didn't know it was done."

"Oh, yes," she murmured. "It's done all over the world in private salons. My teacher told me that I'm one of the few who can perform it. She says I'm able because my childhood dance training gave me grace, and to go with that, my body has become toned from all my outdoor work."

One of my fingers was now on her clitoris, and I asked if she'd like to become a dancer of the nude ballet.

""Oh, very much," she said. "My teacher is going to have me audition for it when I join her."

I was now manipulating her sex in earnest, driving the girl close to orgasm.

And it worked, Bertrand. I had her tell me how she'd feel performing before an audience while she was without clothing, and she went on about the experience in glowing terms, almost raving in her desire to go onto the stage.

I sensed orgasm overcoming her as she spoke of her love for the physical taxations of dance, her warm juices splattering all over my hand as I worked at her pubis, giving the girl what she was seeking. And she was the picture of pure and unabashed sexuality as she writhed on the davenport, slamming her vulva into my grasp.

"You understand what I'm talking about it, don't you, sir?" she asked as her pubis continued in its revel.

I told her that I did.

As mentioned at the beginning of this letter, yesterday I escorted Tarin to do her penance, and I'll say that she had a most trying time of it.

I took her in the four-horse coach, arranging for Hector to drive. I had no idea of what sort of condition the girl might be in on the return journey and felt she might need my attention.

Arriving in the churchyard and alighting from the coach, I saw a few farm wagons and saddle mounts there and learned that several members of the congregation, mostly angry women, had turned up to witness at least the preliminaries of the ritual, much of it, of course, being conducted strictly in private.

Tarin's unshod feet had no sooner touched the weedy ground than two of the elders, wearing black suits and wide-brimmed hats, appeared out of the thick fog, immediately besetting the girl and leading her away by her wrists.

"Perhaps you'd care to come in for a spot of sherry before the start of the proceedings," I heard Vicar Dowling's saying, and I turned to see him approaching from the direction of the rectory. "I know I could certainly use one."

I saw nothing else to do so I joined him, and as we sipped our sherry, he talked about Tarin's penance in a highly animated way, clearly happy to have such a young and lovely girl in his clutches.

"Trust me, Hunter," he said when it was time to go, "by the time I'm done with Miss Tarin Blake, she will be fully purged of all defilement." His smile was broad as he spoke.

The air in the church was so permeated with incense that I sensed its odor even at the door. Candles burned, and the onlookers were seated in pews near the front. Silence reigned.

Then I saw Tarin. The girl was fully nude, and she'd been strapped into a cruel body-harness of supple, mahogany-brown leather. The apparatus fit over her shoulders, crisscrossed her breasts, the straps going beneath her arms and buckling together in the back.

"She won't be doing much frisking about in that contrivance," Vicar Dowling was saying as we walked up the aisle.

He was correct there. Tarin's hands were drawn up behind her, bent at the elbows with the wrists crossed then fastened into a leather belt affixed to the back of the harness.

Rendering the poor girl even more helpless was the fact that she'd been hooked up to a chain that hung from out of the rafters. A thick ring of iron was sewn into the back portion of the harness, and a hook at the end of the chain had been run through it. Thus, they'd left her with the heels of her feet unable to touch the floor. She was swaying slightly in an effort to balance herself in this awkward position.

Perhaps the worst of it was that she would be facing the congregation while being subjected to the ordeals of penance. She'd see their vengeful faces as she endured whatever they might care

102

to inflict on her unprotected flesh.

Tarin was now theirs to do with as they chose.

***

As Dowling stood before the audience, I took a seat behind the others, looking at their faces. The men were scowling, but their eyes betrayed a secret lust for nude girl hanging at the front of the church. Most of the women wore looks of open disapproval, but I believe I detected a certain desire in the expressions of one or two of them. Perhaps they wished it was they who would flog Tarin's bound flesh, or did they have a yen to do more than that? Did they want to get their hands on her or even take her to bed?

"I thank all of you for coming," Dowling was now saying. "The greater the number of witnesses, the greater her shame."

Then he spoke to them of Tarin's guilt, of her working on the Sabbath and exhibiting herself before strangers.

While the vicar spoke, the old woman, Bella, entered from a side door with wooden bowl in her hand. After setting the bowl on the floor, she dipped her hands into it, bringing them out covered with oil. Then, ever so carefully, she proceeded to coat Tarin's body with the shining substance, smearing it in particular over the buttocks and pubis.

Tarin cooperated, even spreading her legs when the woman began oiling her inner thighs.

I had to wonder if the oil was one of Bella's mysterious potions. Would it have an aphrodisiac effect on the helpless Tarin.

When Bella was done, she left, and Brother M., clad in cloak and hood walked in, carrying a leather lash outfitted with a handle of silver steel, long ribbons of scarlet festooning the handle.

"Tarin Blake," Dowling intoned as Brother M. took up a stance behind the dangling girl, "do you confess to the crime of laboring on the Sabbath?"

"Yes, sir," she answered.

"And do you confess to the crime of frolicking nude in the

outdoors while two male onlookers were present?"

"Yes, Vicar Dowling, I do," Tarin replied.

I could easily see that she was doing her best to say what all of them wanted to hear in an attempt to make her penance lighter.

"Tell us what possessed you to commit such foul acts," he asked her.

And that's when Tarin made her mistake, falling into their hands and giving them the excuse they needed to treat her as mercilessly as they'd truly wanted to in the first place.

"I had to, sir," Tarin told him in a humble tone of penitence. "I was obeying my stepmother."

Dowling's face became livid. "You were convicted in a court of law for just those crimes, not your stepmother," he snapped at her, "and you've now compounded your sins by lying to the administrator of your penance. For this, you will receive one dozen extra strokes of the lash."

Dowling nodded some sort of signal, and Brother M. began a whipping of their nude victim, his eyes afire within his hood.

As the lash whistled through the air, I saw that it had hundreds of minuscule leather spikes embedded in it, each one a separate instrument of pain, and when it struck the naked flesh of Tarin's buttocks, she lurched forward in an arc, her pubis thrust forward, the feet raising themselves while her facial features twisted into an expression of both surprise and anguish.

As I've told you, Tarin's a brave girl who's become accustomed to a certain level of physical abuse, if such a thing is possible, but this was plainly a new degree of anguish for her. Her body writhed each time the lash struck, fighting the confinement of the harness. And, try as she might, she couldn't keep herself from crying out as she was punished.

By the time she'd taken the dozen strokes, her bare flesh was quivering, and, even in the dank air of that musty church building, a sheen of her perspiration had mixed into the oil that coated her tawny skin.

When Brother M. had finished with whipping the girl, Dowling again stood before the onlookers. "Tarin Blake will now accept 17 strokes of the lash for the crime of laboring on our Sabbath," he said. "Let us hope that she is thankful for each stroke."

Once again, the sound of the spiked lash reverberated from the stone walls, and again, Tarin shrieked each time the dreadful instrument crossed her unprotected flesh, her body struggling in the inescapable mesh of leather that held her fast as the long tousles of her black hair flew across the jutting breasts.

Brother M., clearly a true whipmaster, used the tool in a way that seemed to be bringing forth a maximum of pain, a stinging that must have penetrated the girl to her very core.

The second whipping finished, Dowling spoke again. "And now, Tarin Blake, your entire body will be flogged for the crime of denuding yourself before strangers," he was saying. "As you have shown your entire body to others, including your most private parts, your entire body will now suffer before others, the number of strokes determined by the good Brother M."

Perhaps it was due to Olford's efforts to bring the lovely Tarin into some mode of submissive living, or it could have simply been that the girl had already suffered so much, but now she pleaded for mercy.

"I beg of you to punish me no longer, Vicar Dowling," she gasped. "I repent, and I will sin no more."

Dowling seemed to enjoy hearing the girl plead as did the audience. "If what you say is true, you will be thankful for the opportunity to serve penance, he told her as Brother M. prepared to begin the chastisement afresh.

The masked flagellator walked slowly around the hanging girl as if appraising her, the gleaming eyes within the hood seeming to size up just how he would proceed with this all-encompassing body-flogging. And just before he began this next whipping, something seemed to come over Tarin, and I suspect that it was due to the mysterious oil that she'd been coated with. I saw her inner thighs shivering, then the vulva itself, a rapid movement that was almost indiscernible at first but soon becoming quite visible.

As the hooded man stood at her side, Tarin glanced over at him, her eyes imploring him to take pity, and as she did, her entire body began quaking with what seemed like fear at the outset but quickly took on the appearance of a sexual arousal.

Brother M.'s very stance was demonstration that he would show the girl no mercy.

I then witnessed a flogging of blatant cruelty. He began walking in a circle around Tarin's bound form once again, but now he let the spiked lash fall with his footsteps, tormenting her exposed body, methodically cracking the leather at first one spot and then another, never giving her a chance to guess where she would next be struck.

The harness was biting into the girl's tender skin as she fought against it, causing the chain she dangled from to rattle. She was losing what little control she might have been able to preserve, grievous whimpers coming from her full lips as her olive flesh turned a reddish color.

How I pitied the girl as I saw the whip sinking its teeth into every facet of her nudity, her breasts, back, the shoulders and legs, and, probably the worst for her, her bare and shaven sex, leather biting into this private cradle while an audience watched.

"The haughty slut's getting her just desserts now," I heard one woman whisper to another. "Look at her. She's being given a flogging she won't soon forget, and well of it."

Her companion chuckled beneath her breath as relished the sight of Tarin undergoing this dreadful treatment. "And just see how she skips to the piper's tune now," she said.

Brother M. was now flogging Tarin's naked feet. As she was already hoisted up, the fire of the whip forced her to dance about on the very tips of the toes, and I recalled the picture of her engaged in the ballet. But this was altogether different. Here her dance was not one of freedom, but one of agony.

It was while Brother M. was giving special attention to Tarin's breasts that the power of everything she was undergoing, and perhaps the oil as well, seemed to rush through her being, a great tremor rippled over her naked body until her sex pounded outward and then started smashing itself back and forth to the rhythm of an invisible lover.

Her bound body had gone into a state of orgasm, and it caused her to let out a scream that was the sound of rapture and suffering combined.

"I've had enough," she cried to her torturer as her legs spread wide open and cocked themselves so high that the feet were grazing the punished buttocks. "How long must I endure this horrid whipping?"

Yet as she pleaded for relief, wet trickles of her ecstasy appeared at the opening to her vulva.

The flogging done, Tarin was let down and off of the chain, but still not released from the tight bindings of the harness. Instead, the elders took charge of her, leading her to the same iron ring where I'd seen Emily West manacled, halting her before it with her back to the pews.

The girl trembled as they made her kneel before the ring with her buttocks resting on the chill floor. Her body now had a high sheen as the oil was mixing with her own perspiration, and her disheveled tresses were falling across her face and down over her heaving breasts.

Further humbling the girl, one of the elders now looped a weighty chain about her neck and secured it with a padlock. He then used another padlock to fasten the free end of the chain to the floor ring. The chain, being of a short length, now held Tarin pulled forward into a pose of contrition. Her face almost touched the ring, the flogged bottom pushed outward as if inviting more punishment, her hands held securely behind her back with the harness belt.

As Tarin was forced into this display of shame, I saw her buttock-flesh clenching itself together, probably in fear of being whipped still more.

Vicar Dowling, with a sardonic expression that could only be interpreted as one of genuine satisfaction, addressed those witnessing this depraved ritual.

"Tarin Blake will now remain in penitential contemplation until the hour of the sunset," he said. "As she recalls her sins, she will be guarded, and the birch rod will be applied to the bare skin of her hindquarters each time her overseer suspects that she might be drifting off into her own selfish reveries. We will now select said overseer."

Each person in the audience raised a hand, holding up different numbers of fingers, and Dowling went into some obscure sort of selection process, calling out numbers at random. Each time he called a number, half of the hands would go down until only one hand was left raised. It seemed to be something like a game of odds-and-evens.

The selected person was a stout and stern woman who advanced to the altar with prayer book in hand and a look of seriousness about her.

"I know the procedure," she said when Dowling handed her a long rod and asked if she knew what had to be done with the girl on the floor. "I will read to her, and I will beat her sinful flesh should she err from her penance."

Dowling again thanked the witnesses, gave them his blessing, and the more public part of the ritual came to an end.

In the churchyard, the parishioners gathered, all of them carrying some smug and twisted posturing of having done their duty.

"We owe you our gratitude," one man said to Dowling. Minutes before I'd seen his face bright with lust for Tarin's bound nudity. "That girl's the worst of the whole lot."

"Indeed she is," the woman accompanying him added. "I've seen her around the village, displaying her legs as a whore would, letting the top of her bosom show. She's a disgrace, and I've suspected at times that she's at the very root of each and every calamity that's befallen these lands."

I stood with Dowling, watching the wagons and horses being driven away and then spoke to him, making sure to keep my voice level and certain.

"I'll stay until the hour of sunset," I told him. "Tarin will need an escort, and I wouldn't want to have any harm come to her."

A look of disappointment crossed his face. He'd probably been looking forward to strapping Tarin down to his bed and using her sexually through the night, but, and this was likely due to Olford's influence, he deferred to my wishes.

Let me close now, Bertrand. I hope you're giving some thought to changes in the disciplinary procedures employed at Rosewood. As mentioned in a previous letter, I've begun keeping detailed notes on the benefits of corporal punishment, and they're adding up to quite a treatise on the subject. It's my belief that a knowledgeable application of the birch to the more unruly bottoms of our academy could be a tool used to raise our academic standards.

I remain your good friend and confidant.

All My Best,

Derek H.

Dear Bertrand,

Neville returned a few days ago but says he'll be off again soon. I've given him detailed accounts of everything that's transpired where Amanda and Tarin are concerned, and he's pleased with their progress, amused at times with the former, impressed with the latter, but he has plans to bring each of them more quickly into the folds of obedience.

Most notably here are the tales he's brought back, although, sadly, fiction they are not. The persecution of young females is running rampant, and he says the situation grows increasingly worse as one goes deeper into the more remote and isolated provinces, making what goes on here seem mild by comparison.

"Many of these village magistrates haven't had the same benefits of travel and education as I have, and they're just as caught up in persecuting these girls as anyone else, making the situation increasingly dangerous," he told me last night.

With a great deal of interest, he's perused my notes on the subject of flagellation and feels I'm onto something, suggesting that I'm amassing enough material for both a lengthy monograph on flogging and sex-torture as well as a manual for teachers that could be employed as a guidebook in using corporal discipline as an aid to better education. It's certainly worth considering as I find the subject matter fascinating to begin with.

On Neville's second night back, he had dinner guests, Mayor Blythe and the County Chancellor, who was travelling the countryside on a tour of inspection.

"This will give me an opportunity to both entertain these gentleman and further Amanda and Tarin's progress," he said during the afternoon. "The perky Miss Smith is far too impetuous for her own safety, and, while I'm pleased with the manner in which Tarin is trying to defer to court rulings, her independent spirit could cause her serious trouble if I should release her from court guardianship any time in the foreseeable future. Things have changed. If she were to walk about in the village now, simply carrying herself as she does, the townspeople would banish her from their midst, and that's the very least they might do."

His plan was to have his guests watch while Amanda received a traditional drawing room birching and then adjourn to the stone out building where Tarin would be given a sex-flogging.

"Thrashing a girl until she spends herself," he said when I asked exactly what sex-flogging consisted of, though I had a fairly good idea. "Then she'll be fucked while still bound up fast, and don't think for a moment that she's virgin. I know everything that goes on in my jurisdiction."

He then went on to tell me that he'd been told by reliable informers that Tarin's stepmother had, on a few occasions, sold the girl to one of Stonehurst's more prominent citizens to be used for sexual purposes. He named no names and told me that even Tarin herself didn't know who the man was as she was always tied and blindfolded when in his presence.

At times, some of what goes on in this forsaken part of the county can be shocking.

That evening, the dinner conversation was mostly carried on by Olford and Chancellor York and concerned the current legal situation in Stonehurst. York was also asking for a complete report on the more distant and dangerous regions that Olford would be journeying to next.

"Now, gentlemen," Neville said when the four of us retired to the drawing room for brandy and some tobacco, "I want to bring in a certain Miss Amanda Smith. Our mayor is already well acquainted with her, but I don't think he realizes how regularly we have to discipline this girl. She was brought into my courtroom for making suggestive overtures in public, not ladylike behavior at any time, and certainly not appropriate in these times."

Ruth was just then escorting Amanda in and standing her in the middle of the room. York's eyes lit up at the sight of the girl, and, I must say, she did indeed look sweet standing there so alone in all of that empty space, the fire highlighting the youthful figure beneath the long dress, the bare pinkish toes peeping from the hem and looking so frail on the hard wood of the floor.

"Good evening, sir," the girl murmured when Olford greeted her.

"Tonight I've decided that Amanda might benefit by having the rod used on her buttocks before a small audience," Olford announced, "and I hope that you gentlemen will be good enough to bear with me on this by watching as she's flogged."

Their interest in seeing Amanda thrashed was plain for anyone to see.

Then York spoke up. "You know, Olford, I often visit the schools of this county, both public and private, and I know something about birch discipline," he said, "and I can tell just by looking at her just what sort of girl Miss Smith is. Perhaps you'd like me to take her in hand. She could probably benefit from my experience as I'm something of an adept when it comes to the use of the rod."

Olford clearly liked this idea and was magnanimously told the Chancellor to feel free in doing with the girl as he saw fit.

"Let's have a good look at you, my little girl," York said to her. "Remove your dress, and then we'll determine just what should be done with you this evening."

Amanda seemed reluctant to bare herself before the imposing Chancellor, the man who was now in control of her immediate fate. Slowly she unbuttoned her dress and then simply let it drop around her ankles.

But Ruth was right there to snatch the garment up and take it away, leaving Amanda truly naked. How fair and delicate she appeared, how vulnerable she was being without clothing while in full view of four men.

"Come and sit near me," York was saying to the girl, pointing to a spot to the left of his chair. "I'd like to get to know you before you're flogged."

With one hand covering her smooth pubis, Amanda walked slowly to him and curled up next to his chair, her rounded buttocks at rest on her heels.

Once she was in place, York stroked her hair and shoulders, talking softly to her, telling her how much help the rod could give her, how it had the power to eradicate the flaws that girls her age were often prone to.

Amanda was staring at the floor, her skin blushing with a bashful glow, a shy smile on her lips. Her hand still covered her sex in attempt at modesty, but her nipples revealed that she was undergoing some sort of odd excitement. They'd become swollen and stiff.

"You're such a precious thing, my dear," York was saying to her as he reached down and stroked her bare breasts, letting his fingers graze the erect nipples, "and you're going to give me your full cooperation while you take your birching, aren't you?"

Amanda nodded. ¡Yes, sir, I am," she said softly.

Then it was time to begin the procedure. York went into action by rising from his chair, helping the nude girl to her feet, and leading her out into the center of the room where he placed her into a posture well-suited for flogging. After ordering her to get down on her hands and knees in a place where she'd be looking at all of us, he told her to spread her knees wide.

While Amanda was getting into the required pose, Ruth was handing him a long switch of birch. "Thank you so much," he said to her. "This is just what this lovely girl needs, but I'd like you to administer the strokes, if you don't mind. I prefer to watch."

It was an intense and strange means of discipline that Amanda endured. York asked Ruth to alternate the strokes between the girl's buttocks and her sex, pausing about ten seconds after each stroke.

"This method of using the birch back and forth from pubis to buttocks is becoming all the fashion in boarding schools," York was saying as her resumed his chair, "and I find the results quite remarkable."

Then Ruth prepared to begin the disciplinary process. She stationed herself in a spot where she could swing the birch from side to side across the girl's proffered behind, and, from that vantage point, she could also bring the instrument upward through the open thighs to strike the exposed pubis.

With her body beginning to tremble, Amanda bowed her head.

"Head up, my girl," York commanded sharply. "Show your face to us. Each time you bow your head, you earn extra licks of the birch for your rump."

With a sizzling hiss, Ruth brought the rod straight across the naked buttocks, causing the Amanda's body to pitch itself slightly forward. Then the woman paused before swinging the tool upward and thrashing at the girl's unprotected sex.

As this procedure was repeated, I saw Amanda's fingers trying to grip at the polished wood of the flooring. She was desperately trying to hold the posture while, at the same time, trying to keep her head up.

As the hapless girl was given this unusual scorching, we sipped our brandy and looked on, watching her fair skin turning pink.

"I'm sure you're familiar with orgasmic flogging, Olford," York was saying, plainly quite proud of this form of discipline, "but I think you'll find this particular method to be invaluable. Notice how her face reflects simple pain when the birch crosses her buttocks and pain mixed with something altogether different when it strikes her exquisitely bare sex-flesh."

As I gazed into the Amanda's eyes, I was able to clearly observe what he meant. Something akin to rapture would filter over Amanda's expression when the birch struck her pubis. Yet, in the same instant, her eyes would beseech me, silently asking for rescue.

I'm not sure how long the birching continued. At one point, I was listening to Olford discuss local politics with the Chancellor when the sound of birch on flesh brought me back to the reality of the harsh discipline taking place.

Looking up, I saw Amanda staring at York as if pleading for mercy, her body noticeably quivering under the birch punishment as her tongue lolled from her mouth.

Then a decided change struck the girl. I saw her upturned toes begin a frantic wriggling just as her rapid breathing turned to ragged gasps of acute suffering. The frisky Miss Amanda Smith was obviously being taken well past what her delicate flesh could endure.

York then looked in her direction. "Something seems to be troubling you, my dear," he said. "I wonder what it might be."

Just as he spoke, a thin rivulet of juice appeared on one of the bare girl's thighs, trickling slowly from her crevice while she blushed with shame, knowing that everyone could see this telltale outer sign of her arousal.

"Ah, now you see what I spoke of, gentlemen," Chancellor York said, a note of pleased triumph in his voice. "This fortunate young lady is deriving all the benefits of a corrective birching, bravely bearing up under her discipline because she's realized the good it can do her, and now her loins are rewarding her efforts. Our evidence, of course, is that tiny stream of juice she's just emitted."

York rose and walked over to stand near Amanda. "Look up here at me," he said to her. "I know you're about to climax, and I want you to thank me while you're about it."

As she looked up, the Chancellor told Ruth that the buttocks had had their share of flogging and that it would now be a good idea to concentrate the birch on the pubis only.

It didn't take a lot. After three more strokes of the rod, orgasm burst through the nude girl in a highly observable manner. Ouching and ohing sounds came from her parted lips while the buttocks hunched themselves back and forth, her pleasure blending with the pain she was still undergoing.

For a moment, she forgot herself and then seemed to remember her instructions. "I thank you, sir, for having this done to me," she said through her sobbing gasps. "This birching has done me so much good."

And we all watched while Ruth flogged the girl through each second of a the body-wrenching orgasm.

Bertrand, I'll gladly admit that it was a rare and wonderful display, and as I watched that luscious girl going through it, I couldn't help but think that the naughtier Rosewood students might benefit from just this sort of punishment.

When Amanda's discipline was finished with, Neville asked Ruth to take the girl to her room. "Strap her out to the four corners of her bed, still naked, but let her rest," he said to the woman.

Then it was time for the second installment of the evening's "entertainment."

The four of us, all carrying lanterns, repaired to the out building.

Immediately upon entering the musty old structure, the low glimmer of lantern light became visible, coming from a far corner, and Neville led us in that direction.

Curiosity as to what might be happening to Tarin was uppermost in my thoughts. I knew, of course, that Neville was planning on having her sex-tortured, but how would we find her? What sort of restraint might she be in?

Hector and one of the guards were at the perimeter of the light's circle, done with binding the girl.

Then Tarin became visible. She was fully nude and strung up between two wooden support posts that were perhaps three feet apart, her wrists and ankles fixed. Her arms were flung up high, long leather straps holding her to the two timbers. Similar straps were fastened to her ankles, the opposite ends tied low on the heavy posts and keeping her slender legs well spread. Her bare feet were able to touch the chill floor, but she'd been blindfolded and gagged, wide buckle-straps being belted over her eyes and mouth.

Thus, both sides of her body were accessible. She could be flogged from front or back, sex-whipped from either direction.

Neville thanked Hector and the guard for binding the girl up, and they departed.

"Ah, I know this one," the mayor was saying. "I remember seeing her flogged in the square. Haughty little thing, isn't she, Olford?"

Neville was somewhat noncommittal in his reply. "Tarin's an independent spirit," he said, "and that doesn't seem to have won her much favor with the populace of our fair village. I'm trying to help her acclimatise herself to the rather trying times we find ourselves in."

The mayor was barely listening. He'd gone over to where Tarin was bound up, a greedy look on his face, openly admiring the girl's unclothed body, looking closely at the smooth triangle tucked so neatly between her supple thighs.

"Do you have her shaved regularly?" he asked.

"Under my guardianship, these girls are required to keep themselves clean and shaven at all times," Neville told. "It's part of their training for a disciplined life. Try examining her with your hands. You'll find her to be firm of flesh and well-scrubbed."

Olford was looking over some flogging devices that had been laid out on a table, looking for a particular one it seemed. Then he found what he was looking for, a short lash-strap with a sturdy handgrip attached to it.

Both the mayor and the Chancellor were now in front of Tarin, each of them feeling the girl as if she actually needed to be inspected. In reality, they were doing nothing more than groping her nudity, and, of course, Tarin could do nothing but stand there

117

and allow herself be fondled. Not being able to see where next she would be grasped, she flinched each time she was touched.

How pleased I became when Olford handed me the lash and asked if I'd be good enough to take care of whipping Tarin's buttocks. The thought of making her writhe beneath a whipping seemed a most gratifying task, and, after taking a grip on the strap's handle, I took up a position behind the girl, waiting for Olford's signal to begin.

I was just admiring the gentle curve Tarin's hips, the perfect shape of the buttocks themselves, when I looked over to see Neville applying a generous layer of oil to a leather phallus.

"We're going to teach this girl something of life's frustrations," he was saying to Blythe and the Chancellor. "She'll crave this tool in the most desperate way before we're done with her."

When Olford had the phallus lubricated to his satisfaction, he walked up to Tarin and inserted it gently into her pubis, wedging it in solidly. Then, after giving her a moment to get used to it, he began working it at her, driving it gently in and out in a simulated fucking.

Once the phallus had begun to stimulate the girl's sex, Neville removed it. "Begin flogging her buttocks," he said to me. "Stop when I raise my hand."

As he stepped back to where the other two stood watching, I raised the whip-strap and brought it across those orbs of perfect girl-flesh three times, pacing the strokes carefully.

That particular strap was a most effective tool. Tarin surged forward each time the leather bit into her buttocks, rising on her toes as her body contorted itself into a arch. The nubile breasts would thrust upward, nipples pointing high as she strained at her bindings. And, as firm as the girl might be, stripes of bright pink rose on the tender skin almost instantly.

When Neville raised his hand, I ceased the flogging, much as I was enjoying having that untamed young creature under my control.

Again, Olford inserted the oiled prong into the girl's crevice and began working it at her. This time muffled whimpering sounds came from under her gag, and she twisted herself in the direction of the phallus, worming her pubis around it.

"The girl seems to like that gadget," the mayor chuckled. "She wants it to give her a proper fucking."

And just when I saw a drop of Tarin's pubic fluid appear, Neville removed the tool and signalled for me to continue whipping her.

Over and over, Tarin was sex-tortured this way. I'd give her about six good strokes of the lash and then stop while Neville worked the phallus at her sex. Thus, she was kept constantly wavering between the suffering of the whip and the ecstasy of being penetrated.

Over the shoulders of Tarin's struggling form, I saw that both York and Blythe were amused at the girl's antics, yet they both had tremendous bulges in their trousers and no wonder. The portrait she made was a classic study of restrained desire, eroticism at one of its most sublime levels.

The sounds from behind the gag were becoming high-pitched, and Neville removed it from Tarin's mouth but left the blindfold in place.

"Uhhh," rushed from the girl's lips as soon as they were free. "Why do you do this to me? Please leave that thing inside of me or I'll lose my mind."

She was swaying about as she spoke, tilting her head back far enough to allow the long, dark tresses to wave about her lashed and glowing rump while her pelvis strained forward as if seeking to capture the phallus within its folds.

I knew that Neville had originally intended to have the girl flogged to orgasm, but now he seemed satisfied with the frustrated and needy state he'd manipulated her into.

"You're going learn to take what others give you and to be grateful for it," he said to her. "You're under my guardianship, and what happens to you is strictly up to me."

Tarin seemed to accept what he was saying, but it was simple to see that having her crevice filled was her paramount concern.

Olford then invited his guests back to the main house. "Miss Amanda Smith should be rested by now, and she's probably grown lonely, strapped to her bed as she is," he said to them. "What do you say to paying her a social visit?"

That seemed to suit Blythe and York, and they made ready to leave, and I could only wonder what they might be planning for Amanda.

Neville spoke to me in a confidential whisper just as he was about to leave. "That girl's desperate," he said, pointing toward Tarin. "You might as well enjoy her situation before you release her."

Then I was alone with the bound and helpless girl, and for a few moments, I couldn't resist just standing there and drinking in the sight of her, relishing the thought of what I was about to do. She was still struggling at the straps that held her fastened out so stringently, breathing rapidly, her feet grinding into the rugged stone flooring. And, most invitingly, the deep need of her pubis was revealed by its highly visible pulsations and the liquid seeping from it.

"Is someone still here?" she asked as I gazed at her.

At first, I didn't say anything. Instead, I simply walked up to her and began running a hand over her torso, my fingers lingering on the warm nudity.

"You're Mr. Hunter, aren't you?" she asked.

"Yes, Tarin," I told her gently.

Then she asked if I'd been the one who'd flogged her, and I told her that I had.

"And what will you do with me now, sir?"

I suppose she'd heard me undoing my trousers and bringing out my erect member. "I'm going to give you what you've been wanting," I said to her as I reached around to get a grip on her

120

buttocks.

I'm not sure if her sigh was one of relief or merely of surrender, but she became willing in my grasp, welcoming my cock as I began poking it into her narrow crevice.

Penetrating that youthful pubis was difficult going, but, with a determination born of desire, I worked at it until I was squeezing my way in a little at a time. Just looking down at the lovely nude who was strapped into so accommodating a posture was inspiration enough. How vulnerable she was, so helpless and yet so ready to be used sexually.

What followed was a coupling of great intensity. Tarin had gone into a series of mild but squealing orgasms as soon as I'd begun entering the hungry and very bare girl-flesh of her smooth mound. And once I was in far enough to begin a stroking of the clutched inner folds, she slipped off into full climactic abandon, her body fighting the leather straps, hips pounding at mine while her entire body rippled with an uncontrolled twitching.

I can only tell you that it was full culmination, and when my satisfaction came, I was propelling that girl far backward in her leather bonds.

Afterward, I realized that a strong case can be made for the theory that, in certain cases, a beforehand flogging, painful as it might be, can enhance the sex act for a greater number of females than one might suspect.

———————

The morning after this intriguing evening, Olford and I met in the library for coffee as he again wanted to look through my notes on flagellation. It seems he's impressed by the information I'm garnering from my studies and firsthand experiences and thinks I'm onto something with the way I plan to cover the subject through the written word. He's even suggested I accompany him on this next journey of his. Apparently, the punishment of suspect girls is far more frequent and severe where he's off to than here. This, of course, would give me a more in-depth look at this most unusual topic, and I'm considering taking him up on the idea. My purely academic research is far ahead of schedule, so far, in fact, that the end is already in sight, so I can well afford the time. As of this writing, I'm only thinking it over, but the idea has its appeal.

I'll sign off now and post this.

In hopes that all is well at Rosewood

Faithfully yours.

Derek H.

Letter 11 PRIVATE

Dear Bertrand,

Neville will be setting off on his next journey within the next three days, and, as of this writing at least, I'm fairly certain that I'll be accompanying him. I've begun preparations, getting together what supplies I'll need and trying to leave my research at a decent jumping off point.

Since the night of Tarin's sex-flogging and my subsequent coupling with her, her behavior's been much the same, but I detect a note of formal subservience in her demeanor. When she's called upon to serve me here in the library, she goes about her duties quietly, but on several occasions she's given me just the hint of a subdued smile, leading me to believe that, dreadful as her whipping might have been, she enjoyed the end result.

Needless to say, I'm looking forward to making love to her so wonderfully willing body again. And I have to admit that I'm also looking forward to having her bound and under my control again. Taking the lash to those ripe buttocks was pure pleasure, and I dearly wish to repeat the experience. Under Neville's rules,

122

I could actually flog the girl at almost any time I choose, but I'm going to handle it much the way we do at Rosewood, enjoying the process only when necessary. Many's the time I've seen a student with an attractive bottom who looks like she's just itching for the birch, but I've always managed to bide my time until that student was truly in need of punishment, and I'm going to handle Tarin in much the same way.

Early this morning, I watched while Amanda was put through an unusual procedure of punishment, one I think we should consider using on Rosewood girls who've committed only minor infractions of the rules.

As usual, I was in the library, just starting my day's work when Neville dropped in, asking if I'd like to watch while Amanda was given something he referred to as a "feathering."

"A feathering is a means of punishing a girl who hasn't done quite enough to warrant a flogging but still needs to be taken to task," he told me when he saw my confusion, "and that's Amanda at the moment. Once again, she's taken to running about and causing a ruckus. Hector's preparing her now in the drawing room. Come along. You'll find this interesting."

A long, wooden bench had been placed in the middle of the room. It was quite sturdy and had iron rings bolted in at the corners, with straps affixed to the rings.

A nude Amanda was lying on the bench, face up, her hands and feet stretched out toward the ends of it, and Hector was in the process of securing her. He'd already tied her wrists into the straps above her head, and now he was drawing her legs out, securing her ankles into the straps at the opposite end of the long bench.

"My thanks, Hector," Olford said when the man was finished with the binding. "I'd say you've got her fixed up just right."

Once Hector had left the room, I admired the appeal of Amanda in that particular fashion of restraint. She was drawn so tightly that each of her muscles stood out, and the strain of the bondage was causing her to splay her fingers wide and stretch her dainty toes into tight little points that pulled inward. Her hair draped over her arms, descending toward the floor, and her legs were being held open just enough to make a man think of entering her helpless pubis.

As I gazed at the girl, her lips puckered in just the hint of one of her saucy smiles. Ever the nymph, she couldn't help but enjoy being forced into making a display of herself.

But she was quick to cease her covert flirting when Neville approached the bench.

He stood over the bare girl, smiling, stroking his goatee, a long and very stiff white feather in his hand. "Have you ever been tickled, Amanda?" he asked as he brandished the feather, a tone of slyness in his voice.

She gave her lips a nervous lick, probably guessing what was about to befall her unprotected flesh. "Why, yes, I have, sir," she replied.

"Who has tickled you, my girl?" he said. "Mr. Hunter and I would be interested in hearing about it."

She was hesitant about her answer. "Well, it was those two women who used to own the farm that borders my family's land," she said. "They no longer live there."

"Tell us, Amanda. What did they did to you."

"They caught me in the woods and asked me to play a game of find-it-where-you-can," she said to him. "Before I knew what was happening, they were tickling me everywhere."

Olford had begun flicking the tip of the feather over the girl's inner thighs, and as he teased her and made her squirm, he demanded that she tell us every detail, leaving nothing out.

Then I saw what was happening. Olford knew the story, probably through one of his informants, and he wanted to shame the girl by making her recount it.

"You'd better do as I say, young lady," he said to her, "and if you're not quick about it, you can look forward to being left alone with Ruth while she flogs your naked cunt. How could they have

124

been tickling you everywhere?"

"I couldn't stop them, sir," Amanda said, her tone plaintive. "They had me naked and tied."

Then she blurted out the whole tale, the words fairly spilling from her lips. It seemed that these two women, who Neville told me later had been run out of Stonehurst for being Sapphic lovers, had come across Amanda while she was out for a walk in the woods. Under the guise of a game, they'd gotten close enough to hold her down to the ground. They then began tickling her, pulling at her clothing until they'd denuded her body fully.

"I really did resist their advances, Mr. Olford," Amanda whined, "but they were quite strong, and they bound me up with rope."

The women had gotten Amanda onto a fallen tree and then tied her hands and feet out to the branches, spread wide for their pleasure, and then they gave her a merciless tickling that had gone on for some time.

By now Neville had begun tormenting the girl with the feather, and, even as she told the story of her woodland adventure, she was giggling. But it was a high-strung sort of giggle, revealing that she found the feather to be uncomfortable.

"Mr. Olford, that's awful," she said. "It's just like what those mean women did to me."

He was standing at her side, running the feather under her arms. "Well, that's just too bad," he replied, "but you should think of these things before you raise such a ruckus around here."

Then he went at it in earnest, using the feather all over her flesh, missing no area. He used the ticklish instrument on her legs, her breasts and midriff, and when he went to work on the small bare feet, they began twitching, and a peal of anxious laughter came from her mouth.

"Not there," she cried out. "Anywhere but there."

Olford's eyes flashed. He'd found her most sensitive spot.

I couldn't help but smile at Amanda's performance. As Olford concentrated the feather on her feet, going from one to the other, she became uncontrollable, giggling and pleading for mercy at the same time. She was thrashing at the bench, bucking up and down, rising so high at times that her buttocks were entirely lifted into air.

"And I'll wager they tickled your cunt as well, didn't they, Amanda"? he said. "Tell us."

She closed her eyes before answering. "Yes, sir," she whispered, "they did."

I'm certain that it was more than coincidence that Ruth entered the drawing room at that time, smiling when she saw Amanda's condition.

Olford prevailed upon the woman to take over with the feathering. "Amanda needs her sex tickled," he said to her. "Will you be good enough to help out?"

Ruth, with a fiendish gleam in her eyes, merely accepted the feather from him hand and went to stand at the nude girl's side.

For a few moments, the only sound in the room was Amanda's rapid breathing. Her entire body was quivering, the little feet still wagging about, and I could see her smooth pubic mound trembling in anticipation of being feathered.

Amused at the situation, Olford told Ruth about Amanda's adventure in the woods.

"Ah, yes, I was acquainted with those two women," Ruth told us. "They seemed to take the greatest pleasure in little sluts like the one we have here. And if I know this girl, she probably teased them into doing what they did."

"It's not true," Amanda whined. "They held me down and took my clothing from me."

But Ruth merely smirked at this and then brought the feather into action, tickling the bare pubis with what seemed to be a practiced touch. She first tickled the girl's crevice, running the feather up and down the now-swelling slit, then brushed the instrument back and forth on the outer mound.

Amanda was reaching the point of being lost to the world,

twisting and writhing in her bonds as if she had absolutely no control of herelf. No longer did she laugh or giggle. The intensity of what she was undergoing only allowed her to moan softly as her lips babbled words that were, for the most part, unintelligible.

With a demonic grin on her face, Ruth leaned down and parted the outer lips of the girl's pubis with her free hand, exposing the swollen clitoris. Then she started using the very tip of the feather to stroke the throbbing nub, inflicting a final and most degrading invasion of her victim.

The moment her clitoris was touched, Amanda's body tensed upward, balanced only on the shoulders and the heels of the feet, and when she collapsed back down to the bench and began her struggles afresh, I saw a thick stream of juice leaking from her tormented crevice.

Quite clearly, the girl had been driven into full arousal.

"I know that those two did more than just tickle her," Ruth was saying to us as she continued working on Amanda. "If she was to tell the whole truth, we'd learn that they were intimate with the same cunt I'm taking the feather to now."

Olford pursued this line of thinking and, using the threat of a sex-flogging, forced Amanda to admit everything.

Ruth had been right. While the nude girl writhed beneath the feathery attack, eyes averted, she confessed what they'd done with her, and they had, in fact, made liberal use of her bare pubis. They'd taken turns licking this private spot, kissing it and sticking their tongues inside until she'd almost fainted.

"Fainted?" Ruth laughed. "Well, perhaps, but probably because she was in climax. A slut like this one isn't particular who or what does the job."

Neville again took this further and made Amanda tell us how the two women who'd stripped her and bound her up had driven her into orgasm with their tongues.

But then she could speak no longer. The feather had taken her into the abyss, and she was temporarily lost to us. That naked lovely was throwing herself at the feather, the very cause of both her suffering and her joy, letting the ecstasy overwhelm her entire body.

Once the girl's quaking had abetted itself somewhat, Ruth departed, and Neville did something I found interesting. He began speaking of his next journey, acting as if Amanda wasn't even in the room. While we conversed, I was aware of her post-orgasmic moaning, and when I'd glance in that direction, I saw that she was still writhing in the leather strappings.

I mention this incident, Bertrand, because I think that this could be an ideal punishment for some of our students. Their shame would become a large part of the chastising experience. Being feathered while bound and nude could be instrumental in humbling a girl who needs that sort of treatment, and I can think of several Rosewood students who do. Perhaps we should think of putting this practice of feathering on our docket of punishments for next term.

Neville wasn't quite done with his captive. He walked over to stand next to the bench, watching while Amanda continued to flutter at the bench. Smiling, her reached down and began squeezing the outer lips of her pubis between his fingertips, causing a low groan to come from her mouth.

"Looks like she's in need of a little more gratification," he said to me and then asked if he might have some privacy.

Even as I was walking out the door, Neville had begun mounting the girl, and she was bending upward to meet him, her ankles and wrists straining at the straps as she sought to be filled.

I'm going to close now, but I'll be sure to write soon and let you know what I decide about going on this journey with Neville.

I hope you'll give some thought to using feathering as a means of discipline for our Rosewood girls.

Sincerely yours,

Derek H.

Letter 12 PRIVATE

Dear Bertrand,

I received a letter from you today and was happy to learn the book I sent has arrived safely. I hope you're getting some useful information from it.

You mention this new student, Priscilla Clark, and, judging by your description of her, she sounds quite fetching. You say that she hasn't taken up residence yet but has only appeared for her indoctrination, but I'm glad you made it very clear to her parents that we use corporal discipline as a means to better learning. I only hope that Priscilla herself isn't too surprised the first time she has to bare her behind for a lesson of the birch.

This letter will be brief of necessity as I'm leaving early tomorrow morning to accompany Olford on his diplomatic and investigative journey deeper into these agricultural regions. I'll still write regularly, but I'm not sure how long my letters will take to reach you. Of course, there will be no way for me to receive my post, but I hope you'll write, sending your letters here to Olford's estate. In that way I can enjoy catching up on the doings at Rosewood as soon as I return. I'll be curious about Miss Priscilla Clark. Perhaps by then you'll have had the good fortune to have taken the birch to her bare hindquarters.

The best to you, and I hope you'll wish me well on this journey

Most Sincerely,
Derek H.

Dear Bertrand,

We've arrived at the home of Thurston Baxter after a grueling three day horseback ride through some of the most desolate countryside I've ever seen. Baxter lives outside the village of Black Oak, where Neville will be conferring with the local politicians and constables for several days. I'll relate more to you of this madhouse in my next letter. Herein, I'll tell you of our journey.

After a half day's ride out of the vicinity of Stonehurst, the landscape began to change dramatically. All the fields were lying fallow and untended, and the dwellings had the appearance of being deserted. But occasionally we'd see people peering at us from the shadows of buildings, all of them with a haunted and desperate look in their eyes.

Our destination for that first day was the village of Langton. By early afternoon, we were seeing far fewer farms, and the roadway began leading us through forests only. It was while we were in one of the more thickly wooded areas that we were approached by a runaway girl.

We'd stopped at a stream that ran parallel to the road to rest and water our horses and were just dismounting when the girl stepped out of the forest. She seemed a bit wary of us, and yet she had a air of bravado about her.

"I'm called Shana," she said when she drew close.

As Neville spoke with her, I was able to take a good look at the girl. Her brownish hair was in tangles, and all she wore was a tiny scrap of what had once been a black skirt and a white bandanna tied over her breasts. Both garments were filthy and torn. Clearly, she'd been living in the forests for some time.

"I've something to offer you," she said to us. "Something that

I'll trade for food. Come and see."

Out of pure curiosity, we followed her into the trees. She took us down a pathway that led into a clearing, and there we met with another runaway.

A thick fog had drifted in, so we didn't see the other girl immediately. But once we were well into the clearing, she became visible. She was naked and facing a wide tree, her arms wrapped around it, her wrists tied together on the other side with a ragged piece of rope.

"This girl is known as Ari," Shana told us, "and she's what I have to offer in trade."

It seemed obvious that these young ladies were using aliases. Olford was asking her what she meant by trade.

"You can do whatever you like with her," Shana said to him. "You can fuck her and flog her as much as you want to. I sometimes give her a flogging just for sport. She's my pet."

Ari was a frail and pretty thing with long, sandy hair and smallish breasts. She seemed frightened, and it was easy to see that she probably depended on her friend to survive the life of a runaway.

As Olford appraised the bound girl's body, Shana was picking up a bundle of switches that were lying on the ground near the tree, fresh saplings tied together with a piece of cloth. After getting a steady grip on the bundle, she drew it back and then brought it down fiercely over Ari's shoulders.

"Shana, please," the naked girl whined as the force of the blow slammed her into the rough bark of the tree.

"Well, well what do you say?" Shana asked. "Will you exchange some food for the use of this girl's body?"

Olford stared at her for a few moments, looking quite imposing in his long, black cape and high riding boots, then accepted her offer. I suppose I shouldn't have been surprised at this as his interest in the flagellation of young female bodies seems to have heightened greatly since we were colleagues at Rosewood.

After he'd gone back to our mounts and come back with a generous amount of our provisions, he took the switch bundle from Shana's hand and approached the girl who was fastened up to the tree.

Shana came over to stand near me, munching on a piece of fruit.

"Selling you friend's body for a little food isn't bothersome to you?" I asked her.

"She wouldn't last a day out here without me," she replied, unconcerned. "Besides that, she likes it. There've been times when she's begged me to whip her."

Somehow, I found that hard to believe. When I looked back toward the tree, Ari was peering over her right shoulder at Olford with an abject look of fear in her wide eyes. Clearly, she wasn't looking forward to being flogged.

Olford stood directly behind the girl with a look of anger on his face. Then he began striping the switches across her buttocks, furiously drawing an X pattern over the bare flesh, the red stripes standing out brightly in the gray fog.

Again and again the switches struck, and in no time, Ari was shrieking, her shrill cries echoing through the silent forest. She was grinding her naked body at the tree, scraping her breasts and pubis at the bark as her wrists tugged at the piece of rope that held her fast. Her head tilted itself backward as her cries grew louder, and her buttocks were swinging themselves back and forth, vainly trying to escape the flogging.

"Please, good sir," she begged when Olford began to whip at her shoulders, "it's only a bit of food we're asking for."

"I'm trying to teach you something," he said to her. He'd finished with the shoulders and was now beating her upper thighs.

He then told them his identity and of his position as a magistrate.

Ari grew even more frightened, and Shana's air of nonchalance disappeared.

"Are you going to turn us in?" Shana asked.

"No, but you'd best return to your homes before it's too late," Olford replied. "If a group of irate citizens should apprehend you, they'd give you far worse treatment than you'd receive in any courtroom."

Satisfied with the flogging he'd given the bound girl, he tossed the bundle of switches aside and stepped close to her, gripping her shoulders with his hands.

Ari's shrieking became different as Olford mounted her. But with his cape spread out and the fog swirling around, it was hard to tell exactly what he was doing to her. However, it's safe to say that he was invading her body with his manhood.

Ari's feet kicked at the ground as Olford pounded at her, quickly taking his pleasure, with no thought of hers. Within a couple of minutes, he was done with her.

As we walked away from the two runaways, Olford warned them once again of the folly of their ways, and then we were mounting up and heading back to the roadway.

During the rest of that afternoon's journey, we passed through two smaller villages as we rode toward Langton. The first was not much more than a crossroads with a few shops and two taverns. But at the very outskirts of this outpost, a tall, thick post had been planted into the ground at the side of the road, and a just-recently-whipped girl was fastened to it.

The post I speak of had four wooden pegs embedded in the sides of it, two high up, two about 12 inches from the ground. The girl, a well-proportioned young beauty with reddish hair, was naked and tied to the post with leather straps. Her arms were raised high above her head, wrists lashed to the upper pegs, and her ankles were fastened to the lower pegs, keeping her bare toes several inches from the ground.

"Well, that one's certainly been rendered immobile," was Olford's dry comment as we rode by her.

She was twisting herself at the pole, pulling weakly at the

straps. Fresh welts from the lash marked her well-shaped buttocks, and, even from the roadway, I could hear soft groaning sounds coming forth from her lips.

We stopped in at one of the taverns for a quick drink, and here the local townsfolk had gathered to congratulate each other on the treatment they'd given the girl on the post. There is much talk among these people concerning what they refer to as "Doing the Work of the Good," and, in their opinion, whipping that helpless and naked girl had been just that.

"We beat the evil spirits from her," I heard one man saying as he toasted those around him.

Neville and I kept to ourselves, had our drink, and got back to our travels.

In the other village we passed through before reaching Langton, we saw yet another hapless girl in the clutches of these superstitious fanatics. Out in the square stood a platform constructed of wooden planks, and, in the center of the platform, there was a barrel that had been sawed in half lengthwise and nailed down to the planks. A crowd of people was gathered around the platform, seemingly waiting for something to happen.

Just as we rode near, two constables were hauling a half-stripped girl toward this platform and pulling the rest of her clothing from her body while she screamed out her innocence.

"I didn't offer my breasts to that man!" I heard her saying. "No man has ever touched me there!"

The two constables paid no attention to her protests, and by the time they'd gotten her up onto the platform, she'd been stripped to the full nude.

They laid her face down on the barrel, her arms and legs straddling it at each side, and, as they did, I saw that there were four long straps nailed down to the platform. To these, the constables first attached her wrists, she struggling all the while. Then they grabbed at her flailing feet, gripping her by the ankles and tying them to the other two straps.

Even though the nude was now helplessly strapped out, she still continued to battle, wrenching herself at the straps, squirming about atop the barrel.

While the crowd cheered him on, the larger of the constables took a birch rod from one of his belt loops and proceeded to thrash the captive girl. He didn't seem to be counting the number of strokes. Instead, he simply birched her in a furious manner, randomly using the wooden instrument on every part of her body.

The poor girl continued to proclaim her innocence. "This is too cruel," I heard her cry out as she fought her restraints. "I'd never do such a thing."

Having to be on our way to reach Langton by nightfall, we rode away, but even as we left the village behind, I could still hear the sound of the rod on bare flesh.

    ***

In this part of the letter, Hunter relates the journey into Langton and gives a description of the impoverishment of the town. Their accommodations at one of the local inns are less than comfortable, so he is glad when Olford's meetings are over the next morning. At this point, they set out for Evanshire, their last stop before Black Oak, where they'll stay at the home of Thurston Baxter for several days.

    ***

Let me say here, Bertrand, that the deeper we travelled into these outer provinces, the lonelier the landscape became. We passed through no smaller villages on the trip to Evanshire, and we saw no one on any of the farms. I'm sure there were people about, but they seem to be staying in hiding.

It wasn't until the late afternoon, while we were still an hour's ride from Evanshire, that we encountered a human being. We'd stopped in a churchyard to rest our horses in the shade of large tree. The stone church building was in such bad need of repair that we'd assumed it was no longer in use, so we were a little surprised when a man of the cloth emerged from it and approached us. He was heavyset, his clothing in tatters and he seemed excited about our presence.

"I hope you gentlemen have stopped by to make a donation to our humble church," he said to us after introducing himself as Rev. Talbot. "We've grown quite needy in these trying times, you know."

We gave him a few coins for the use of his shade tree, and the man seemed disappointed at such a small donation.

"Perhaps you'll care to offer more when I show you what's going on down below the church building," he said. "I've a girl at penance there, and she needs additional attention. You might want to assist me, for a donation of course. But come along, and you'll see what I'm talking about."

We followed him to the back of the old building and down a short flight of stairs that brought us to oaken door. With an iron key, Talbot opened the door to still more stairs. Here, he led us down to a large vaulted room, supported by low stone arches. Tallow candles mounted into the walls furnished a dim, wavering light.

"This dungeon was condemned and sealed up long ago," he told us, "but with all of these evil harlots creating such trouble, we've been given permission to reopen it."

Then I saw the girl at penance. She was standing in the middle of the chamber, naked, her arms raised high above her. Two thick chains with manacles welded to their ends hung from the arch directly over her, and her wrists had been clamped into these manacles.

"This is Bridget," Talbot was saying to us. "As you can see, her behavior has been less than pure lately."

Bridget's body was smoothly molded, lush, and she had a mane of dark tresses that tumbled over her shoulders and breasts. Her bare feet were on the stone floor, but she was hanging limply in the iron fetters, her head bowed. Stepping to a place where I could view her backside, I saw the reason for her exhaustion.

She'd just recently been flogged; her buttocks bearing fresh whip marks.

"Bridget's had the good sense to confess to me that she's had lewd thoughts concerning men, thoughts of fornicating with strangers," Talbot told us. "So, in order to cleanse her mind, I've made her available for fuckings between her whippings. For a small donation, you gentlemen are welcome to her."

It was incredible, I tell you. He was actually selling a girl who'd come to do penance!

I glanced over to see Neville taking a whip from a hook, a thin, flat lash-strap with a wooden handle. He then stood at Bridget's side, swinging the whip in readiness to use it on her buttocks.

"I see that she's already had at least one good thrashing," he said, peering at her.

"Yes, Bridget was somewhat reluctant to confess the whole of her wrongdoing," Talbot said. "I had to use the whip to wrest the whole truth from her."

The girl was looking around the chamber now, her eyes growing wide with a dull sort of fear. Apparently, she'd been through quite a hard time down in that dungeon.

"Do you think you deserve such a severe penance, Bridget?" Neville asked her.

"Sir, I only came to..." she started to say.

Then Talbot interrupted her. "You'd better not tell any more of your lies, my girl," he said to her, his tone quite stern. "Things could go much worse for you if you should."

She looked at Talbot and then back to Neville. "Yes, sir," she said meekly, "I deserve this penance."

It was clear that she was afraid of Talbot and didn't want to tell the whole truth of what he was doing with her. After all, we'd soon be gone, and she'd be alone with him, completely at his mercy.

"Very well," was all Neville said, but he was wearing an amused sort of grin.

Then he began flogging the girl, but oddly enough, he did it in a very mild way. It was no harsh beating but rather a stinging and teasing with the whip. He was snapping it at her, making her dance in place and causing little red spots to flare up on the naked flesh.

"Ouch," was all she was saying by way of expressing her pain.

After he'd worked on the buttocks for a few minutes, he stood in front of the girl and began pinching her nipples with his free hand, twisting them until the brownish buds grew stiff. Even the breasts themselves became swollen and started heaving slightly upward.

A soft moan of contentment came from the captive girl's mouth when Olford transferred his hand to the wispy pucker between her legs and fondled it gently.

"Your little puss is positively humming," he said to her with a chuckle. "I think that being flogged must agree with you."

Bridget said nothing. She simply wormed her sex into his hand, arching her pelvis forward and rising slightly on her toes.

"I believe you could use a few more strokes of the leather," Olford said as he took up a stance at her side again.

"No sir, I've had enough," she murmured beneath her breath.

"You'd best behave yourself Bridget," Talbot piped up at this comment from her. "You've a long way to go before your penance has been fully served, you know."

She bit her lip as if trying to hold back from speaking.

This time Neville used the lash in a somewhat more forceful manner, searing it straight across the nude buttocks in quick, cruel strokes that made the girl cry out and hop from one foot to the other, but he only gave her about a dozen licks. Then he laid the whip aside, finished with her.

He walked over to me and told me to enjoy Bridget's body. "I had a turn with that runaway yesterday," he said to me in a confidential tone. Then he turned to Rev. Talbot. "What say you and I go outside and discuss our donation to the your church while my friend gets better acquainted with Bridget."

Talbot's eyes lit up at the mention of money, and the two of them quickly departed.

Then I was alone with that whipped and fettered beauty, and I must say that I'd developed a terrific yen for her by that time. The semi-darkness of the stone chamber made the soft curves of her figure stand out, and the iron restraints made her flesh appear all the more pliant.

I already knew, of course, from watching Neville fondle the girl, that she was at some stage of sexual arousal, but I wanted to test her myself. I walked up to her and placed my right hand on the mound of her sex and felt it carefully, running my fingers up and down the opening to the crevice. Yes, it was pulsating and moist as well.

She looked at me through hazy eyes. "Are you going to stick yourself into me?" she asked.

"I thought we both might enjoy that," I replied with a smile.

She merely nodded.

Already, I was loosing the front of my trousers and taking out my erect member, and as I did, Bridget was spreading her thighs ever so slightly, clearly in need of sexual relief.

As I stepped close and began prodding at the girl's youthful pubis, I reached behind her and took a firm grip on her whipped buttocks, drawing her toward me and ramming my member into her slot. She winced at having her punished flesh grasped so tightly, but she helped by thrusting her hips forward, the pubis wiggling at my penis.

When I managed to sink myself in right up to the hilt, Bridget's feet lifted themselves from the floor, her legs wrapping around me. This left her dangling from the wrist manacles, her only other support being my hands holding her buttocks. But she didn't seem to mind a bit. Her bare body wormed itself about, her pelvis slamming back and forth.

"I'm having my climax already!" she cried out.

It was certainly more than one climax that she was going through, and I let the girl enjoy herself for as long as I could. But finally I wanted the same sort of satisfaction myself, and I unleashed my lust into her warm and willing sex.

I kissed her goodbye before leaving. "I hope the Reverend Talbot isn't too hard on you during the rest of your penance, Bridget," I said to her.

"I'm afraid he will be," she said in a weak voice, "but this small part of it has been delightful, and I thank you."

Outside, I found Neville already mounted up, and I did the same as the good reverend told us to come back anytime. Neville must have made a generous "donation."

Then it was time to be on our way.

***

Hunter gives a lengthy narrative here of their stay in Evanshire, where their accommodation at one of the local inns is much more comfortable than in Langton. Neville spends much of the next morning in a meeting with the local magistrate; conferring on the best ways to handle the unusual times they find themselves in. Hunter explores the village and finds that the stocks, pillory, and whipping post are in place, but on this particular day, they're not in use. They aren't able to get away until almost noon. They reach Black Oak at sunset, and by the time they're riding up to Baxter House, darkness has fallen.

***

I must say, Bertrand, that the sight of Baxter House looming up out of the darkness was an eerie one. It's a great and rambling place, and I've learned that it was a convent at one time. Perhaps the nuns kept it up, but it seems to be falling apart now.

Baxter had retired for the night when we arrived, but a housemaid showed us to our quarters, and as soon as we were settled in, I sat down to write this letter. I'll post it in the morning and write to you as soon as possible.

My best to you
Most Sincerely,
Derek H.

Letter 14 PRIVATE

Dear Bertrand,

Much has occurred since my last communication to you. Thurston Baxter's home is a strange one, and what goes on here is reminiscent of a darker time in history.

There are at least a dozen girls living under Baxter's domain, but only some are wards of the court, the rest being captured runaways. Two of them haven't been found guilty of any crime. They're simply awaiting trial, and in the meantime, Baxter can do as he pleases with them, including trying to wrest their confessions by means of ordeal or the whip.

The tumbledown old building itself is just as dilapidated inside as it is out, but it's filled with all manner of centuries old furniture that would be priceless if it weren't in such bad need of repair.

Baxter's in his late fifties, a large man with head of frazzled hair who dresses in tattered but formal clothing at all times. Surprisingly, the man's happily married to a tall, gaunt woman who goes by the name of Maude, and the two of them share a blissful union, mostly, I suspect, because of their common love for the flagellation of girl-flesh. It's a perverse household they run, and their victims suffer daily.

Neville went into the village on our first morning here, to meet with the local magistrate, and, after I'd written to you and made a few notes in my journals, I found myself just wandering about, first within the house and then out on the grounds as it was one of those rare days filled with sunshine and warmth.

Two unusual events came about during my explorations. The first happened when I was only about a hundred yards from the house, walking down a flagstone pathway that had become moss-covered. As I was rounding a turn, I caught a glimpse of something colorful from the corner of my right eye. Stopping, I looked in that direction, at first thinking I'd been mistaken, but then I saw what had caught my attention. There, standing atop a boulder, was a young girl of golden hair and body, her only covering being a scrap of brown cloth—perhaps silk—tied around her hips. The cloth barely concealed her pubis and only the smallest portion of her buttocks was hidden.

The girl stared straight at me as I began walking slowly closer, approaching her carefully, much the way one would stalk a wild animal. She was fairly ample of breast, the breasts standing high and taut, her body lean and sun-burnished.

When I was close, she jumped to the ground, landing softly on bare feet, a veritable child of the forest.

"Are you from the Baxter house?" she asked, her expression flat. "If you are, don't think you'll capture me. I won't be taken back there to be flogged yet again."

"I'm a guest there," I told her, "and I've no intention of harming you."

Then she asked if I had any food with me, and as I was telling her that I didn't, I realized that I knew her. She was the same girl I'd encountered while riding on Olford's estate, the one girdled in field flowers and calling herself the whore of the woodland!

As soon as she learned that I could offer her no help, she turned and disappeared into the forest, blending into the landscape as quickly and quietly as a deer.

I thought for a moment of pursuing her, but it was easy to see that she'd acclimatised herself to living in the forest. I'd be at a

142

loss.

Still puzzled, I went back to the pathway and continued on my way.

A few minutes later, the second strange incident came about. The pathway had become wider, broadening into an arbour paved with flagstone and surrounded by stone benches. Entering the arbour, I could see two people at the other side. One I recognized as Maude Baxter, sitting on a bench. The other figure was also female, much younger, naked and kneeling on the ground. Having no idea of what might be going on between the two, I started to leave, but Maude saw me, smiled, and beckoned for me to join her.

"I'm glad you came along, Mr. Hunter," she was saying as I took a seat on the bench. "You're just in time to see Karen being put through the paces."

I was staring at the lovely bare creature kneeling sideways a few feet before us. She was clean of limb; her hair longish and auburn, and her pert breasts had softly rounded contours. With her hands folded demurely across her lap, she appeared the picture of docility, prepared to obey.

"Karen was just about to go and pick me a bouquet of fresh switches," Maude was saying while I admired the girl's nudity. "You may go and fetch them now, dear. Pick five or six very long and very thin ones."

Without a word, the bare girl arose and scampered off into the wood, her flesh so alluring against the verdant backdrop.

"Karen's just come under our guardianship," Maude said to me when we were alone. "She's a darling thing, and I'm in the process of making her into my personal pet, if you will. But you'll see. She was an excellent performer last night, and now she's going to be rewarded. Do you enjoy seeing a girl being flogged, Mr. Hunter?"

"I suppose I do find it interesting," I had to admit. "I teach at Rosewood Academy for Girls, and we often use the birch rod on

143

our students, the errant ones that is."

"How I envy you," she said with a laugh. "My mind positively reels when I think of an entire school full of naughty bottoms."

Within two minutes, Karen was back with six newly picked switches in her hand, stripped of all twigs and leaves, thin and long. And when she handed them to her mistress, I saw that her fingers were wet with fresh sap.

"You're such a dear," Maude as she took the switches. "Now give me your hands."

When Karen obeyed, holding her hands out to the woman, wrists crossed, Maude removed a short leather belt from her satchel and cinched the wrists together, drawing it in a full extra notch and pulling it tight enough to make the girl wince and bite her lip.

"Now you may step back several paces and get down on your hands and knees," Maude said to the girl. "Face in the direction of Mr. Hunter."

With her hands fastened, Karen had a bit of difficulty in assuming this posture, but she managed.

Maude had taken out a white ribbon of satin, and now she was tying one end of the bundle of switches together with it, making it into a neat efficient flogging tool. When she was done, she stood and went to stand at the kneeling girl's side, readying the switches in her hand.

"Now, Karen, I know we didn't plan on having a guest with us this morning," she was saying, "but since Mr. Hunter's happened along, I think it's your duty to entertain him properly, don't you?"

"Yes, ma'am," the girl replied. "What would you like me to do?"

Twice the switches flew through the air, hissing over the nude buttocks. "You must tell him of how you pleasured Miss Waverly last night," Maude told her. "Tell him how you used your mouth on her, and look at him as you do."

The girl tilted her head; her face blushing as she looked into my eyes, and when she spoke, the switches began slowly striping her exposed buttocks.

"I was upside down," the girl stammered between strokes, "and Miss Waverly put her sex to my mouth. Somehow, I managed to make her climax."

At Maude's urging, Karen was forced to tell me exactly what had happened to her. It seemed that this Miss Waverly was an old friend and partner in depravity with the Baxters. She'd visited the previous evening, and while she and Maude sipped sherry in one of the drawing rooms, Maude had had two manservants suspend a nude Karen from a ceiling candelabra by her ankles, her mouth at waist level.

At first, the two women had paid no attention to her. They'd talked of old times while Karen hung in the middle of the room. But finally Miss Waverly wanted to see the girl flogged, and Maude used a strap on her victim, warming the bare skin.

"But you're not telling Mr. Hunter how good you were," Maude said as she continued switching Karen's nude hindquarters. "If you don't tell him everything, I won't give you the reward I promised."

"It was when Mrs. Baxter completed my flogging that I was able to bring her friend to happiness," Karen told me, becoming unnerved at having to repeat the lurid details of what she'd done. She was licking her lips even as she trembled beneath the punishment of the switches.

This Miss Waverly had raised her skirts and dropped her undergarments once Karen's body was striped, and then she'd pressed her sex directly to the girl's inverted lips. Karen had no choice but to lick and kiss at the pubis, and, under the threat of another flogging, they'd kept her doing it until she brought Miss Waverly to climax.

"Karen's lips were shining with juices," Maude laughed. "She looked so beautiful."

145

As I said Bertrand, the Baxters are a most depraved duo.

But Maude was by no means done with her "pet." Finished with using the switches on Karen's buttocks, she brought out a white silk scarf and blindfolded the girl and then told her to lie down on her back.

Karen had to comply slowly, the flagstone biting into her raw and punished flesh, but she did as she was told, and once she was on her back, Maude handed her the bundle of switches.

"It's time for your reward, my precious girl," she said as Karen gripped the switches. "You may now flog your cunt until you spend yourself. Won't that be nice?"

"Oh, it will, Mrs. Baxter," the girl exclaimed in all sincerity.

Already Karen had opened her legs, feet flat on the ground, knees drawn up and spread wide. Then, with the switches in hand, she began a light flagellation of her bare pubis, squirming under the mild strokes.

"Karen becomes excited after her rump's been disciplined," Maude said to me in a hushed tone. "The switching I just gave her has made her puss quite needy."

I could well see that she was telling the truth. Karen had a lopsided grin on her lips that conveyed the level of her excitement, and her sex was rising to meet the switches, her buttocks sometimes lifting themselves into the air.

"Does this reward make you glad that you've been so obedient Karen?" Maude Baxter was saying, her face alight with joy.

"Yes it does," the girl managed to say even though she was moaning in rhythm to the self-flagellation. "It feels so refreshing to my puss."

Karen's expression of shame had disappeared. Rather, she was smiling in unabashed delight, loving what she was doing to herself, and I think I have an idea as to why. It seems that a blindfolded girl loses certain inhibitions because she feels as if she's off in a private world of her own. This, of course, releases sexual behaviors that she might not otherwise practice. I believe that this might be an aid for helping our students in the acceptance of their punishments. Blindfolded, they would probably be less reluctant to admit the nature of their wrongs.

"It's so pleasant to see such a pretty little thing wallowing in her own body," Maude was saying. "She simply looks so darling lying there, so naked and so aroused. See how fine her flesh is, how the sun dapples on it."

Karen was twisting herself into the stones of the arbour, her body trembling, cream leaking from her whipped pubis. And then she shuddered while giving out a long groan and cresting herself upward on the tips of her bare toes.

"Uhhh!" came from her lips. "Everything is tingling inside of me."

"Your sex is having a climax, isn't it Karen?" Maude asked in a syrupy-sweet voice,

"Oh, yes, it is!" the naked girl exclaimed as she drove her tender skin at both the switches and the stones beneath her.

All I could do was watch and wonder as Karen orgasmed for what seemed like over a minute, making herself into the picture of self-gratification.

The three of us walked back to the house together, Karen still in the nude, and I asked Maude if she knew anything about the girl I'd seen earlier.

"Yes, that's Gwendolyn, a runaway," she told me. "We had her in custody until she made an escape, but she won't be on the run much longer. Our groundskeepers are searching her out, and when they bring her to me, I pity her rump."

———

I spent the afternoon with my notes, concentrating mostly on the material I'm gathering for the manual on the art and science of corporal discipline. I'm obtaining much valuable information concerning the psychological aspects of the subject through observing extreme flagellation during this sojourn. Combining this with the histories of the many young ladies we've dealt with at

Rosewood, it could be a case-by-case treatise, each case illustrated with information on how we've handled our students.

Neville returned by early evening, and we dined with the Baxters, the meal served by two of the girls being held here. The girls wore nothing but scraps of cloth tied around their hips and through their crotches, leaving their intimate portions scarcely covered and their youthful breasts fully nude. They served silently, both seemingly in fear of the Baxters and the uniformed housemaid who watched over them, arms folded across her chest.

"I think you gentlemen can well see that we're doing something about the harlots here in Black Oak," Baxter said to us after we'd been making polite and general conversation. "Anyone can see that they're all a pack of sluts who've let some sort of diabolical menace take charge of them. The only way of dealing with them is by the whip or worse, and that's just what we're doing."

Olford was mostly noncommittal on the matter, but he did mention that his primary concern for Stonehurst was the prevention of civil unrest.

"But I've heard that you send your fair share of girls to the pillory and the stocks," Baxter replied.

"Indeed I do, and, for many of these young ladies, it's just what they need," Olford told him. "Those of us in authority are engaged in a real balancing act these days."

As they were speaking, one of the half-naked serving girls almost tripped, her bare toes catching in a frayed spot of the carpet. It was really nothing. Oh, I suppose she might have spilled something, but she didn't.

Maude however, grew livid at the girl's mistake and immediately called the housemaid to her side. "Bind this clumsy thing hand and foot, Ida," she said. "Then strip her naked and give her 17 strokes of the birch.

The serving girl, a fair young miss with hair the color of sand, became frightened, her eyes opening wide. "Please don't have me flogged, Mrs. Baxter," she pleaded. "I'll be more careful."

148

"Don't talk back to me, Alice," Maude snapped at her. "Just for that, you'll receive an extra 5 strokes of the birch, and you'll be tied into a bowed position when your flogging's done with.

Ida, apparently happy at the opportunity to birch the girl, took Alice well away from the table, where all of us could see her. Then she ripped the girl's scrap of covering away from her.

"Lie face down on the floor, Alice," she said to the now-naked girl. "Hands behind your back."

While the girl obeyed, Ida went to a closet and returned with several lengths of sturdy, tightly-woven silken cord.

The worn, burgundy-red carpet served to enhance the unblemished texture of Alice's skin, and when Ida stood over her in her maid's uniform and sturdy shoes, the girl appeared ever so frail and vulnerable.

After tying Alice's wrists securely behind her back, yanking at the rope and making her captive whimper, Ida then trussed the ankles together, and once she had the girl bound up, she went to a corner where a birch switch was propped and brought it back with her.

"Begin whenever you're ready Ida," Maude was saying, a thin leer on her lips. "Do her hard and do her slowly. Make her wait for each lick."

That's exactly what Ida did. She raised the birch high and held it there for several moments, relishing the girl at her feet, making the victim anticipate the fire that would soon singe her unprotected nudity.

Then, as the flogging began, the Baxters went back to conversation even as the sound of the rod on bare buttocks crackled through the air.

"The time for mollycoddling these young strumpets is over and done with," Thurston said as he sipped his wine. "Alice probably doesn't know it fully, but right now she's getting just what she needs."

I was listening, but I kept glancing at the flogging taking place

149

a few feet away. Alice was grinding herself at the carpet, her feet bucking up and down, her wrists fighting the rope. And the poor girl could hardly help but moan her discomfort.

"We've two girls that we're going to work with this evening," Maude said to us. "One is being held here until she's brought to the pillory, the other we need a confession from."

It seemed that Thurston had brought the girl who was to be flogged in the pillory home, telling the magistrate that he'd "toughen her up" for the lash. The other girl had yet to stand trial, but she was planning to proclaim her innocence to all. The Baxters had been given the task of wringing a confession from her by any means they chose, a most enjoyable endeavor for both of them.

"Yes, of course, I'd be honored to watch you working on the two young ladies in question as I'm certain Mr. Hunter would," Olford told them. "Thank you for your invitation."

Ida had finished giving Alice the prescribed number of stripes with the birch, and now she was cinching the girl's ankles to her wrists, drawing her into a severe arch, the strained toes touching the fingers.

"That should keep her out of harm's way Ida," Maude said with a chuckle when the woman was done with the binding. "Thank you."

As we enjoyed a light dessert course, pretty Alice was worming about on the floor, tiny moans still coming from her lips. I could see that Ida had been most thorough with the reddening of her buttocks, the stripes glowing brightly.

Yes, Bertrand, I felt sympathy for the girl, but I also found her appearance quite alluring in such stringent bondage.

When dinner ended, we adjourned to another room, simply leaving the unfortunate Alice lying there bound, and I had to wonder when someone would come to release her.

Olford and I had a few minutes alone before we were to view the girls that Maude had been speaking of during dinner. "It's my opinion that the Baxters are half-mad," he said to me in the shadowy hallway, "and it's anyone's guess what they're planning on doing with these two girls, but, in the interests of diplomacy, we'll have to go along with them. They've been getting away with this sort of behavior for some time, and it's likely they'll be allowed to continue."

The Baxters led us to probably the largest room in their home, a vast, high-ceilinged chamber that had probably once been used as a meeting hall. Two rows of stone columns led through the center of it, and it was partially lit by tall candelabra and several lanterns.

"Let us introduce you to Lenka first," Thurston was saying as we walked in. He was rubbing his hands in anticipation. "She's the one we're toughening up for a public whipping."

Lenka was bent over a square wooden table that measured about four feet across. She was fully naked, feet on the floor, her upper body lying atop the table. Long straps were tied to her wrists, the opposite ends attached to two of the table legs. This, of course, left her hindquarters displayed and most available to anyone who might want to use them. Her ankles were spread and strapped to the table's other two supports, a pose ideal for buttock punishment.

I saw that the girl, although well shaped, had a lean and hungry wolf-like appearance about her that was somehow rather attractive. Her hair was a lustrous chocolate-brown color, but it hung about her shoulders in disorderly strands as if she'd been there for some time.

Maude was quick about getting close to the captive nude. "Doesn't she have a most fetching little bottom," she said to us as she ran a hand lovingly over the buttock-flesh, letting her longest finger slide between the two globes. "I'm sure she'll be proud to show it to the townspeople when she's strapped into the pillory posts."

As the woman's hand continued its adoring explorations, I was able to see that the buttocks were already well punished.

They had a deep pinkish hue about them, but the color was beginning to fade, making it clear that she probably hadn't tasted a flogging for an hour or so. Instead, she'd been forced to wait for whatever might befall her next, bound to the table and ignored.

Lying on the floor was a flat, leather strap with a wooden handle. "This is one of my favorite tools for flogging a guilty rump," Thurston was telling us as he picked up the lash-strap. "It covers a wide area of flesh and induces a rather all-inclusive sort of pain. Good for use on the back and shoulders as well."

Maude stepped out of the way, and Thurston stood directly behind the bare girl, planting his boots solidly on the floor, and then swinging the strap back and forth across Lenka's buttocks.

A shriek came from the girl's mouth the moment the lash touched her bare buttocks. They were likely sore from who knows how many previous thrashings.

Olford must have noticed the same thing. He asked Maude how long the girl had been strapped out to the table.

The woman let out a sadistic laugh. "She's been there since late afternoon, and she still has a ways to go," she said. "You can believe that she'll sleep with her welts tonight. I've informed my staff that anyone who wants to can have a turn at flogging her, and several have had a go at her already. She'll think twice before she acts like a whore in this town again."

After he'd given the girl a dozen strokes or so, Thurston put the strap aside. "That should hold her for a while,î he said. "Now I must show you the girl who won't admit to her crimes."

Maude stayed with Lenka, and I looked back to see her applying oil to the girl's punished rump, cooing to her as if she was concerned, but it wasn't long before I heard the strap striking flesh yet again.

At the other side of the room, a girl of youth and beauty with strawberry-tinted hair was just being prepared. She was lying face up, nude on a long iron ladder had been propped between two heavy stone blocks that stood at about the height of a person's knees, while a pair of the Baxter's manservants tied her down with leather straps, her hands and feet spread to the ladder's sides. She appeared frightened in the ghostly candlelight, her body quivering, her hair falling about the stone block behind her head.

"I'd introduce you to the lovely Miss Allyson if she weren't quite so busy with being strapped into place," Baxter said to us as we entered the circle of light, "but, for what she's about to go through, being bound is an absolute necessity."

As he spoke, the two butlers finished with the bondage and stepped to one side, where a low charcoal brazier was burning, ominous waves of heat rising from it.

Baxter walked slowly toward the prone nude. When he was next to her, one of his hands went to her right nipple and twisted until she let out a soft whimper.

"You're in for much worse than a mere pinch of the nipple if you're not willing to admit to wrongdoing," he said to her in a level tone.

He explained to us that this girl had been observed in the act of divining the future with playing cards but wouldn't confess to what she'd done.

"More than likely she was engaged in a game of patience," Olford whispered to me as Baxter went back to toying with the girl.

"Come now, Allyson," he was saying as he ran his fingers down her abdomen and rested them in her pubic area. "You'll feel much better once you've confessed. Then you can go to the village courtroom for sentencing, take your punishment, and be done with all of this."

Now he was tweaking the sensitive outer folds of her pubis, making her tug at the bindings and writhe her bare body at the ladder.

"Has this girl's cunt been flogged tonight?" Baxter asked the taller of the two butlers.

"Yes, it was given a nonstop birching of ten minutes duration while she hung upside down by the ankles, the feet well apart," the man answered. "Then we gave it 17 strokes of the three-thonged lash."

"Very thorough," Baxter replied. "She's wet in her crevice already, and we've barely started."

He was running his hands over every portion of her nudity now, quite plainly enjoying having this lovely girl bound and at his mercy.

"I'll give you another chance before we begin, Allyson," he said in a patient voice. "Admit that you were divining the future with those playing cards."

"I know nothing of fortune telling," she cried out. "Why won't you believe me?"

He paid no attention. Rather, he nodded to the butlers and each of them picked up a long set of tongs. Then they used the tools to begin sliding the fiery brazier toward the ladder!

I'll tell you, Bertrand, I watched with an increasing sense of horror when I realized that they were about to put that container of red-hot coals directly beneath the bound and naked girl.

They slid the brazier to a place directly beneath the center of Allyson's body, the coals not two feet from the bare flesh, nothing between her and the heat but the iron of the ladder.

"Since you have no clothing on, you're probably a little chilly," Thurston said to her as stepped back from the heat. "Perhaps if we warm you up a bit, you'll be more apt to tell us the truth." He had a cruel and maniacal gleam in his eyes.

The girl was able to withstand the heat of the coals for only a few moments before she began struggling at her bonds, an anguished moaning erupting from her lips just as a coating of perspiration formed on her taut skin.

"How can you do this to me?" she cried out in less than a half minute. "I'm on fire."

They couldn't leave the coals under her for very long. She was sure to faint or much worse. I could see her flesh glistening with heat, her perspiration dripping down into the fire, causing a hissing steam to rise.

"Now will you confess, or shall I have these men place the coals beneath you once again?" Baxter snarled at her. "I've plenty of time to torture you, you know."

"Have pity, sir," she sobbed. "I've done no wrong."

Her words fell on deaf ears. Thurston was already nodding for the brazier to be replaced beneath the ladder. And again, Allyson was forced to suffer, unable to escape the fiery heat of the coals no matter how she wrenched at her bindings.

I watched as they repeated the procedure again and again. The heat would sear through her vulnerable flesh until she was about to lose consciousness. Then Baxter would have it removed ut only long enough for her to recover. Then it would be under the ladder again.

The vast hall was becoming a veritable cacophony of sound. Allyson's screams and pleas for mercy echoed through the dark shadows, and from the other side of the chamber, I heard the sound of Lenka's flesh being flogged yet again. She, too, was shrieking as her body reached the limits of its endurance.

"I'm going to go over and watch Lenka being flogged," Olford said to me. "I find her rather pleasant to look at, and I might even take a hand at using the strap on her."

Allyson, by now, had gone off into delirium. Her screaming had the high-pitched sound of a banshee, and her struggles were so violent that the leather straps were actually biting into her skin.

Baxter was becoming exasperated at not being able to wrest a confession from the girl, even though he was enjoying the torturing of this girl. To subjugate her even more, he began using a thin birch on her sex. The naked flesh-hillock was already ablaze from the heat the coals, and when the birch began snapping at it, it was enough to finally drive the girl to do as she'd been told."

"I'll say anything you wish," she cried out, "but please give me relief from this awful torment."

"Did you divine fortunes with playing cards?" Baxter asked.

"Yes, yes, yes!" she replied. "Will this torture stop now?!"

"Yes my dear," Baxter said, calm now as he laid the rod aside, "and you shall be rewarded handsomely for your honesty."

I saw what her "reward" was going to be. After the brazier was taken from under the ladder for the last time, Baxter and the two servants began surrounding the girl, clearly preparing to take turns with using her defenseless body for sexual purposes.

"Do join us Mr. Hunter," I heard Thurston saying as I walked away from this scene of medieval torture. "Can't you see that the fires have well-prepared this young lady for some first class fucking?"

I thanked him but continued on my way, heading in the direction of the girl being table-flogged.

The so-called toughening up of Lenka's buttocks seemed to be at an end, at least for the time being. As Neville looked on, Maude was oiling the red and punished flesh, speaking in soothing tones that made it sound as if she was truly concerned about the girl that she'd just beaten.

"I know that these preliminary floggings must be a little hard on you, Lenka my dear," she was saying as her hands devoured the young buttocks, "but you'll thank me when they're strapping you into the village pillory for a real whipping. When that time comes, your pretty rump will be ready to withstand the rigors of the punishment they're going to give you."

Lenka managed to thank the heartless woman, and as she did, I saw that a light trickle of juice was appearing at the top of her thighs. Then I glanced at Neville to see that he had a true yen for the bound girl.

"I'm off now," Maude told us abruptly and left the room.

Olford smiled his thanks when I told him that I was leaving too. He'd now be alone with the nude and tethered girl he was lusting for, and from all indications, she was primed for just that sort of thing.

Once back in my room that night I certainly had my share of scribbling to do on the subjects of sex-torture and question by ordeal but very little on corporal punishment where schoolgirls were concerned, although the position Lenka had been fastened into gave me something to think about, and I eventually wrote a bit about it.

The way Lenka had been bound up might be something for us to think about, Bertrand. Just the position itself would be a humbling experience for a student guilty of pride. We'd have her nude, of course, and one of us could sit at the end of the table to lecture the girl, looking into her eyes, while the other administered the birching. I'm not sure which I'd enjoy more, but it's one more thing we might think of.

We'll be here at the Baxters' residence for a few days more, and I'll write before we're off on the next leg of our journey.

Most Sincerely,
Derek H.

Letter 15 PRIVATE

Dear Bertrand,

I'm relieved to say that we'll leaving Baxter House early to-morrow morning. In a perverse sort of way, it's been quite entertaining and even informative staying here, but there are times when this place conjures up images of the worst sort of lunatic asylum.

During our stay, I've been able to fully explore this place. Being quite proud of the lifestyle they've accomplished, the

157

Baxters gave me free rein to poke around wherever I chose, and you can believe that what I found would be shocking to most people.

All of the girls being held captive here sleep in a large common room on one of the upper floors. They take their slumber completely naked, their beds consisting of nothing more than thin straw pallets. When they retire for the night, their wrists are locked into chains mounted in the wall, and their ankles are locked to chains embedded in the floor.

The Baxters allow their staff members to use these girls for sexual purposes. Anyone who wants to is permitted to go there in the night and fornicate with the girl of his or her choice. Yes, I've seen several of the female staff going there, and shortly afterward I'll hear the sound of a young female voice moaning in pain or pleasure or both.

The girls go about in nothing more than scraps of cloth that conceal very little, and the Baxters are forever forcing them out of even these paltry coverings in order to better flog them.

On one afternoon, I came across a very curious room at the end of a long hallway. After opening a wide door, I went in and found that the large space contained various pieces of discipline equipment—a whipping stool, wooden restraint chairs, and hooks and rings with chains affixed to them. In the very center of the room, a steel trapeze hung from the ceiling. The floors were uncovered as were the tall windows. I learned later that the Baxter's call this their "corrections room."

At the opposite side of the room, a tall wooden ladder was leaning against the wall, and much to my surprise, I saw that a nude girl had been tied to it with leather straps. Needless to say, I couldn't resist going closer to investigate, and as I drew near, I saw that it was Lenka, the girl I'd seen table-flogged on our first full evening here. I suppose I really shouldn't have been surprised as the Baxters are always leaving these girls bound up after whipping them.

I said hello to Lenka and asked if she knew who I was.

She turned to look at me. "I'm not sure, but I think your name is Mr. Hunter," she said.

"That's right," I told her. "I suppose we weren't properly introduced the first time I saw you."

She knew what I was talking about and turned her face from mine, shamed by what I'd seen her go through.

Lenka's hands were tied to an upper rung, one wrist at each side of the ladder, and her ankles were tied in the same way to the very bottom rung. Her naked toes were unable touch the floor, probably a very uncomfortable position, and I could easily see that her buttocks had been recently flogged. Fresh stripes laced the girlish flesh.

As I inspected her, she asked if I'd come there to give her a flogging, and I told her no, that I'd come upon this room by accident.

Lenka seemed quite relieved to hear this, and then she asked if I'd rub some oil into her punished areas. "The oil makes my bottom feel ever so much better," she said to me. "I think Mrs. Baxter left some on that whipping stool."

Sure enough, there was a large bottle of oil where she'd said it would be, and I picked it up and poured some onto my right hand. The prospect of fondling Lenka's buttocks while oiling them was most assuredly a pleasant one.

I oiled her gently, rubbing the liquid thoroughly into her youthful skin. The flesh was still warm from whatever had been used on it, and her body squirmed from my touch.

"I don't mean to do that," she said, "but I can't help it. Mrs. Baxter thrashed me horribly with a leather strap. I'm very sore."

I told her that I understood and continued my ministrations, still enjoying the feel of her nudity.

"I'd release you, but I don't have the authority to do so," I said to her while I stopped to douse my palm with more of the oil.

"Oh no, you mustn't do that," she gasped with a note of panic in her voice. "If Mrs. Baxter should come back and find me loose, she'd begin my punishment all over again."

When I went back to work on her, I noticed that her lips were moving as if she was rehearsing something she wanted to say, and I asked her what was wrong.

"Well, I just wondered if you'd rub some of the oil into my puss," she said. "Mrs. Baxter used the strap on it. I know I shouldn't ask a stranger to touch me there, but it's so very itchy and sore."

Reaching between her legs, I rubbed the downy cleft. Again, she pulled involuntarily from my touch, but I told her that I'd try to be more gentle with her, and she was soon relaxed, even helping me a bit by worming her mound into my hand. This area was even warmer than her buttocks, and I could feel a slight pulsation in it that hinted at sexual arousal. Naturally, this gave me ideas, and I was soon yearning to step up onto the lowest rung and plant my member into her. Of course, I knew it wouldn't be a problem. As I mentioned, the Baxters make these girls available to everyone under their roof.

"Being flogged seems to have done something to your puss," I said to her as I ran my longest finger into it, finding that it was quite juicy.

She became open with me then, telling me that much of her burning was coming from within. Her breath was coming faster, and she'd begun to wiggle about on the ladder.

"Tell me the truth, Lenka," I said to her as I diddled with her swollen clitoris. "You'd love to get a good fucking right now, wouldn't you?"

She closed her eyes and sighed. "Yes, I would," she said ever so softly.

Suddenly, I wanted to possess that girl in an odd sort of way. I wanted her to admit that a flogging had made her pubis ache for sexual contact.

After pulling my manhood from my trousers, I stood on the

ladder's bottom rung, sticking myself between her thighs and teasing the outer lips of her pubis.

That girl was more desperate than I'd thought. "I thought you were going to put it inside of me sir," she murmured.

"Why do you need it?" I asked her. "Did you get excited while the leather was being used on your flesh?"

"I guess that's when it started," she said to me.

"Was it the pain that aroused you?" I said.

By questioning her this way and teasing her with my penis at the same time, I got her to reveal some most interesting facts. She claimed that it wasn't the pain that was arousing but a combination of two other factors—the feeling of being needed and the sheer warmth that ran through her flesh when it was whipped.

Once she'd made these admissions, I rewarded her by ramming my member deep into her, and the moment I did, that girl's body lurched at me, the pubis tightening in orgasm. Her buttocks hammered back and forth as she received what she seemed to need so badly, and her wriggling at the ladder became positively frantic.

Needless to say, I fully spent myself into her, and it was a union that I found to be highly gratifying.

That evening I told Neville about this strange room and the incident with Lenka, and his interest was keen. In his library there's a ladder similar to the one in the Baxters' corrections room. It's used for putting books on the higher shelves, and Neville seemed to think that it would be a perfect implement of discipline for Amanda.

"I believe an hour or so strung up like that with a birching or two thrown in for good measure would do the naughty Miss Smith a world of good," he said, smiling and stroking his goatee. "We'll have to put her on the library ladder as soon as we return."

The Baxters' cruelty and their creativity when it comes to

putting their girls into restraint seem to know no bounds. Since being here, I've seen every form of bondage and punishment possible, but one of the most unusual punishments occurred just yesterday.

Gwendolyn, the wood nymph, was captured during the late afternoon. I was looking out of a window when I saw her being dragged out of the forest by two groundskeepers. Her hands were tied together in front of her, and a long rope was attached to the wrist binding. The groundskeepers were on horseback, and one of them had the other end of the long piece of rope attached to his saddle. Thus, Gwendolyn had to trot right along to keep up. Her piece of covering was still on, but it hung precariously loose, and she was dirt-splattered from living out of doors.

Maude emerged from the house as they drew near, a triumphant smile on her lips. She was accompanied by three uniformed housemaids, and she immediately told them to strip the girl and get her cleaned up for punishment.

"I wouldn't sully a lash-strap on that girl," I heard her saying. "The whore's filthy."

The housemaids untied Gwendolyn's wrists, grabbed her by the forearms and hauled her over to a washtub while ripping her one piece of clothing from her. They put her in the big tub, filled it with cold well water, and then proceeded to clean her up with a stiff-bristle brush, two of them holding her while the other did the scrubbing. Surely it had to be a quite uncomfortable way to get washed up.

When they were almost done with her, one of them went into the house and returned with a shaving mug and a razor. Then they stood her up, lathered her pubis and shaved it down to the bare skin. Being wet, the little mound gleamed in a most attractive way. She had no hair anywhere else on her body, but the maid with the razor flicked it over the girl's body anyway, making sure that Gwendolyn was entirely smooth.

Once they were done with cleaning her, they pulled the girl

into the house, and that was the last I heard of it until the dinner hour.

"The escaped girl was brought in this afternoon," Maude said to Neville and me just as we were finishing the meal, "and this evening she'll be punished in the main hall before everyone in this household. I do hope that you two gentlemen will be in attendance."

We assured her that we'd be there.

I suppose I hadn't realized just how many people the Baxters have working for them. With the maids, butlers, the kitchen staff, the groundskeepers, and the coachmen, there were probably a good 25 people in the hall when we arrived. I'm referring to the large room where I saw Allyson and Lenka flogged.

Straight backed chairs upholstered in maroon velvet had been set out in wide semi-circle, and we took our seats with the others. Thurston was present, but Maude and the runaway girl were nowhere to be seen. A hushed air was about the hall, and many candelabra had been lit, making the whole atmosphere one of formality.

From somewhere far off I heard the sound of a large bell being struck one time only. And then, from out of the shadows, Maude led Gwendolyn into the light, holding the girl by one arm.

Gwendolyn had been dressed in a white towel-like garment that was simply wrapped around her. Her hands were in front of her, and a short chain with manacles at the ends of it held her hands together, her wrists being clamped into the manacles.

Maude brought her victim to a halt when they were in the center of the semi-circle. "I bring before you the girl who didn't appreciate our hospitality and chose to live in the woods instead," she said. "She's here to take punishment for this, and, hopefully, to apologize for her lack of good manners."

With that said, Maude pulled the towel-like garment away from Gwendolyn's body, revealing her fully. The girl wore nothing beneath, and her smooth nudity stood out in a most pristine manner in the shimmering light of all the candelabra.

Maude said something to her that no one else could hear, and Gwendolyn got down on her knees, her buttocks resting on the stone floor between the upturned soles of her bare feet. Then she leaned forward until the palms of her hands were flat on the floor. This left her rump pushed outward in a perfect posture for accepting a flogging.

When the girl was in position, Thurston rose from his chair, a long birch rod in hand, and stood behind her.

"Let us all hope that this ingrate has the good sense to convey her regrets to us," Maude said as she sat down in the chair that her husband had vacated.

Thurston began using the rod in a manner that was entirely heartless. He started with the buttocks, drawing the birch back and forth across them so ruthlessly that the hall reverberated with the sound of flesh being switched. He wore a smile of pleasure as he went about this task, clearly enjoying the girl's suffering, and, when I took a glance around me, I saw that the audience was taking an equal enjoyment in what they were witnessing.

Gwendolyn's lips were parted in a silent cry for help, and her head nodded downward after about the fifth or sixth stroke.

"You will face the onlookers," Thurston said to her. "Keep your head up and your eyes open."

Gwendolyn obeyed quickly, probably knowing that the flogging would get worse if she didn't.

After doing a more than thorough job on the girl's naked posterior, Thurston turned his attentions to her back and began striping a crisscross pattern over it with the birch.

It was at this that Gwendolyn seemed to reach the limit of her endurance, and she broke down and began shrieking her pain each time the rod struck. Her flesh trembled as the tip of her tongue hung out of the side of her mouth. The bare breasts heaved themselves up and down to her gasping breath, and I could hear little half-sobs coming out of her.

"That's enough," she was able to say. "I've learned my lesson. I'm so sorry that I ran from your house. It won't happen again."

"It certainly won't," Thurston said with a snort. "You're going to be kept in chains at all times."

And even as the girl continued to plead with him and express her regrets for having escaped, Baxter went back to flogging her buttocks, going at them as if he had no thought of ever stopping.

When the girl was raw and red, Maude stood, and her husband ceased the horrid birch punishment. She ordered the girl to remain in the kneeling position but to sit up straight while putting her hands on her sex.

"You will now open your knees wide and masturbate your cunt to orgasm," Maude said to the girl. "While you do it, you will continue to look at my staff, the people who tried to make you welcome."

Gwendolyn's whole body blushed with shame at the very idea of what she now had to do, but she began to manipulate herself, fearful of the tool in Thurston's hands. He was standing at her side, the birch at the ready.

It was quickly obvious that Gwendolyn was highly sensitive to sexual stimulation. A shudder ran over her as soon she touched her sex, and her tongue emerged from her mouth to lick at her upper lip. The little pubis was moving itself onto her searching fingers while the chain that linked her wrist manacles made a soft clanking sound.

The entire hall was very quiet, but then Thurston brought the birch down on the girl's back, and the smacking sound filled the air.

The combination of being flogged and masturbating at the same time had an immediate effect on the kneeling girl. Suddenly she rammed her longest finger deep within herself and let out a long groan as her shaven mound started pounding at the finger.

A wailing sound came forth from Gwendolyn's mouth as she

looked from face to face through dazed eyes. The girl was being overwhelmed by orgasm and not just one. She seemed to be going through a series of them, one following another. And she didn't seem to mind being subjected to the birch yet again. Her pleasure was so great that she was oblivious to all else.

It was quite a performance, I'll tell you Bertrand, and as I watched I couldn't help but wonder how many of our Rosewood girls have been right on the brink of this sort of behavior when undergoing punishment.

As I mentioned at the beginning of this letter, it has indeed been entertaining staying here at Baxter House, but I'll be glad to depart in the morning and be done with this madhouse.

Also, I find myself looking forward to seeing Tarin. Neville is of the firm opinion that I should remain her chief disciplinarian—at least as long as my visit lasts—and it's a task that I see as quite enjoyable. It won't be long before I have that girl trussed and nude for the lessons in humility that she so needs. Needless to say, I still ache for her lovely body, but time will tell how that aspect of her training goes.

We're on a circuitous route, so we won't be passing through Langton and Evanshire again. We'll only visit one major village, where Neville will meet with the local magistrate, so if we ride long and hard, we could possibly be back at his estate in just a little over two days, a prospect that suits me fine.

I probably won't write during the journey, but I'll get a letter off upon our return though that might also take a day or two. I'll need time to get settled in, meet with Tarin, and get my research back into motion.

My best to you and everyone at Rosewood

Sincerely,

Derek H.

—

Letter 16 PRIVATE

Dear Bertrand,

I'm happy to be able to write and tell you that I'm back at Olford's estate. We arrived two days ago in the late afternoon following a hard ride, and I must say that when this house came into sight, I felt a true sense of homecoming.

Immediately upon our arrival, I went to my quarters and slept soundly through the night and well into the next morning.

Neville and I had a sumptuous breakfast together, and then I repaired to the library to get my work in order. But I wasn't alone there long. Within the hour, Neville came in, telling me that we needed to get a report from Ruth on the behavior of Amanda and Tarin.

A few minutes later we were joined by Ruth, and her report was not a good one. On several occasions, Amanda had upset the household by playing with Neville's dog in a most raucous fashion, and she'd also been negligent in her chores. Ruth had sent her out to pick a small basket of berries one day, and when she hadn't returned after an hour had passed, Ruth had gone to look for her only to find the girl frolicking in a stream, naked.

"Amanda's such an irritating child! I gave her a few hours on the platform after the berry picking incident, but I'm sure she knows that that won't be the end of it."

"No, it won't," Neville replied, and even as he spoke, he was glancing at the ladder propped against the bookshelves.

But it was Tarin who'd been truly rebellious in our absence. As I've told you, Bertrand, these girls aren't given a lot of chores. Their chief occupation while here is simply to learn to conduct themselves in a ladylike manner.

Tarin had been doing her chores satisfactorily, but Ruth claimed that the girl had done so with a certain aloofness.

"She thinks she's too good for honest work," the woman said to us. "The girl's nothing but haughty."

I knew that this couldn't be entirely true. After all, Tarin was used to living on a farm. It seemed that, once again her dignity and her way of removing herself from things had gotten her into trouble. This was the very sort of behavior that caused the people of Stonehurst to dislike her.

"Thank you, Ruth," Olford said to the woman when she was done with her report. "I'd greatly appreciate it if you'd fetch Amanda now."

While Ruth was gone, Neville told me that he wanted to leave the problem of Tarin in my hands. "But I do believe her situation warrants serious discipline," he said. "Tarin has a fine spirit, and you know I admire it, but if she continues to act like this after I give her her freedom, there's no telling what the jealous women of Stonehurst might do with her."

I told him I'd handle it, already savoring the thought of having that young beauty nude and bound up for punishment. After all my reading on the subject of punishment, I was anxious to employ some new techniques.

Olford was quite curt with Amanda when Ruth brought her into the library. Without elaborating as to why, he told her that he wasn't satisfied with the way she'd been conducting herself. Then he ordered her to remove her dress.

Amanda seemed a bit confused, but she quickly did as she'd been told, revealing that fair and delicious body of hers, and while she was stripping herself, Neville asked Ruth to get some belts and straps from the drawer where they're kept handy.

"Fix Amanda up to the ladder," he said to her. "Hands together at a top rung, ankles together at a lower one. Make sure her feet are unable to touch the floor."

Ruth smiled, eager to victimize the now-nude Amanda. She belted the naked girl's hands together in front of her and then had her stand on the very bottom rung of the ladder with her arms

168

raised high. Then she used a strap to fasten Amanda's wrists to a rung near the top, cinching the leather tightly.

"Step off the rung you're standing on Amanda," she said once she had the girl's wrists secured.

When Amanda complied, she was left dangling; her wriggling toes unable to find a footing as the floor was several inches below them.

Ruth then belted the girl's ankles together and fixed them to the bottom rung with another leather strap. Thus Amanda was left hanging on the ladder, tied to both the top and the bottom of it.

Neville decided to administer the flogging himself and dismissed Ruth.

Once she'd left the room, he picked up a birch rod and stood behind Amanda. "I understand that you've been somewhat remiss in your chores during my absence," he said to her, snapping the switch in the air with an ominous cracking sound. "What do you have to say for yourself?"

"It's not true," she said in a tone that was almost indignant. "I did everything I was told to do."

"I see," he said to her, "and were you told to frolic about naked and go for a swim while you were at it?"

Amanda didn't answer for a few moments. She'd been found out, and her bare buttocks clenched themselves together in fear of the birch.

"Well, I wasn't exactly told to do that," she answered slowly, "but I got terribly dirty while picking berries, and I thought it would be a good idea to clean myself up before returning to the house."

Olford burned the rod straight across the middle of Amanda's buttocks. "You're going to learn to follow directions," he told her in an angry tone, "and you're also going to pay for telling these little fibs of yours."

"But I've told no fibs, sir!" she whined, truly frightened now.

169

She could see that this was to be no light birching.

Olford paid no attention to her. Already he'd drawn the birch back to begin her punishment in earnest. Then he started swinging the wooden instrument back and forth across those fair and naked buttocks with a force that would surely teach the girl a good lesson.

Amanda made no attempt at false bravery. The light red stripes appeared on her flesh almost immediately, and she shrieked with each lick of the birch. Her body struggled at the straps that held her in place, toes straining themselves toward the floor, her pelvis worming about while her hair flew around her shoulders. This wasn't one of the schoolgirl-type thrashings she'd undergone in the past. This was genuine punishment.

I saw that her delicate body had broken out in a blush that was probably caused by both shame and suffering, and her shrieking became mixed with a sort of half sobbing sound.

"Please don't beat me any longer, Mr. Olford," she cried out at one point. "You have my promise that I'll always do as I'm told."

"Yes you will," Neville replied, "but that doesn't exempt you from paying for your past misbehavior. You neglected duty, and you'll take your birching for it."

He kept it up until Amanda was gasping, and, even after he'd laid the rod aside, her body continued in its uncontrollable writhing.

Then he told me that he'd be going into the village to catch up on things at the courthouse. "I'll spend the night at the inn," he said. "Court will be back in session early tomorrow."

Gesturing toward Amanda, he said that she needed to stay right where she was for at least an hour and asked if I'd give her another birching before releasing her. Of course I was glad to oblige.

"And I'll tend to Tarin this afternoon," I said to him.

Olford was all for that. He wanted the girl's behavior modified as soon as possible. "I've an idea," he said just as he was leaving the room. "Loose Amanda's ankles during the last fifteen minutes of her hour on the ladder. Perhaps it would do her good to dangle by her wrists for a while. If she should try to step up onto that bottom rung to rest herself, take the lash to her until she learns better."

After Neville's departure, not five minutes had elapsed before Amanda underwent a rapid change, as that girl tends to do. While I was going over my notes, her voice abruptly broke my concentration.

"Do I look pretty on this ladder, Mr. Hunter?" I heard her saying, and, when I glanced up, I saw her looking over her shoulder at me, a mischievous grin on her face.

"I believe we've been through this before Amanda," I said to her. "Now you'd better behave yourself or your second switching will go even harder than the first."

I could tell that she was trying to rub her thighs together in a effort to stimulate her sex, and that made her bare rump gyrate itself in a manner that was most appealing.

No longer able to focus on my work, I went to the ladder and unfastened her ankles in order to fondle her. "You may stand on the bottom rung, Amanda," I told her. "It's only during the last fifteen minutes of this hour that you're required to hang by your wrists."

When the girl stepped up onto the rung, she placed her naked feet at each side of it, leaving her legs open. She might as well have come right out and asked me to put my hand on her pubis.

I trickled the fingers of my right hand very slowly up the inside of her left thigh, teasing her, and then cupped her shaven mound with my palm. She was quite warm, faintly moist, and she pushed herself into my grip.

"That feels so good sir," she whispered. "It makes getting tied up and punished worth it."

I quickly realized that my caress could ruin the disciplinary

171

nature of her session on the ladder and removed my hand. She needed to suffer, not enjoy herself, if she was ever going to learn to behave in a manner that would keep her out of trouble. But I again touched her, this time spanking on the pubis. In her state, she was quite sensitive there, and she started to pull her thighs together.

After telling her to stay as she was, I gave her a thorough puss-spanking, sending her into a fresh torrent of shrieking.

When I was done, I gave her a strict admonition to remain quiet for the duration of the hour and told her that if she disobeyed me, she could expect to have the lash used on her. That was enough to silence the girl.

Becoming immersed in my work, I was surprised when I noticed that it was time for Amanda to hang by her wrists. "Step off of that bottom rung," I said to her, "and you'd better not let me catch you trying to get your feet back on it."

She did as I'd told her, and it made for pleasant viewing. Because of dangling by the wrists only, Amanda couldn't seem to keep herself from fidgeting about. As she wiggled, her wrists twisted at the leather bindings, and this made her luscious buttocks swing themselves from side to side as the toes of her little feet curled under, the soles crinkling from the strain.

But she managed to cease her flirting, keeping herself quiet while she hung there, and for this reason I made her last birching a fairly easy one.

Once I'd released her, I told her that she would now be permitted to go to her room and rest up.

She stood there for a few moments, still naked, lost in thought, so I asked her what was wrong.

"Oh, nothing, Mr. Hunter," she replied quickly. "I was just wondering if you'd allow me to masturbate before I put my dress back on."

I suppose the way I smiled at her carried an air of benevolence. "Of course you may, my dear," I told her patiently. "I believe you've earned that right."

Actually, the idea of watching her in the act of masturbation had a great appeal for me.

Amanda hurried to the floor, lying on her back and spreading her legs as her hand fairly leapt into action.

Leaning back on the desk, I relaxed as she went into the motions of self-satisfaction. She was grinding her punished buttocks into the ornate Oriental carpet, the fingers of her free hand clutching at the thick fabric. And she was biting her lower lip, half-closing her eyes as full arousal surged through her youthful loins. Again, her breath started to go in and out with a short gasping sound. She was arching her back, her rump occasionally rising from the floor to leave her teetering on her toes and shoulders.

It took the girl almost no time to reach orgasm, and when I saw that it was overcoming her, I stood at her side staring down into her eyes.

"What seems to be happening inside of you, Amanda?" I asked.

She smiled up at me. "I'm having climax, Mr. Hunter," she exclaimed. "Many of them."

"But doesn't your bottom smart?" I went on.

"Yes, it does," she said, "but I hardly notice it right now."

Then she seemed to drift away, floating in orgasmia.

Putting her dress on when she was finished, Amanda looked somewhat sheepish, and once she was covered, she hurried from the room, promising she'd be better behaved in the future, but I hardly took much stock in that statement. Amanda's much too impetuous to be able to keep such a promise.

———————

That afternoon, I put Tarin thorough a vigorous and most interesting session of punishment. I don't have time to describe it here, Bertrand, but I will in my next letter as I'm sure you'll be interested in the details.

My Best Wishes,

Derek H.

P.S.

Two of your letters arrived during our journey. Thank you. I was enthralled to read about Priscilla Clark's first encounter with the birch. It sounds as if she might be a perfect subject for some of the new punishment methods that I've been describing.

Letter 17 PRIVATE

Dear Bertrand,

As I said in my last communication, I punished Tarin during the afternoon of the same day that Amanda was given a ladder-flogging. I'll describe it below, but first I must tell you of some new developments here.

When Neville returned from his first day of reopening the court, he was most distraught. He'd found the citizens of Stonehurst to be up in arms about both Amanda and Tarin. First of all, Vicar Dowling had circulated a petition among the people, a petition demanding that Amanda serve penance for her overt flirtations. There were so many signatures on it that Neville had no choice but to comply with Dowling's wishes. With Neville being so busy, I was saddled with escorting the girl to penance on the next day.

Secondly, the people were demanding that Tarin receive yet another public flogging.

"It's all due to that rum-soaked stepmother of hers," Olford told me. He seemed quite angry. "She's been going about the village saying that Tarin committed two crimes and, therefore, should receive two punishments. The people so want it that I've no choice but to grant them their wish. It's that or a civil uprising."

So, he and I will escort Tarin into the village tomorrow for her second trip to the pillory or whatever the people choose. Neville, wishing to remove himself from the situation as much as possible, has left the details of her flogging in the hands of a committee appointed by the villagers themselves.

But let me now tell you of how I handled Tarin on our first full day of being back. If you'll remember, Ruth's complaint was that Tarin did her few chores but did them with an air of disdain. My task was to instill an attitude of humility into the girl. I'll admit that I was savoring the idea of having her at my command, but I can also truthfully say that I have an affection for the girl that makes me concerned for her. Neville is absolutely right when he says that Tarin would be in grave danger if she should walk about Stonehurst with her present manners. Judging from what he tells me, the people are in an ugly mood these days.

When it came time to attend to Tarin's chastisement, I asked Ruth to take her to the out building, and when I went there myself, I took Hector along. I wanted him to do the binding and flogging. In that way, I'd be free to give the girl more personal attention.

I made sure that we arrived well ahead of Ruth and Tarin so I could look around and decide just which piece of equipment to use for this sort of punishment.

With lantern in hand, I poked about until I came across an iron trestle that had obviously been designed for bondage. The trestle was shaped like a small stepladder, padded at the top and standing about as high as a man's waist. Heavy iron rings were built into it at each end, and leather straps were tied to each ring. As soon as I saw the device, I knew it was just what I needed.

A few minutes later, Ruth brought Tarin into the building, holding her by one wrist. "Here's the haughty Miss Blake," she sneered. "I sincerely hope you can whip some sense into her."

I thanked her and told her that Hector and I would handle things from that point on.

"Not so smart now, are you?" Ruth said to the barefoot girl as she stalked away.

But Tarin gave no reply. She simply stood there, waiting to see what was going to happen to her.

I told her to remove her dress, and when she was naked, her forest-green garment lying next to her in a velvet heap, I nodded to Hector in a signal to fasten her to the trestle, telling him that I wanted her facedown, buttocks propped up.

Tarin appeared so girlish and frail in the powerful hands of Hector. He bent her over the iron device, her pubis on the piece of padding at the top, her arms hanging down one side of it, legs down the other.

Deftly, the man fastened her wrists to the straps at that side of the trestle, then cinched her ankles to the other two straps, drawing her out fully, pulling at the leather until her flesh was strained. This left her rump at the very apex of the trestle and in an ideal position to be flogged.

While he finished with the restraint, I walked to a rack, where several tools of the flagellator's art were hung, and selected a quirt of braided leather.

When I returned, Hector, done with strapping the girl down, was proudly surveying his handiwork. The knots were tight, neat and inescapable.

"I hope you'll take care of flogging this young lady," I said to him, handing him the quirt, and his broad, leering grin told me that he'd be more than happy to.

"No, not him Mr. Hunter," Tarin blurted out when she saw what was going on. "He can't be the one to punish me. He's a cruel man. He'll beat me terribly."

"You'll get exactly what's required for this situation Tarin," I explained. "Your only task here is to learn a lesson from this experience."

Then I told Hector to give her buttocks five licks of the quirt.

The leather instrument flashed through the air five times in rapid succession, each stroke leaving a pinkish line on the tawny buttocks.

"Do you know why you're being punished Tarin," I asked her.

"I truly don't," she said. "I've been nothing but obedient to the wishes of others since I've been here."

"Yes you have," I said to her, "but some people say you seem to think you're too good for honest work. Is there any truth in that?"

"I've labored since I was a little child," she said. "I know what work is."

"Perhaps, but you need to modify your way of carrying yourself," I told her in no uncertain terms.

Then I told Hector to begin her flogging, specifying that he was to give her slow, well-paced strokes that weren't to stop until I gave the signal.

I seated myself on an upturned wooden box and watched as Hector administered a most expert flagellation of that rounded and oh-so-lovely bottom. He seemed to know how to use the quirt in a way that produced a maximum stinging and heating of the flesh, and he soon had Tarin writhing at the trestle.

With her face hanging downward, some of her long, dark hair was spread out on the stone floor, and as she twisted herself under the leather punishment, those tresses were sweeping back and forth on the stones. Her buttocks were able to wag slightly in a feeble attempt at avoiding the quirt, but this did her no good. Hector found his target with ease.

After Tarin had received perhaps a dozen stripes, she lifted her face, looking in my direction, imploring me for mercy. But her eyes had a look in them that I've seen in the eyes of several Rosewood girls, the ones who misbehave on purpose because of some hidden desire for the birch. You've observed them Bertrand. They've committed some infraction of the rules in order to receive punishment, but when the time comes to take it, they're frightened and regret their actions. Still, they find their way back again and again, and I'm convinced that some deep yearning in their young loins drives them to the very thing they dread.

Tarin was wearing that same sort of expression, and I could easily see that her pubis was becoming excited. Now, rather than wagging to and fro, it was humping up and down, moving with a phantom lover.

Suddenly, my desire for that girl took on a new dimension, and I desperately wanted to wield the quirt myself, to be holding it in my hands and driving that naked young thing into the orgasms of flagellation.

"I'll take care of her from here on," I said to Hector and then dismissed the man. I wanted to be alone with the girl, to possess her fully.

"Will you go easier on me Mr. Hunter?" Tarin asked as she tried to catch her breath. "That man has already set my bottom on fire."

"Stop trying to bargain with me Tarin," I said as I gave her a sound lick of the quirt. "You're a ward of the court. You're here to be disciplined, and I've been given the responsibility of doing just that."

Standing at the side of the trestle, I began whipping her buttocks red, seeing only those dusky globes before me.

Tarin's pelvis pounded at the iron apparatus, while the rest of her body struggled mightily at the straps, the strain causing her sinews to knot beneath the skin. The girl was trapped in the web of pleasure-pain, eros and suffering.

But again she pleaded with me. "Take pity sir," she gasped. "Surely I've paid my debt."

I let out a short laugh as I ceased the flogging and reached between her thighs. "Don't be coy with me," I was saying as I took a grip on her shaven mound to find that it was absolutely soaked. "We both know what's going on inside of your puss. Your juices are dripping all over my hand."

"The quirt is forcing those juices from me," she said to me. "I can't control it."

"Then you can climax for me," I told her. "You'll be flogged until you do."

She became silent as I went back to laying the quirt across her glowing rump, but within a half minute, she was moaning in the ecstasy of her pain.

I couldn't help but congratulate myself. This was just what Tarin needed. Not only was she suffering physical punishment, but her psyche was also being laid bare, her needs being brought to light, thus humbling her far better than any sort of prolonged torture.

And I'd learned something valuable. The girl had developed those first faint yearnings for the lash.

"I'm doing as you said!" she shrieked as her buttocks drove themselves up and down with a new fury. "My puss is climaxing!"

I could see orgasm rushing through her whole body, the flesh rippling with an unseen bliss.

"Love your punishment Tarin," I said to her when it seemed she was at her zenith. "It can help you."

For the rest of that day, the picture of Tarin writhing and orgasming on that trestle was in my imagination, and late that night, after the rest of the household was asleep, I went to her bed chamber. The room was in darkness, but she was awake, naked beneath the covers.

"I was hoping you'd come," she whispered as I climbed in with her.

I'm sure you can imagine that it was a coupling of great intensity. I found that I couldn't get enough of her physical charms, and she certainly had no lack of willingness. So long was I immersed in the partaking of her body that the sun was rising when I finally left the room.

_____

As I said at the beginning of this letter, I was the one who brought Amanda to Vicar Dowling in order for her to serve penance. The poor girl was duly frightened. She'd heard all the stories of the bizarre rituals that Dowling conducted, and she wasn't anxious to be in his clutches.

Hector drove us in the four horse carriage, and on the trip there, I did my best to comfort the troubled girl, trying to tell her that it would all be over with soon, but I found it hard to muster up a sincere tone. I was worried about her. Amanda might be an impertinent little thing, even daring at times, but I didn't think she was quite strong enough for the sort of penance ordeals that Dowling inflicts on his victims.

As we alighted from the interior of the coach, I saw a great number of farm wagons and saddle mounts. Many people had come to see Amanda serve penance, and I knew the reason. Her crimes had not been private ones. She'd flirted publicly with many Stonehurst men, and she'd been branded as a harlot. These people felt as if they had a vested interest in seeing the girl pay for what she'd done. In short, she was seen as being openly evil.

We were barely on the ground when two staunch church-women approached Amanda. One of them unbuttoned her dress while the other yanked it roughly from her, leaving her completely naked. Then they grabbed her wrists and hauled her toward the church building.

As she was being taken away, Amanda turned her face back toward me, a look of silent terror on her delicate features.

Dowling came up to me, again inviting me into the rectory, but I refused.

"Amanda's a rather fragile girl," I said to him. "I'd at least like to be present while they're preparing her."

Inside the church building, I found that the pews were almost completely filled with those who'd come to witness this vicious spectacle, but I was still able to find a seat that gave me a good vantage point.

As I sat down, I saw Amanda standing at the front of the

church, and the two women who'd dragged her into the building were still holding her wrists.

Sideways to the pews was a huge and sturdy sawhorse constructed of rough timbers. Lying across this was a thick, cylindrical object. It was most likely part of a large tree trunk, but I couldn't tell for sure as it was covered with dark burlap. Leather straps were tied to the four corners of the horse.

Then I noticed the most interesting feature of this ominous-looking contraption. Protruding from the very center of the cylinder and angled forward was a prong covered with an oiled leather sheath.

The old woman, Bella, entered from the side door, carrying a stone jug. When she was close to Amanda she whispered something to her and the girl spread her legs as the two churchwomen tightened their grip on her.

Bella poured a shimmering, almost golden, liquid over Amanda's naked body. Then she set the jar down and massaged the oil into all areas of the girl's flesh.

As the ancient woman was about these ministrations, Dowling walked up to the front of the church and began addressing the congregation.

"The girl you see before you is guilty of disrupting this community with shameless and conspicuous sexual overtures," he said in the monotone sometimes used by the clergy. "She has been responsible for men neglecting their work, thus contributing to our crop failures. Fortunately, she has seen the error of her ways and has come forward to serve penance for this evildoing."

Bella was almost finished. Her finger was within the girl's sex, applying the potion to the inner flesh, and as she did, I saw a dazed look come into Amanda's eyes. The potion was having its effect on her.

"You may proceed," Dowling said to the women holding Amanda's wrists when Bella was done.

Amanda gave not the slightest resistance as they pulled her

181

...horse and helped her to mount it. As she sat down on ...pparatus—it stood only about two feet off the floor—the ...omen made her position herself in a way that put her pubis just over the leather-covered prong. Then they pushed her downward by the shoulders, forcing her to accept the prong into her sex.

I know firsthand that Amanda has quite a small crevice, and so I didn't wonder that she grimaced as the prong invaded her. She couldn't stop herself from putting up a bit of resistance, but those two women were much stronger than she, and they got her seated, the phallus firmly imbedded in her sex.

"Lie down girl," I heard one of them say. "Do as I tell you."

They soon had Amanda lying flat, face down on the burlap-covered cylinder, hands outstretched. And when she was in place, they wrapped a long belt under the cylinder and buckled it together at the small of her back, firmly holding her into place against the burlap. The audience now had a full side view of the girl's nude body.

With each of them taking hold of a wrist, they tied her into the straps at one end of the sawhorse, pulling her tight. Then they did the same with her ankles. The bare girl was now stretched into an X, tied to the four corners of the horse, fastened to the cylinder and filled with the oiled prong. Surely, it was a most degrading position for the unfortunate Amanda to find herself in.

It didn't surprise me to see Brother M. entering the candlelit room, wearing his traditional black robe and hood and carrying a whipping tool, a lash-strap with a handle of carved ivory.

"Good people," Vicar Dowling was now saying, "perhaps Amanda's youth prevents her from understanding the full implications of what her sort of seductive behavior leads to. It is hoped that the penance of being scourged by the whip will help her to undo the evil that lies within her."

Then he nodded to one of the black-suited elders, and the man stood before the congregation. In his hand was a thick book. Opening it, he began reading some sort of obscure chant that was in the same unidentifiable language that I'd heard read during one of Emily West's penances.

As his monotonous voice filled the room, it was joined by the sound of leather striking naked flesh. Brother M. had begun flogging Amanda's buttocks in a ceremonious manner, slowly, solemnly.

At the very first stroke, Amanda pulled at the strappings that held her, and this, of course, drove her pubis at the prong buried in it and caused a shudder to run through her glistening body.

The audience murmured their approval, and a woman near me spoke to her husband in a whisper. "She won't come around batting her eyelashes at you again, will she?" she said.

"No she won't, and a good thing that is," he answered. "It's her sort that are ruining our community."

I tell you, Bertrand, I could barely conceal my anger. I've observed these hypocrites long enough to know that this man was probably flattered beyond words by Amanda's precociousness, and given half a chance, he probably would have delved his member into her on the spot if he could have.

With those same methodical strokes, Brother M. was giving his victim a full body-flogging, using the lash up and down the length of the girl's nudity, whipping her back and shoulders, the thighs and calves, even striking the undersides of the twisting feet and turning the sensitive skin red.

Yes, Amanda's struggles had become animated, and she'd begun yelping every few seconds. The birch is barely tolerable for her, but the lash is something that her tender flesh simply can't bear.

"You mustn't whip me with that thing!" she cried out after she'd endured maybe a dozen licks. "Stop or I will surely faint."

She might just as well have not spoken. The penance of the lash went on, the leather mercilessly punishing her unprotected flesh.

But it wasn't long before a change came over the girl, and I'm certain that it was due to the potion. That dazed look in her eyes became even more pronounced, and she began pushing her sex at the prong, almost imperceptibly at first but the momentum increasing until she was openly hammering at the thing.

"Little whore," a stern-looking woman near the front muttered under her breath. "She doesn't care how much she's scourged as long as she has something up inside of her."

Finished with running the lash over the length of Amanda's body, Brother M. was now concentrating his attentions solely on the bare buttocks, turning the flesh to the color of roses, and through one of the slits in his hood, I could see his lips twisting themselves into a smile of sadistic glee.

It was inevitable I suppose that the burlap directly beneath Amanda's sex should turn a darker hue with juices running from within her young loins. The lash was heating her while the prong stimulated her insides, and it was certain that the potion was working some sort of aphrodisiac magic.

"Uhhh," she groaned when she was engulfed with the mixed pleasures. "You must stop this."

But her words came out weakly, and, as much as she might have truly wanted the whipping to be done with, her physical rapture was great. Plainly, she'd gone through orgasm.

The reading ended and Brother M. stopped lashing at Amanda's body. Then Vicar Dowling stood before his flock.

"This girl will now suffer further and make amends," he said flatly. "Any woman whose husband was accosted by this harlot may now come forward and give her three strokes of the birch rod."

As some of the women began standing and walking toward the sawhorse, Dowling produced a long rod and handed it to the first one in line.

Almost every woman in the audience came forward, and as they took turns flogging their victim, I was certain that Amanda couldn't possibly have flirted with that many men. Those women

184

probably just felt like inflicting pain on her. The senseless perse-cution that's running rampant hereabouts seems to be bringing out the worst in just about everyone.

One by one, they gave Amanda's already well-chastised but-tocks the allotted three strokes while she wriggled at the horse. The poor girl was still deep in agony's throes, and this new round of flogging was causing her to grind her sex into the prong once again. And by the time the fourth or fifth woman was finished with her, Amanda had clearly started orgasming yet another time.

"Serves you right, slut," one woman said as she swung the birch viciously at the captive buttocks. "I only wish I could give you as many licks as I'd like to. You'd get a proper thrashing then, one you wouldn't soon forget."

Amanda was babbling now, saliva dripping from the corner of her mouth. I couldn't make out what she was saying, but it sounded as if she was pleading for mercy and meaning it fully.

When the churchwomen were done with birching the girl, Dowling stood again before the congregation, thanking them for both witnessing the penance and helping with it.

"She is done now," he said, holding his hands skyward. "Let us hope she has learned the way of goodness and chastity."

When he was finished, the audience rose and walked sol-emnly from the church, all of them wearing the smug expression of people who consider they have done their duty.

Neville had warned me that I'd have to leave Amanda there for the night if Dowling should suggest it. "Amanda's crimes were public ones," he'd said. "For this reason, her penance must be fulfilled completely."

But Dowling made no remarks to this effect, possibly due to the fact that I'd insisted on taking Tarin away after her turn at penance.

"Release her and take her back to Olford," was what Dowling said to me on his way out. "He'll know how to handle her from this point on."

185

It was an exhausted Amanda I escorted back to Neville's estate. On the one hand she seemed bewildered. After all, she'd done nothing to warrant treatment so harsh, but on the other hand I felt she'd learned a valuable lesson. I think she saw the importance of learning the ladylike behavior that Neville was striving to instill in her. She'd had a sample of just how fanatical these people have become where girls like her are concerned.

As I said, tomorrow we take Tarin into the village for her second public flogging, and I must say I feel pity for the girl. Things have gotten worse, and I'm certain that the people of Stonehurst will show her no mercy.

Olford has told me that he may be taking another girl into his guardianship, but I don't have any of the details on this matter as yet. I'll let you know when I write to you of Tarin's punishment.

> Most Sincerely,
Derek H.

Letter 18 PRIVATE

Dear Bertrand,

I received another of your letters yesterday and was glad to hear of the doings at Rosewood. Yes, I'm well acquainted with the student you wrote of, Faith Gordon, and it doesn't come as a surprise to me that you had to treat her to a fresh taste of the birch. I had occasion to administer a punishment to this same student last term, and her reaction to having her rump brightened up a bit led me to believe that she'd be back for more. You say you made her strip to the bare and submit to the blindfold, but you didn't elaborate as to how she responded to these treatments. I hope you can go into this matter in your next correspondence.

Neville has indeed taken in another girl as a ward of the court, a Miss Jennifer Ware, a runaway and a genuine spitfire. She was apprehended just outside of Stonehurst, where she was attempting to sell her body. This attempt wasn't greatly successful as the first person she approached was an out of uniform constable, who promptly had her arrested. But if I know anything of these peacekeepers he more than likely had his way with her before taking her into custody.

Jennifer is a handsome girl. Her body, just budding into womanhood, is ample enough of bosom and molded into fine curves. Her face is set off by a thick mass of sunstreaked, blondish hair that has hints of strawberry in it. An altogether pleasing package.

The problem with this particular young lady is that she has no intention of changing her ways and has made it quite clear that she'll escape if given half a chance. She was brought before Neville on charges of vagrancy and prostitution and sentenced to a whipping in the pillory. He tells me that the whip, rather than humbling the girl, simply made her angry enough to denounce the villagers as hypocrites.

"She represents a real challenge," was the way Neville put it when I asked how she would be handled as one of his wards, "but I plan on taming her one way or the other."

Miss Amanda Smith was given two days to rest up after her most grueling session of penance, then she quickly returned to her saucy and impertinent ways. Twice Ruth has had to put her on the platform for a few hours, and she's been birched several times for flaunting herself.

On the day after I last wrote you, Tarin submitted to another punishment in the public square. Neville and I escorted her to Stonehurst in the four horse carriage. Hector drove, while we remained inside with the girl, doing our best to boost her spirits.

At one point, Tarin asked what was to be done with her by way of punishment, but Olford honestly could offer her no information.

"A committee was appointed to decide on the method of your punishment," he told her. "They met last night and I don't know any more than you do Tarin."

I can say truthfully that the whole affair was an ugly business. Anyone who believes in the basic goodness of human nature has never been to this region to see these people venting their unfounded hate and fear.

Our carriage had no sooner stopped before the courthouse than two bailiffs flung the door open and dragged Tarin out. Looking backward, she gave Neville a pleading look, but of course the matter was out of his hands at that juncture in time. Still, he followed the bailiffs and Tarin into the courthouse.

"There are no cases to be tried before me this morning," he told me, "so Tarin's punishment should begin shortly. I'm going to supervise while they prepare her. I'll see you in the square when all is ready."

Left on my own then, I wandered about the village, finding that Stonehurst's populace was in a foul and vindictive mood. Everyone present seemed to be greatly looking forward to seeing a naked and helpless girl displayed for public chastisement. And I learned that Tarin's reputation had taken on a dangerous new perspective. People were blaming her solely for all of their misfortunes, claiming that the all of the original evil had emanated from her in the first place.

"I'm convinced that all our misfortunes have their roots in Tarin Blake," I heard one woman saying. "That girl infected the others."

"I've suspected her of consorting with the dark side for some time," another was muttering. "Just the way she walks has a hypnotic effect on men. I've seen my husband become entranced at the very sight of the whore. If I had my way she'd be hung in the pillory and left there until the vultures disposed of her."

You can well imagine Bertrand, what a chilling effect these

word had on me.

Stopping in at one of the taverns for coffee, I heard still more gossip about Tarin. One man claimed that he'd seen her just two nights ago in a wood near his farm. According to him, Tarin had been leading three other girls in a strange dance. They'd all been naked, and during this dance, they'd been chanting at the moon.

"It was eerie," this gentleman said to his listeners, "and when the dance ended, they flogged each other with bundles of thin switches until all of them collapsed right there. And it was Tarin Blake goading them through this ritual, I tell you."

The gentleman relating this absurd tale obviously believed his own words. The hysteria so prevalent hereabouts had caused him to actually see this event, though it was probably nothing more than a few shadows filled in with the details of his imagination. I knew for certain that there was no truth in it since Tarin had been in service to me two nights previously.

A commotion outside caused all the tavern's patrons to make for the door. Tarin was being led from the courthouse and toward the pillory platform by two bailiffs.

I hurried outside in time to see the girl being taken through the crowd. She was almost naked, her only covering being some soiled rags tied low on her waist and through her crotch to form a sort of makeshift loincloth. A leather collar had been fastened around her neck, and one of the bailiffs was leading her by a strap attached to the collar while. Outside of that she'd been left unbound.

The throng parted as Tarin was brought forward, but several people spat out curses at her, and most were mumbling about her getting her just desserts.

Tarin looked straight ahead, seemingly impervious to these verbal slings and arrows.

How frail and defenseless that girl appeared once she was stationed on the platform and standing between the tall and heavy posts of the pillory. At a command from one of the bailiffs, she put her hands at her sides and her feet together. Then the man removed the leader strap but left the collar on her neck.

Emerging from the courthouse was one of the clerks, attired in his black robe and white, curled wig. He stepped up onto the platform and unfurled a parchment.

"The convicted and sentenced girl before you, Tarin Blake, will now serve sentence for the second of her crimes, that of cavorting outdoors while stark naked and in the the full view of two male onlookers," he read from the parchment. "For this crime she will be hung by the ankles from both posts of the pillory and flogged. This flogging will consist of 17 strokes of the lash applied to her sex with an equal number being applied to her buttocks simultaneously. After she has received said strokes of the lash, 21 strokes of the birch rod will then be applied to her sex and an equal number applied to her buttocks and back, again in a simultaneous manner. This sentence written and delivered by a committee of the good citizens of Stonehurst. So be it."

Even as the clerk was exiting, another bailiff mounted the platform and strode purposefully toward Tarin. Gripping her around the waist he turned her upside down and hoisted her upward, her feet pointing to the sky.

Quickly, the other two bailiffs secured her ankles into the straps attached high on the heavy posts, and once she was fastened, the one holding her about the waist released her, leaving the almost bare girl in the air, swinging slightly to and fro, her long hair spilling all over the rough planking, her sex at about the height of a man's waist.

Now that they had Tarin hanging from the posts, two of the burly men grabbed at her flailing arms and tied her wrists into straps attached at the bottoms of the pillory timbers, drawing her out in a most stringent manner as they knotted her into the leather bindings.

Thus she was left suspended in this inverted position, drawn out into an X configuration. Her upside down face wore an expression of surprise and shame, and each muscle in her lean and supple body was stretched, the sinews visible beneath the taut, youthful skin.

Finished with their work, the bailiffs dismounted the platform. And then, to my great surprise, Mayor Blythe and Chancellor York climbed up onto the platform, each of them carrying a lash strap and a birch rod.

"Yes, those two are going to carry out the flogging," Neville said to me as he appeared by my side. "They went before the committee and insisted that they were the best for the job, and needless to say, they could hardly be refused."

"I'm sure they'll enjoy themselves," was my answer to this. Already, I could see both of them lusting to punish girl-flesh.

"No doubt," Neville was saying, "and they're concerned, shall we say, about both Jennifer and Amanda. They're coming out to my place tomorrow night to see how the saucy Miss Smith is getting along, and York tells me that he has some sure-fire discipline techniques that Jennifer can benefit from. What it amounts to is that the good mayor wants another amorous union with Amanda, and York simply feels like flogging a fresh body, that of Jennifer Ware. I suppose I'll have to accommodate the lechers."

As Olford spoke, I watched as Mayor Blythe waved to the audience and then turned toward Tarin. Laying the flogging instruments aside for a few moments, he ripped the rags from the girl's body, leaving her fully naked. There she dangled, the most intimate flesh of her loins open to the gaze of all present.

Then York came forward. "Ladies and gentlemen of Stonehurst," he intoned in a most pompous tone, "let us hope that this girl learns the way of the good and the upright from this punishment. Let us hope that she mends her ways and that her pain will chase the evil from her being."

As the onlookers applauded his words. Blythe took up a stance behind the naked girl, standing slightly to one side of her, while the Chancellor stood in front of her, he too standing to one side.

191

The mayor delivered the first stroke, a resounding lick to Tarin's buttocks. Immediately afterward, York swung his lash-strap down on her smooth pubis. The moment the leather touched the flesh of the pubis, I saw a hint of moisture begin to leak from the tender crevice.

"The bailiffs stimulated her with a leather prong while they prepared her," Olford whispered to me.

I merely nodded, not surprised.

York and Blythe administered this first installment of the flogging in a slow manner, alternating the blows between the buttocks and the sex, but each time one of the straps fell, it was in a most forceful way, and even a girl like Tarin couldn't help but cry out with the agony of it.

Her cries seemed to please the audience, and a light smattering of applause arose from their midst and I even heard a few cheers.

"Whip her still harder," someone shouted.

"Yes," came from another, "whip the whore until she passes out."

"Look at all she's done to us," a woman near me shouted. "Nothing's too horrid for the likes of her."

Looking sideways, I saw a look of worry come over Neville's face.

Blythe and York were still lashing at their victim, taking a seeming interminable length of time to administer this part of the sentence. When they were done, they immediately laid the straps aside and picked up the birch rods in preparation to flog the girl again.

Studying Tarin's countenance, I could see that the lashing had taken a considerable toll on her, perhaps because of having to accept such dreadful punishment before so many people. Her flesh was shuddering, and she was jerking at her bonds, but this seemed to be involuntarily rather than a sincere attempt at escape.

Looking closer, I saw that the liquid was now draining freely from her pubis, glistening on the reddened flesh. Her youthful breasts were heaving themselves up and down as she gasped for breath, and her body had tightened itself in the stricture of the leather bonds, her fingers splaying open, her toes arced.

And still, she had 21 strokes of the rod yet to endure, to the buttocks, back and the sex.

No longer able to conceal their glee, Blythe and York birched the nude girl with a vengeance, smiling in satisfaction and licking their lips, the bulges in their trousers revealing their lust. They were still flogging her slowly but with such force that the rods whistled as they flew through the air and cracked sharply when they landed on the bare flesh.

"Take pity!" Tarin shrieked. "There's not an ounce of evil spirits in me and you know it."

At this, the citizens shouted their disagreement, and Tarin's two torturers took to birching her still more soundly.

At long last it seemed to be over, but then Tarin's body suddenly convulsed and began spasming in a most animated fashion as she let out a long moaning sound.

"I don't believe my eyes," someone said. "That slut's actually gone into climax. She's climaxing from being whipped."

Everyone stopped in their tracks and watched in silent awe as Tarin shook and shivered through a long orgasm that seemed to come from the very core of her loins.

This intense convulsion left the girl just as abruptly as it had overcome her, and then she went limp in her fastenings as the audience walked slowly from the square, shaking their heads in astonishment and muttering over what a harlot the girl was.

But by the time we'd collected Tarin's dress and bundled her into the carriage, the crowd had had time to talk among themselves and were congregating in angry little groups. Then, as Hector began driving the coach out of town, they began gathering around us, hurling insults toward Tarin and shouting about banishing her from Stonehurst forever. As the throng became thicker, Hector was forced to bring the horses to a stop.

Clearly disgruntled, Olford emerged from within the carriage and faced the mob, looking quite magnificent with his boots planted firmly apart, the wind blowing his long cape about him.

"Tarin Blake has most lawfully received sentence for her wrongdoing," he said to them in no uncertain terms, "and she will now be escorted to my home in the same lawful manner. Anyone blocking this carriage, will be arrested on the spot and stand trial before me on the morrow."

With that, he climbed back on board. The crowd dispersed, but they did so reluctantly, still talking of the evil within Tarin.

"Dangerous times," Neville said to no one in particular as we left Stonehurst behind us.

I still have much to communicate to you Bertrand, but it will have to wait until my next letter as I've become quite occupied again. My research is all but wrapped up, and my flagellation manual is beginning to take some sort of shape. There's also the matter of Amanda Smith. As soon as I lay my pen aside, I have to give her young rump a sound birching. Once again, she's behaved in such a way as to warrant flogging.

Again, I ask you to inform me as to how Faith Gordon responded to taking punishment fully bare and blindfolded as I'm still planning to add these treatments to Rosewood's discipline program.

Take care of yourself.

My Best Regards,

Derek H.

194

Letter 19 PRIVATE

Dear Bertrand,

As I mentioned in my last letter, Blythe and York scheduled themselves to visit here at Olford's estate. Admittedly, York actually wanted to see Neville's final report of our journey into the nether provinces of this region, but, of course, both men were just looking for an excuse to come out and toy with Amanda and Jennifer.

The night of their visit was one of the gloomiest I've seen here. A severe north wind was howling around the house, there was no moon out, and the fog was thicker than usual. Before the two of them arrived, Neville had the lamps well-lit and fires started in most of the rooms, but even so there seemed to be a shadowy and almost ghostly pallor hovering about the house. Still, with a determination born of yearning, I suppose, Blythe and York made their way here, regardless of the weather..

The four of us took seating in the main drawing room, and Amanda served cognac, wearing a tiny, white dress that Neville had furnished her with. The dress was quite short, tucked at the waist and sleeveless, and it was easy to see that she was wearing nothing beneath it. Indeed, she made a lovely sight with her pale legs glowing in the firelight and prancing about so prettily on her little naked feet.

I'm afraid I made the mistake of mentioning Tarin's ability to dance the nude ballet, even remarking on how agile and accomplished she was at it. I say mistake because Neville's guests were highly interested in this and even expressed an interest in seeing the girl dance. Right then, I knew that, sooner or later, poor Tarin would have to perform for these lustful gentlemen.

Finished with seeing to everyone's needs, Amanda was just about to leave the room when Mayor Blythe spoke to her. "You certainly make for an enchanting picture this evening, my dear," he said. "Come closer and let me have a good look at you."

She minced his way with a mischievous on her lips, stopping before his chair and giving him a little curtsy that exposed an inch or so of her bare buttocks.

"Yes, you look quite fetching in that little costume," Blythe said to her, "and you have such well-shaped legs."

"Thank you, sir," she said, giving him another impish curtsy, one foot behind her.

"Don't be so formal, my child," Blythe was saying as he opened his arms. "Come sit on my lap and tell me how you've been getting on."

That nymph frisked right into his arms, curling up into his laps and snuggling close to the large man.

York had gone into conversation with Neville, but I wasn't listening to what they were saying, Instead, I watched unobtrusively while the mayor played with young Amanda. Somehow, I felt like he was setting a trap for her. He was teasing her and giving her a tickle here and there, and she was playing right into his hands, giggling and encouraging his affections.

"Tell me, sweet girl, is your little puss still bare?" Blythe was asking as his fingers flickered about the hem of her dress. "I certainly hope so."

"Oh, yes sir," Amanda exclaimed as she lifted the little garment to exhibit her sex. "Just see how smooth it is."

"So it is," he said to her as his fingers went to her pubis and began caressing it in a most intimate manner.

Amanda loved the attention. She opened her trim thighs to accommodate the man, pushing her pubis at his fingers as she blushed the blush of arousal and giggled still more.

"You're being ever so fresh with me, sir," she said, but it was clear that she wished for him to continue.

Suddenly, Blythe's demeanor changed. "You're quite a naughty little thing, Amanda," he said to her sternly. "No wonder the people of Stonehurst had you tried for flagrant seductive behavior." Then he turned toward Olford. "Do you see how this girl's behaving?" he asked.

"Oh, don't thing I haven't been keeping an eye on her," he said, his tone level, "and don't think she won't be birched soundly for her antics."

Blythe considered this a moment. "Perhaps I can lend a hand," he said. "I'll be glad to punish her right here and now."

As Neville rose and brought a long rod from where it stood in a corner, I watched Amanda's expression change. She'd fallen neatly into the mayor's snare, and she seemed quite surprised by this turn of events. It was plain to see that she hadn't counted on being flogged on this particular evening.

Neville had resumed his chair and gone back into conversation with the Chancellor as the punishment got started. They were speaking of Jennifer Ware, and York seemed to think that she represented a special case, one that had to be dealt with both quickly and severely.

But my main attentions were on Blythe's handling of Miss Amanda Smith.

"You'll stand in the middle of the room and strip your clothing, what there is of it," he said to her.

Amanda leapt from his lap to obey. "I was merely trying to be hospitable to a guest," she whined as she got into place and began removing the dress.

Blythe wanted no back talk, and as soon as the girl was standing fully nude, he went to her side and ordered her to get down onto her hands and knees. Then, once she was in this posture, he gave her three sharp licks with the rod and ordered her to crawl toward the piano bench.

As Amanda complied with this demand, the mayor walked along behind her, snapping the birch at her naked buttocks as she made her way across the room. Each time the rod struck, she let out a plaintive yip.

Once she was near the grand piano, Blythe pulled the padded bench out and told her to climb up onto it. As she did so, he urged her into position with the rod, placing her on it lengthwise, face-down with her arms dangling over one end, her thighs straddling the sides. Then he had her to hold tightly to the two legs near her hands and to turn the soles of her feet upward, toes resting on the floor. Thus, she was posed in a manner that made her rump quite available and exposed her spread sex somewhat from behind.

"Must I call Ruth in to bind you up?" Blythe asked.

"Oh, no, sir," she said quickly. "I promise to stay just as I am."

"Very well," he said to her as he stood to one side of the bench, "but should you release your grip or try to slip away, I'll have Ruth strap you into place, and your punishment will begin afresh, and you'll take twice the number of licks that you would have otherwise."

I could see Amanda's knuckles turn white as she grasped the piece of furniture for all she was worth.

Believe me, Bertrand, the flogging that Blythe gave that unfortunate girl was nothing like anything we would ever even consider inflicting on a Rosewood student. He trounced her in way that was positively inspired, thrashing away at her with absolutely no regard for her dignity or feelings.

No sooner had four or five licks crossed her bare posterior than Amanda was shrieking and moaning both, completely forgetting that anyone was witnessing her humiliation. And the rod was falling with such intensity that each time it landed a fresh stripe would appear on the fair and delicate skin.

Out of one ear, I could halfway hear Olford and York talking, although their words were becoming mixed with Amanda's shrieking sounds. They were laying plans for giving Jennifer a severe dose of discipline within the hour. York wanted her in line as soon as possible.

Hector was summoned and dispatched to fix Jennifer to the whipping platform in the out building. "Strip her and chain her out to the four rings," Neville said to him. "Then round up as many of the guards as you can find. We'll join you shortly."

Blythe had taken a short break from his endeavors. He sat down, breathing heavily. "I'll let those stripes sink into her sassy behind and then give her a fresh measure," he was saying.

Looking over at Amanda, I saw that he'd done considerably more than merely flogging her behind. He'd reddened her from the shoulders all the way down to the bottoms of her fidgeting feet. She was still holding tight to the piano bench, soft sobs and moans coming from her lips.

York had changed the subject to that of Tarin. "Her situation is the most distressing of all," he was saying to Neville. "Two villagers came to me yesterday and suggested, in all sincerity, mind you, that she be staked out naked in the forest and left to the wild animals. And I've heard that Dowling's congregation is talking of trying to revive the Medieval practice of putting whores to the branding iron."

Sufficiently rested, Blythe resumed his position next to the bench, smiling in readiness to flog poor Amanda yet again. "You seem to be in need of more birch," he said to her. "Is that so?"

"No, please, sir," the girl wailed. "Don't flog me any longer. I can't bear it."

Now, now," he said in a patient tone, chuckling, "we both know how beneficial this is for a girl like you. Just be brave and take what you're in such need of."

Then he was flogging away at her buttocks, restoring the crimson to them and causing Amanda to begin wiggling and moaning all over again. I'll say it was harsh treatment to give a girl so young and tender of flesh, but Blythe was relishing each second of it, licking his lips each time he brought the rod across her nude form.

By the time the man was finishing up this most dreadful flogging, Neville and York were preparing to leave for the out building, Neville beckoning for me to join them.

"Will you be coming along to see Jennifer disciplined, Mayor Blythe?" York asked as we were taking our leave.

Even as he spoke, Blythe was laying the rod aside and loosing the front of his trousers. "This girl needs something to settle her down," he said, "and I have just the thing for it."

Then he was clambering atop the prone Amanda, his huge member going between her thighs on its way to her pubic crevice. I'm sure she welcomed the relief of being filled, but Blythe's hulk seemed to dwarf the fragile and youthful girl beneath him.

And as I was closing the door behind us, I could hear Amanda squealing, the squeals seeming to reflect both pain and ecstasy.

With lanterns well-lit, the three of us made our way through the shrouds of fog, approaching the gloomy shadows of the old out building. Once inside, we could see flickering lights coming from near the far west wall, and we picked our way carefully in that direction.

Lanterns had been lit around the whipping platform, and Hector and three uniformed guards were standing to one side of the apparatus. This platform is constructed of roughhewn wooden planking, Neville told me that it had once the bed of a hay wagon, and it stands about a foot high. Embedded in the stone floor near the corners of the platform are four rusted iron rings, animal tethers at one time, and steel chains are attached to the rings.

There, in the center of the platform was a fully naked Jennifer, her strawberry-blonde hair forming a thick pillow beneath her shoulders. Her wrists and ankles had been padlocked into the free ends of the chains, and she'd been pulled out until her flesh was taut in the steel fetters.

The girl made a picture that was purely and classically erotic, bringing to mind the dungeons of yore, damsels in the clutches of inquisitors. Her breasts stood upright, the nipples high, and her back formed a concave arch just over the curve of her buttocks. How flat her midriff was. Like the other girls, she'd been shaved to the bare skin, and her pubis formed a smooth hillock. She was in a state of slight movement, writhing and testing the chains that held her fast. And she was looking around herself, a naked youth surrounded by seven fully clothed adult men. How could she not know that we desired her chained nudity?

York had taken a three-thonged whip from a hook mounted on a pillar, and he was standing at the end of the platform in a most threatening manner.

"I understand that you think of yourself as a prostitute," he said to the girl. "Is that true?"

I was astounded at her answer.

"I am," she said boldly, "and I plan to continue plying that trade once I'm free of this wretched place."

"You look far too young and innocent to be a streetwalker," York laughed as he dangled the whip over her, letting the thongs drape across her pubis.

"But that's what I am, sir," she told him, "a streetwalker."

"I see," York replied. "Well, perhaps this will prevent you from walking the streets."

He stepped back and began whipping the soles of her bare feet, first one and then the other, and he did it a most ruthless manner, brutally flagellating this sensitive flesh until it turned scarlet. The little feet fluttered about in attempt to avoid the punishing leather, but that was all for naught.

"Will that keep you keep from walking the streets?" Blythe asked. He was laughing at her.

"Perhaps, sir," she gasped, "but only temporarily."

"Then I'm going to give you a taste of what the life of a whore is like," the Chancellor snapped at her. "I'll show you what it's like to earn a living by spreading your legs for all comers and letting them do whatever they like with that delicious body of yours."

With that said, he gave her bare pubis several sharp licks of the whip, causing the captive nude to wrench at her steel bonds and open her mouth with a loud and plaintive scream.

"Now," York said, turning to Hector and the guards, "which one you gentlemen wants to be the first to enjoy this so-called whore's body?"

The four of them glanced at each other, pleased with their good fortune, and then they conferred among themselves, apparently deciding that Hector was to be given the privilege of having the girl first.

"Very well," York said to him. "Give her cunt a good fucking, and don't worry about her pleasure. That's not what we're here for." Then he turned back toward Jennifer. "And you'll be fucked by all of these men, and you'll take a sex-whipping between each."

Jennifer's eyes grew wide. She was plainly not ready to endure anything like this, and I could easily see why. Even with all her bravado, it was easy to tell, just by looking at her sex, that she was highly inexperienced. Her pubic crevice was tightly puckered, making it clear at the most cursory glance that she'd perhaps been entered once or twice at the most, if at all.

Hector had pulled a most mammoth member from his trousers, making the helpless girl redouble her vain efforts at escape, and he was mounting her defenseless body, smiling in gratification before even inserting himself into her feminine slot.

Jennifer shrieked and wrenched at the chains when the man plunged into her pubis. And as he began pumping away at her, she squirmed in a most uncontrollable way beneath his bulk. I could see her flesh grinding itself into the rough wood and chafe marks appearing on her wrists and ankles as she struggled.

But it was all to no avail. Hector stroked at her until he was satisfied and then rose to stand over her with a broad grin. "She's a regular stick of dynamite, this one," he told us.

York seared the whip into the Jennifer's mound once again, and this time her tongue lolled from the side mouth as she suffered the lashing, garbled sounds coming from her lips.

"This is how whores are treated," York said to her, sneering, "and you're just getting started."

One by one, the guards took their turn at coupling with the chained girl, and York gave her a sex-flogging after each one had finished with her. By the time they were done, every inch of that girls's flesh was quivering, and a coating of perspiration had formed on her skin. Her eyes were partially closed, and she was breathing heavily, apparently out of touch with her surroundings.

"Do you still enjoy the life of a whore, Jennifer?" York asked her.

She didn't seem to comprehend what he was saying. "I don't know what's happening to me," she managed to say, her voice sounding weak and distant.

"No, you don't," York was saying as he put the whip aside, "but you're going to learn to act like a proper young lady. If you don't, you'll stay in the court's custody for some time to come."

Oddly, Neville seemed intrigued by this entire episode, inhuman as it had been, and he nodded his approval when the Chancellor was done.

"Give her water but leave her where she is for about an hour," he told Hector. "Let her see what a whore's bed is like."

As we left the out building, Jennifer's moans were still floating through the air.

Even with things as busy as they are here at Olford's, I plan to write soon as I'm certain you'll be intrigued with everything that's happening here.

Again, please let me know how Faith Gordon responded to taking her flogging fully nude and blindfolded.

My Best To You.

Derek H.

Dear Bertrand,

Lately, I find myself working until well after midnight, poring over my notes and scribbling away. During the days, there always seems to something that calls for my attention, but I'm still ahead of the schedule of work I set for myself, and I'm making forward progress on my side project, the manual of flagellation and punishment techniques.

Neville is away in Stonehurst almost every day, leaving the three girls in my hands much of the time, a responsibility that I don't find altogether unpleasant, if you know what I mean.

Soon after the night of Blythe and York's visit, Neville came to me with a written outline of progressive discipline that he wanted Tarin to undergo. The mood of the village populace concerns him, and he wants Tarin's behavior corrected as soon as possible.

"I know I told her that she'd mostly only have to suffer the birch while here," he said after I'd remarked that the disciplines he'd outlined were quite rigorous, "but her situation is perilous. Being subjected to these ordeals is to her benefit."

Since then, Olford's concern has become still greater. Whenever he returns from the village, he broods over the increasing dissatisfaction of the people. "They've taken to having midnight rallies, complete with huge bonfires," he's told me, "and they talk constantly of Tarin being the original cause of everything that's gone wrong hereabouts. I've never heard such nonsense, but it's frightening just the same."

I can't be certain, but I believe Jennifer Ware has had some sort of awakening to good sense. Ever since she was sex-tortured on the whipping platform, she's become quite cooperative and a bit reticent. She goes about her few tasks in a humble and quiet manner and spends the rest of her time alone, reading or taking walks. Olford feels that she doesn't need too much more than an occasional light birching, and she accepts these floggings willingly and without question.

The brightest spot in recent developments has been that of Amanda Smith turning over a new leaf. Apparently the severe flogging that she suffered at the hands of Mayor Blythe finally got the message across to her.

"I know that I must learn to behave myself, and I'm going to do just that," she said to me the day after that particular flogging.

A daily dose of the rod has been enough to keep the naughty Miss Smith in line since that time.

Coincidentally, Tarin came to me shortly after Neville had given me the schedule of her discipline program. At the time, I was at work in the library. Tarin came in quietly, bringing my coffee, but after she set the tray down, she remained standing there as if she wanted to say something.

Glancing up, I asked her if something might be wrong.

Without speaking, she went to stand in the middle of the Oriental carpet, removed her dress, and got down into a kneeling posture, buttocks resting between the heels of her bare feet, hands on the floor. Then she surprised me completely.

"I'd like to be flogged, sir," she said.

Astounded, I rose and went to stand at her side, telling her that I didn't quite know what to make of what she was saying.

"Jennifer has told me all about what the people of Stonehurst are saying about me," she said, "and she's also told me what was done to her by Chancellor York. I feel it's to my advantage to learn humility even if I only learn to act it."

I couldn't help but see this as a step in the right direction for the girl, and I fetched a rod from the corner. Returning to her side, I gave her nude posterior three quick but very sharp stripes.

"I see no reason to give you a harsh flogging," I said to her. "The very fact that you're volunteering yourself for this shows me that you're making progress."

"You must help me, sir," she whispered. "Flog me well. It's the only way I'll learn."

As I've mentioned to you, Bertrand, Tarin's tawny rump is most adorable, the sort of rump that seems made for corporal chastisement, so I surely couldn't resist granting the girl her wish, and I proceeded to thrash her in a most thorough manner. But as I birched her flesh to crimson, giving her probably more strokes than she'd counted on, I gave pause to wonder. Was this girl, in fact, actually becoming addicted to pain's bittersweet kiss? Had she developed a need to suffer at the hands of others? Od did she realize how much pleasure she was furnishing me and simply wished to gratify another human being?

When I was done with birching those sweet buttocks, I told Tarin to remain as she was. Then I sat down in a wingback chair that was in a spot where I could look into her eyes, and I'm certain that she could see the affection that I've developed for her in my expression. But I felt the need to put it into words and did so.

"I feel the same about you, Mr. Hunter," she told me once I'd voiced my feelings, "and I have for some time." She was still breathing a bit quickly from the birching I'd just given her.

Reaching over to the desk, I picked up her discipline schedule, telling her what it was as I glanced over it.

"Our couplings have been magnificent, Tarin," I said to her gently, "but I'm afraid that I have a certain responsibilities to both Mr. Olford and to you."

Then I went on to tell her that I was obligated to put her through the disciplines that Olford had spelled out. "In the end, this could keep you from a lot of trouble," I said to her.

"I understand that, Mr. Hunter," she replied softly, "and I'm ready."

Two days later, I began working on Tarin's new schedule, starting as soon as she'd had time for her morning wash and body-shave. Many of the disciplines that Neville had prescribed for the girl were designed to humble rather than simply inflict physical pain. The first was a variation on ladder-flogging that displayed the victim's buttocks in a most shaming fashion. But let me describe it for you, Bertrand.

Once I'd summoned Tarin to the library, I, of course, had her strip herself to the full nude. Her manner was pleasing to me. She was silent, docile, and obedient. Without a word, she removed her one garment, put it aside and then stood with her hands behind her back, ready for her discipline.

I then had her stand before the tall ladder, facing it, and once she was in place, I hoisted her wrists up to about the height of her shoulders and strapped them to the sides of the apparatus.

"You're going to begin walking the ladder, Tarin," I said to her. "Put your feet on the first rung."

When she complied, I told her to stand on the second rung and then the third. By the time she was on this third rung, her buttocks were propped well outward. With her feet at the sides of the rung, those lean and well-defined rump-apples were clenched tightly together, but her sex was openly on exhibit. And here I strapped her ankles to the sides of the ladder. This posture made the girl blush and her buttocks tremble with the strain.

"Your lovely behind seems to be inviting the birch," I said to her as I ran my hands over it. "I believe it's time that Ruth came in and flogged you."

"No, Mr. Hunter," she exclaimed. "I beg of you not to let that horrid woman see me displayed so. Flog me all you care to, but please don't bring her in here."

Actually, her reaction vexed me somewhat. Questioning authority was the very thing I was trying to cure her of. Admirable as her spirit is, it's also the cause of many of her troubles.

"You're going to learn to accept the demands of others," I said to her as I signalled to Ruth with the bell rope.

Minutes later, Ruth entered the room, her leering expression telling me that she'd guessed why I'd summoned her.

"This girl needs a taste of the rod," I said to her. "I hope I can prevail upon you to flog her well."

"Oh, of course," the woman answered as that leer grew even wider.

She retrieved a birch rod from the corner and stood to one side of Tarin, chuckling at the position the girl was bound into. "With the way you're so attractively proffering your little bottom, you seem to be just asking to have it attended to," she said. "How can I not oblige you? I'd feel absolutely guilty if I didn't provide you with a decent beating." Then she turned to me and asked how many strokes the girl was in need of.

"I was going to recommend only a dozen," I said from behind the desk, "but this young lady questioned me, so I'm going to leave it up to your discretion, Ruth. Give her as much as you thinks she needs to learn that her place is to serve."

I could see that Ruth was pleased with this prospect. She now had free rein to flog Tarin as much as she pleased.

And then Ruth began thrashing those bare and defenseless buttocks, bringing the rod across them in swift, methodical strokes that were more forceful than they appeared. A thin pinkish stripe rose on the flesh each time the sound of birch on naked skin echoed through the room.

Trying her best to retain her dignity, Tarin was biting her lip in effort to not cry out, but it wasn't long before she broke down and began moaning each time the rod gave her buttocks its fiery caress.

"Please, Miss Ruth, not so hard," she said between moans.

"This impertinent thing needs the lash," Ruth said to me.

I didn't speak but merely nodded and Ruth fetched a lash-strap.

"Now you're really going to get it, m'lady," she said once she was standing near Tarin again, lash in hand and raised.

"I've done nothing to deserve a leather-whipping," the girl pleaded. "You can't use that on me."

Ruth laughed. "Oh, I can't, can't I?" she said. "I believe I'm the one making decisions here, not some naked girl who's bound up to a ladder with her bare bottom sticking out."

It was a cruel lashing that the woman administered, and Tarin did not bear up well under it. She was tugging fitfully at her bonds, her buttocks wagging back and forth, her long, dark hair swaying to and fro as she struggled.

The girl had the good sense not to plead with her tormentor any longer, but she couldn't restrain the moaning sounds that were coming continually from her full lips.

Tarin surprised once again during that session. While Ruth was resting her whipping arm for a few moments, the naked girl spoke up.

"This is what I need, isn't it, Mr. Hunter?" she asked.

"I'm afraid it is, Tarin," I told her. "I'm glad you understand that."

As I spoke, I was peering closely at her sex, and, sure enough, it was moist with arousal. And then I knew for certain that the girl had developed a need to be disciplined, to suffer for others. Truly, her loins were addicted to what her flesh feared.

After Ruth had given her only a half dozen more licks, I told her that the girl had had enough to learn a lesson and dismissed her.

For the next hour, I attended to my paperwork, leaving Tarin on the ladder. She said nothing, accepting of whatever might befall her. But the second time I glanced up, I saw that her pubis was trembling violently. Without moving or being touched, the girl was orgasming.

For the next several days, I put Tarin through several such disciplines, all of them clearly designed to shame her, following Olford's outline closely.

On one day, I had Ruth order her to perform all of the most menial household chores, scrubbing floors and such, and I specified that the girl was to do these chores without a stitch of clothing. Thus, she had to go about the house all day completely nude, kneeling and cleaning.

One of the disciplines required that she be taken to the forest and fixed up to a tree with straps, naked. Simple but effective bondage was employed in this procedure. I stood her with her back to the trunk of a very large tree and strapped her wrists together behind it. Then I tied the end of a long strap to her left ankle, wound the strap about the tree and fastened the other end to her right ankle, leaving her feet held apart.

Of course, Tarin has become accustomed to the rigors of restraint, but there was more than just that in store for her. Once she was bound up, I left her, knowing that two of the guards would soon be passing by.

I took up a position on the crest of a small hill where I was hidden by a thicket and the wisps of fog drifting by. Yet I still had a clear view of the girl, and I was close enough to hear whatever the guards might say about her. Seating myself on a large boulder, I waited to see what would happen.

Sure enough, within minutes, the two guards came trotting by on horseback, making their usual rounds. I recognized both of them, Olaf and Warren. Olaf had been present for Jennifer's sex-torture, and I knew him to be quite a lusty gentlemen. He was the first to spy Tarin.

"What have we here?" he said as he reined his horse in. "Look over there, Warren."

The two men simply stared at the bound and naked girl for a few moments, dumbfounded, I suppose, by this pleasant turn of events in their day. Then they rode closer and dismounted.

"What's happened to you, my pretty girl?" Warren said when they were near her. "You seem to be in somewhat of a predicament."

Both men were chuckling with glee. They'd come across quite a prize, after all.

"She's probably being punished," Olaf said, "so we might just as well enjoy her body as long as she's been made so available."

He put his hands on Tarin's shoulders and kissed her full on the mouth. Surprisingly, the girl responded with what seemed to be genuine ardor, straining forward in her bonds kissing him back.

When he was done with her mouth, Olaf stepped back, and both men began groping the girl, exploring her captive nudity with their hands. Olaf fondled her breasts while Warren ran a hand up the back of her left thigh, bringing it to the lower portion of her left buttock. Then he began squeezing and pinching the bare flesh, making Tarin rise up on her toes and squeal.

Voyeurism was more enjoyable for me than I might have thought. I found that I was highly entertained by watching these men take advantage of Tarin.

Their attentions to her were becoming more intimate. Olaf was suckling on her breasts, one by one, and Warren had transferred his hand to her smooth pubis, at first simply cupping it in a caress and then letting his longest finger slide up inside of her.

Still, I remained hidden, content to merely observe for a while longer. Tarin was obviously getting caught up in being a plaything in restraint. Her moans were ringing through the woodland, and she was writhing in their grasp. As she contorted her naked body about, I could see that she was scraping herself at the rough bark of the tree, but that didn't seem to bother her. She'd abandoned herself to being used.

Before things went much further, I appeared on the scene, startling the two guards.

"Sorry, sir," Olaf said to me. "We just assumed that Mr. Olford was having this girl punished."

I assured them that it was quite all right. "You're giving her just what she needs," I told them, "but I'm afraid that I must loose her and take her back to the house now. She's due for a birching."

Olaf and Warren went on their way while I released Tarin from her leather bindings.

211

"If having those men sex me is supposed to be a part of my discipline, I'm ready," she said.

I was pleased with her willing attitude but told her that that wouldn't be necessary as I handed the girl her dress.

"May I walk back naked, sir?" she asked.

I merely took her hand and led her back down the pathway.

———————

These mild but shaming disciplines have been having a humbling effect Tarin, and she seems happy with the new approach to life she's been given. I believe she senses that what she's learning will keep her from future travail.

The shaming process has also made the girl quite amorous. She constantly asks me to visit her bed chamber, and on most nights I've gone to her.

Tarin's lovemaking has taken on a new dimension. She's responsive and ever so willing to comply with whatever I choose to do with her. She seems to think only of my pleasure, and she makes every orifice of her body available to me. Having such a submissive lover at my fingertips is probably every man's dream come true, and I'm fully enjoying myself.

———————

An interesting side note to recent developments has been the irrepressible Amanda's reaction to all the time I'm devoting to Tarin. Today she came into the library, wearing the little dress she wore for Blythe and York's visit. It seems she asked Olford is she could make it her regular house garb, and he's permitted it.

I hadn't disciplined her in several days because of being busy and also because her behavior's been exemplary.

"No one has switched me or even given time on the platform in I don't know how long," she said as she fidgeted in a nervous manner.

"Well, that's due to your ladylike behavior," I told her with a smile. "Good girls don't to have to suffer quite so much as those who are always misbehaving themselves."

212

She licked her lips, choosing her words carefully. "But won't I become naughty once again if I'm not regularly birched?" she asked.

Then I saw her motive. The girl was actually jealous of Tarin getting all of the attention. She wanted to strip down and be attended to even if it meant taking a flogging.

I decided to reward her. "Perhaps you're right, my dear," I said to her. "I believe I'll put you on the platform for a while."

"Must I remove my clothing?" she said, her hands already going to the buttons of her dress.

"Of course you must," I told her in the stern tone that she probably wanted to hear. "In fact, you can take that dress off right here. You'll be nude as I march you through the hallway."

The girl was fairly glowing with a strange sort of happiness as I took her to the room where the platform was located, and she jumped right onto the contraption once we were there, even stretching her hands and feet out toward the straps hanging from the heavy corner posts.

I fastened her tightly into place by her wrists and ankles, hauling her arms and legs up into the air, leaving only a portion of her buttocks touching the wooden planks of the platform.

"Miss Ruth often straps me to this thing when I misbehave," she said softly.

"Yes, I know that, Amanda," I said as I sat down next to her and began caressing the naked flesh of her pert breasts, making the little nipples rise to my fingers.

"Perhaps you do, but I'll wager you don't know that she licks my puss and puts her finger in me once she has me bound up like this," Amanda said. She was twitching her girlish rump mischievously about. "And there's nothing I can do to stop her. She does as she likes with me."

Quite obviously, the girl needed some tending to, and I told her that she'd been so good lately that I just couldn't bring myself to take the birch to her.

213

"Then what will you do to me?" Her words came out in a rushing gasp because I'd taken a firm grip on her smooth sex.

"I'm going to do is have you orgasm for me," I told her.

And then I proceeded to give her pubis a thorough fondling, first running my fingertips up and down the outer lips until I had her squirming frantically. Then I slipped a finger in and located her clitoris, finding that it was already moist and swollen.

"That tickles so," the girl giggled as she fought the straps. "You make me feel so foolish."

I was certainly enjoying the contortions of that little nymph. As she writhed within the strictures of her bindings, she was biting her lower lip, breathing rapidly and humping herself at my finger. That's when I decided to do a bit of an experiment with her. I removed my finger from her love nub and began giving her pubis a light hand-spanking instead, playfully slapping at the shaven flesh.

That did it for Miss Amanda Smith. Being puss-spanked did even more for her than having her button played with, and she shot off into a series of orgasms that seemed to make her half-delirious. She was howling with delight, kicking and clawing at the air and making an absolutely delightful exhibit of herself.

Once she'd calmed down a bit, I made ready to leave, telling her that she could probably do with spending some time in the strappings. "I'll send Ruth by to check on you," I said to her.

"Please, Mr. Hunter, I don't want to be alone with that woman," she exclaimed. "You've been so kind to me. Miss Ruth will birch my puss and sex me." Once again, the impish girl had gotten herself a little too deep.

"I believe you know better than to question authority, Amanda," I said to her, stern now. "You'll stay where you are and do as you're told."

Then I left her. She's learning and learning well, but she still has that need for guidance and direction.

I'll continue to write as the chance presents itself. I'm hoping that all is well at Rosewood, and I'm looking forward to my return to its hallowed halls.

Most Sincerely,

Derek H.

Letter 21 PRIVATE

Dear Bertrand,

I'm sorry it's taken me this long to get a letter off, but I trust you understand my busy situation.

I received your last letter yesterday and was much taken by your description of Faith Gordon's second session of birch punishment. Bravo on binding the girl up for it. It sounds like she more than deserved it. I appreciated your comments on her reactions to being flogged while bound, blindfolded and without clothing. It sounds as if she'll be back for more, and I hope that, once I return, I'll be fortunate enough to give her a good bottom-crisping myself.

Punishing our students with these new methods serves two purposes. Those who don't want to be treated this way will buckle down to serious study, and those who wish for a taste of this forbidden fruit will make themselves available to us through their misbehaviors. In either case, it's a winning proposition all around.

Amanda's deportment continues to be of excellent quality, but I haven't forgotten the scamp that exists in her being and still subject her to the birch regularly.

I've taken Tarin into a new phase of strict and severe discipline that's geared to eradicating or at least disguising her so-called haughty nature as quickly as possible. Neville and I have both begun to worry seriously over the girl's safety as the frenzy of the people of Stonehurst grows. They stage angry rallies each night, and, when I gaze out of my bed chamber windows after dark, I can see the bright glow of bonfires burning in the village. Neville tells me that the accusations toward Tarin are growing increasingly preposterous and numerous. For this reason, the unfortunate girl must accept harsh discipline. I'll elaborate on the methods I'm using on her later in this letter, but first I must tell you of another matter.

Jennifer Ware has turned out to be not the spitfire she portrayed herself to be. She's attentive to others and obedient, and I'm certain she values her freedom enough to avoid the path she'd started on. Olford, however, seems to think that she bears watching and feels she needs harsh discipline. Just two night ago he put her on the post with the phallus mounted atop it and called several guards in to take turns using the strap on her. She weathered the discipline well and even expressed her thanks to Olford, but he still left her in the hands of the guards when her flogging was done with. I can only imagine what they did with her once he and I'd departed.

Vicar Dowling circulated one of his petitions, this one demanding that Jennifer Ware serve penance for her errant ways, the petition being successful enough to pressure Neville into sending her to pay the church its due by submitting herself to the scourge of the whip. Again, I took on the responsibility of escorting the girl to Dowling.

The penance that Jennifer suffered was a very private one, administered by Dowling, three elders, and Brother M. only with no members of the congregation present. The ceremony itself was the most strenuous penance I've yet witnessed, and I'm convinced that it was because Jennifer was foolish enough to denounce these people as hypocrites when she was flogged in the public pillory.

Like Amanda and Tarin, Neville permits Jennifer only one

garment, a dress, and hers is quite short, frayed and ragged, dark blue in color. The elders beset the girl the moment I brought her into the murky, candlelit church building and fairly ripped this dress from her body.

Jennifer trembled in their strong hands as they half-dragged her to the area before the altar. How naked and girlish she appeared in the hands of those sturdy, black-suited men, all of them scowling at their victim. Yet, at the same time, I could see them lusting for her youthful flesh. Clearly, they were overjoyed at having this nude and exquisite creature under their control.

At the front of the church stood an old and battered set of stocks, and Brother M., wearing his long robe and hood, was standing next to the forbidding apparatus, arms folded across his chest.

As I was seating myself in one of the pews, the elders were shoving Jennifer's head and hands into the slots intended for them, leaving her bent over. Then Brother closed the top half of the stocks, trapping the girl by the wrists and neck. He fastened it with a hasp and secured this with a large and cumbersome padlock. The stocks were set at right angles to the pews, giving me a side view of the nude girl. I could also see her face.

Dowling took his place behind the pulpit. "We are duty bound to purify this girl," he said ceremoniously, "and to teach her the ways of the good and the just." He opened a thick book before him and began reading. "The unclean must be cleansed," he chanted.

At his words, one of the elders picked up a jug and poured water over Jennifer's shoulders, back, and buttocks. The water must have been cold because the girl howled when she was doused with it.

"The unclean must endure the pain of constancy," Dowling read.

The elders began applying iron clamps to Jennifer's bare flesh. They fastened a few to her toes, tightening them enough to make

217

the girl hop about, two to her breast nipples, and one to an outer lip of her sex.

"The unclean must be scourged until they are cleansed," Dowling went on.

At this point, Brother M, picked up a long, leather quirt from the stone table and stood behind the captive, raising the instrument of flagellation high.

"Whip her," the vicar said, his tone excited, "whip her until she mends her ways. She'll confess her wrongdoing and promise to enter into the folds of goodness."

"You don't have to whip me," Jennifer shouted in a desperate attempt to save herself. "I'll confess to everything I've done, and I'll enter your flock. I will be of the good."

No one heeded her.

Brother M. began a precise and well-ordered flogging of Jennifer's hapless buttocks, striking her flesh with powerful strokes of the quirt, each stroke causing her to struggle in the captivity of the heavy stocks. Her clamped feet skittered about on the floor as her rump wagged to and fro beneath the leather punishment.

Brother M. had probably given the girl well over a dozen licks of the cruel instrument when Dowling ordered the flogging to be temporarily brought to a halt and went to stand before her, raising her chin with the tips of fingers.

"Now do you regret your evil ways, my child?" he asked her.

"Oh, I do," Vicar Dowling she whined plaintively. "I swear to you that I only sold myself once, and that was only out of desperation. Never, never will I do it again. I wish to be of the good."

"Did you denounce us, we of the good, as hypocrites when you were in the public pillory?" he asked.

"Yes, and I was wrong," Jennifer wailed. Clearly, she wanted to escape being whipped further. "I've seen my errors. Release me, and I'll walk the true path."

Suddenly, a look of livid anger came over the vicar, and he stepped back from her, hands on his hips. "You're lying to me, slut," he exclaimed, "and you'll be made to suffer for it." Then he nodded to Brother M. "Whip this girl until she's ready to faint," he said. "She's going to pay."

A fervency came over the churchmen that was so intense that they seemed to almost forget my presence, and they went into an orgy of self righteous lechery. As Brother M. flogged their victim, the elders and Dowling used her body to satisfy their warped carnality.

Firstly, each of them approached her from the front, freeing their members from their trousers and wedging themselves into her mouth. One by one, Jennifer was forced to suck them to erection.

Dowling again called a halt to the flogging. Then he stepped in back of the girl to slip his penis through her thighs and into her sex, screwing into her until he'd spent himself.

All of the others took a turn, Brother M. continuing to use the quirt on the girl's now-red rump between each screwing.

As for myself, I was transfixed by the tableau unfolding before my eyes. Dowling and the elders were fully engrossed in the pillaging of Jennifer's youthful loins, their faces aglow with a twisted sort of rapture, while Jennifer was all but lost to the world. She was continually groaning at the degradation she was being subjected to, her nude body writhing under both the whip and the male members invading her sex. Yet it was impossible to discern whether her actions were being brought about through the pain and shame of her ordeal or what was occurring within her smooth pubis for she'd quite plainly gone into an ongoing orgasm.

When Brother M.'s turn at sexing the girl was at hand, he parted his robe and mounted not her pubis but her buttocks and inserted his member into her anus. Certainly, she was virgin in that orifice, and as she was filled, she moaned as if she would pass out.

"I've never been touched there," she shrieked, but I could see that this special treatment was having a magical effect on her. She was one of those rare girls capable of buttock-orgasm, the climax spreading from her anus and into the flesh of the rump-globes.

But they still weren't done with her. Once Brother had dismounted the girl's buttocks, he released her from the stocks, and the elders seized her and chained her to the ring embedded in the stone floor, making her kneel in the posture of penitence.

"I've seen my wrongs," Jennifer was sobbing. "Please don't put me in these awful chains."

"And I still detect insincerity in you," Dowling barked at her. "You'll kneel in penitence through the rest of the day and through the night, supervised by the good elders of the church."

Neville and I had agreed that, if Dowling chose this course of action, I would acquiesce to his wishes. It seemed a gesture of good will that would appease the irate citizens of Stonehurst. So, with a great deal of misgiving, I left Jennifer in their hands, promising that I'd return for her early the next morning.

She looked at me, beseeching my mercy with her eyes, but there was nothing I could to help her, and I took my leave, wondering what the unfortunate girl would suffer in the night.

_____

As I said at the beginning of this letter, I've begun a new phase of Tarin's discipline. Daily, I take her to the out building as it affords the means for applying the intense sort of discipline that Olford's prescribed for her. I usually enlist the aid of either Ruth or Hector, and my preferred method of restraint is to hang the girl from the suspension chain, naked, only the very ends of her toes touching the floor. Then Ruth or Hector will give Tarin a slow flogging with a lash-strap while I lecture her on the importance of carrying herself demurely. She takes her discipline well, quietly and obediently. Apparently, she understands that the danger she's in is quite real.

These sessions give me mixed feelings. On the one hand, I have to admit that the sight of Tarin hanging in such stringent bondage is an erotic one. The appearance of her supple and youthful flesh is greatly enhanced by the taut suspension. Hanging as such, her rib cage is outlined beneath the tightened skin, and her breast blossoms stand out so proudly. She seems to glow in the lantern light, and I greatly enjoy watching her writhe beneath the lash. On the other hand, my growing affection for the girl makes me want to go leniently with her. If she was truly mine, I'd probably keep her in line with the birch only most of the time.

When Neville returned from the village this evening, his mood was a bit more disgruntled than usual. In addition to dealing with the citizens' growing anger, he'd been beset by requests from York and Blythe to have Tarin perform the nude ballet for them.

"I had to accommodate the lechers," was his comment on the situation, "and, of course, they'll want to see more than just dancing, but I have that problem solved as well. Just to keep our guests entertained, I'll have Jennifer and Amanda put on some sort of lewd exhibition while Tarin dances. That should keep them satisfied."

So, two nights from now, we'll be entertaining these noble guardians of the public trust.

Olford feels as if it's time to see how both Amanda and Jennifer behave themselves in public. On the day after Blythe and York's visit, he'll be taking these two to a village that's about a half day's ride from here to watch them interact with others. Of course, it's much too dangerous to allow Tarin to be seen anywhere.

I'll be sure and get a letter to you shortly after Tarin's performance. I don't know what Olford's planning to have Jennifer and Amanda do to entertain, but I'm sure it will be something that's highly engaging to the senses.

My Best Regards,
Derek H.

Dear Bertrand,

I pen this letter by the midnight oil after an evening that was low key in tone but lurid to the point of being surreal. Blythe and York were here to watch Tarin perform the dance, and the entire night was charged with an otherworldly sensuality.

The two pompous gentlemen arrived around 8 p.m., and the four of us adjourned to the main drawing room, where Tarin would perform for us. After a glass of brandy all around, Neville began speaking of taking Amanda and Jennifer over to the next village, assuring the mayor that the two were ready to begin mingling with polite society once again.

"I've even arranged for a display of their obedience to show you what I mean," Olford told them. "Ruth should be bringing them in any time now."

Only moments later, Ruth escorted Amanda and Jennifer into the room. The two girls were naked and blindfolded. Their hands were strapped together in front of them and leather collars had been buckled around their necks. Ruth was leading the two by long straps attached to the collars, taking them over to the far side of the room.

"Well, they're certainly dressed for obedience," York chuckled.

At Ruth's curt command, the girls got to the floor, side by side and lying facedown, their bound hands outstretched before them.

"Please begin whenever you're ready, Ruth," Neville said when the two nudes were in position.

The woman took up a position at Jennifer's side, doubling the leader straps over and gripping them in her right hand. Then, after eyeing her targets, she began a furious lashing of both girls. She whipped at them in an indiscriminate manner that included the whole of their backsides, the straps blazing across the girls' buttocks, thighs, and shoulders.

"How highly efficient," Blythe remarked. "Getting two in line with one flogging."

Under Ruth's practiced hand, both Amanda and Jennifer were already wriggling about on the polished wood of the floor, both of them letting out mild shrieks as the straps punished their bare flesh.

The vicious flogging didn't last long. Once the girls were reddened, Ruth ceased whipping at them and told them to turn over. The blindfolded duo obeyed quickly, rolling over onto their backs.

"Now both of you can begin masturbating yourselves," Ruth told them, "and I'll be standing right over you with these straps in my hand to make sure you do a thorough job of it, my precious sluts."

The girls swung their hands over their heads and down to their groins and then began manipulating themselves. I could see a blush of shame wash over Jennifer nakedness, but I thought I detected just the slightest hint of a delighted smile cross the lips of the irrepressible Amanda Smith.

The room became quiet as the bare girls stroked their most intimate portions. Neville rose and took a seat at the piano, first trickling his fingers lightly over the keys and then beginning a formal piece, striking a few low and somber chords.

And then Tarin walked into the room and stood in the wide and clear space before us, her hands poised well above her head, her right foot flat on the floor, the left foot en pointe.

That girl had never looked quite so lovely to me as she did at that moment. She was nude, freshly washed and shaven, and her flesh glistened with a coating of oil.

As Neville went deeper into the piece, playing louder now, Tarin began to dance the ballet. She moved slowly at first, matching the subdued tone of the music. Her dark and tousled hair swayed about her back, but the motions of her body were filled with the animal-like grace of a panther, fully controlled. It was classical ballet to be certain, but the girl seemed to be able to put her own interpretation into it, making the dance her own, and a thing of erotic beauty it was.

"Magnificent," I heard York murmur the first time Tarin pirouetted on the bare toes of one foot.

Then, as the music picked up slightly in tempo, she was flying through the air, arms outstretched, one supple leg flung out behind her. She was a creature of the ages, a timeless nymph ruled by music, her body a servant of her art.

Moaning sounds drew my attention from this dance of Eros Fantasia. Glancing to the other side of the room, I saw that Amanda had quite clearly gone into the throes of an ongoing orgasm, and Jennifer wasn't far behind her. Both girls were twisting and turning about at the floor as their fingers worked frantically at their pubic mounds.

Ruth's eyes were afire with a perverse elation. She'd begun whipping her bound victims as they masturbated. The leader straps were flying through the air and landing with crackling noises on all areas of the girls' exposed flesh.

"That's it," the woman snapped at them. "Finger yourselves like whores. You know you love it."

York and Blythe were glancing back and forth between the sight of Amanda and Jennifer masturbating and Tarin's dance of solo passion. Altogether, it made for a tableau of pure sexuality.

But most of my attention remained on Tarin. Such a nimble thing of beauty she was as she pranced about the room. How purely agile she was on her toes, her nudity expressing each note of the music.

It wasn't until near the end of the piece that the tempo became truly rapid, but Tarin was easily able to keep herself exactly in time, her body seeming to respond with a mind of its own.

When Neville sounded the last crashing chord, Tarin was on

her left knee, her right foot stretched out in front of her and in the air, her head thrown back so far that her dark hair touched the floor. Her hands were straight up in the air, and here she remained motionless.

Something quite amazing happened when she was done. Rather than rise when she was applauded, Tarin got onto her hands and knees. The room was silent as Amanda and Jennifer had finished orgasming and Ruth had ceased the whipping.

Tarin kept her eyes to the floor when she spoke. "Might I be flogged before Mayor Blythe and Chancellor York, Mr. Olford?" she asked. "I wish to prove to them that I've erased my false pride."

"Of course, Tarin," Neville replied as he rose from the piano bench and fetched a birch rod. "I appreciate your willingness to demonstrate your improvement as I'm sure our guests do."

York was rising from his chair. "I'd be honored to administer this girl's flogging," he was saying.

Neville handed him the long, thin wooden whip.

York stood beside the bare girl, licking his lips at the very sight of her delicately proffered body. Before starting, he tapped the rod gently on the buttocks as if drawing a bead on them.

It was a mean-spirited and sadistic flogging that York issued. He didn't count strokes or pause. Rather he simply birched the girl without mercy, flailing away at the unprotected flesh of her twitching rump and turning it a bright crimson.

Tarin looked up at me once, and I could see the faraway look of a strange and removed sort of agony in her eyes, a look that conveyed that she'd entered the netherland of pleasure-pain, the entranced landscape of rapturous suffering.

No matter how brutally she was flogged, Tarin never cried out, nor did she try to escape or beg for pity. She simply accepted the fate that she'd brought upon yourself.

She only spoke when York was finished with her. "Thank you, sir," she said humbly.

As things drew to a close, Blythe insisted on escorting Amanda to her bed chamber to "tuck the poor girl in," but, of course, he was planning on tucking his member into her sex.

The hour grows late, Bertrand, and the rest of the household is at rest now. As soon as I finish with penning this letter, I'll go to Tarin's bed chamber. After her most erotic ballet, I'm filled with desire for her.

Before leaving, Mayor Blythe told us to keep a close eye on Tarin. "I've heard talk among the villagers of kidnapping the girl," he told us. "They want to rid Stonehurst of her presence in any way they can."

I don't doubt his words. Twice today I've seen groups of men on horseback riding in this vicinity, and the bonfires burn bright tonight. All of this worries me as I have the distinct feeling that they'll do far worse to the girl than simply banish her from the community should they lay their hands on her.

I'll be keeping a careful eye out tomorrow while Neville takes Amanda and Jennifer over to the next village.

Wish me good fortune as I do you.

My Best To You,

Derek H.

Letter 23 PRIVATE

Dear Bertrand,

I write to you with Stonehurst behind us. I say us because Tarin is with me. We've found refuge at the home of a friendly farmer and his wife after a ferocious ride of two days. But I get ahead of myself. Let me tell you of how we come to be here.

It was Hector who brought me the news just shortly after I posted my last letter to you. He rode in from Stonehurst, anxious to speak with me. Once I sat down with the man, he told me that the villagers had reached the point of uncontrollable mob hysteria, and that they were planning to come for Tarin at dusk. When I asked him what they wished of her, he didn't really know for certain, but he told me that the entire populace was in the darkest of temper.

At that moment, I knew I had to take Tarin from that place.

As it was almost dusk then, there was no time to waste, and I told Hector to hitch up the four-horse carriage as quickly as possible. Then I dashed about the house, gathering provisions, some clothing and personal effects. After getting all my notes, books, and papers together, I went for Tarin, telling her that we must leave at once. She didn't question me.

Outside, the carriage was ready to go. I went to the livery and took two saddles from their hooks, and when I came back, I told Tarin to get inside the carriage and to lie down on the floor. Once she was in place, I covered the scantly attired girl with blankets.

"Stay down," I said to her. "I'm afraid we're in for a rough ride."

At the last moment, I ran back into the house and returned with two of Olford's dueling pistols and a musket, all fully loaded. I also brought along one of his swords. There was no telling what we might encounter.

227

When I climbed up into the driver's seat of the carriage, I could see the glow of fire coming from the village, and it seemed to be moving toward Olford's place. The villagers were on their way, lanterns and flares lit.

Snapping the reins, I cantered the horses away, saving them up for what I felt sure would have to be a mad gallop.

Half a mile from Olford's estate, I caught sight of the angry mob, their shouts faintly reaching my ears.

Knowing that the speed of the carriage could greatly effect the outcome of our escape, I drove the team to a place atop a fairly steep hill where a flat stretch of roadway lay ahead, and there I stopped, waiting for the crowd to draw near. Their shouts became clear once they'd reached the level stretch of the roadway.

"We want Tarin Blake! Seize the evil one!" they were crying in unison and sending chills through me. Who knows what they might be planning on doing with the innocent girl concealed within the carriage.

"Are you all right?" I yelled to her, and she assured me that she was fine. "Very well," I said. "We'll be making a run for it in a moment."

Drawing one of the pistols, I cracked the reins and sent the horses down the hill, galloping them for all they were worth, their hooves sounding like a stampede.

Halfway the distance to the mob, I fired the pistol into the air, and it gave out a mighty roar that stopped the people in their tracks. But many quickly recovered the shock and stood to block the roadway.

"Someone's trying to make off with the evil one!" a voice shouted. "Stop that carriage."

Several of the braver ones blocked our path, but I kept the horses at a fierce gallop, determined to run through anyone who remained in my way. It was a test of wills, but at the last moment, when the steeds were bearing down on them, those in the road scattered, shouting in fear, several scrambling and falling into the ditches. We'd made it through.

For the next hour, I kept the carriage moving at a brisk clip, finally stopping in a thick wood where there was a stream to water the horses. While I explained to Tarin the reason for our flight, I loosed two of the horses and saddled them. Then I turned the other two back in the direction of Stonehurst and sent them on their way. More than likely they got Olford's carriage back to him.

After strapping my gear onto the two saddled horses, I helped Tarin to mount up as she assured that she knew how to ride. I must say that I took a moment to admire how lovely she looked on horseback, her little dress climbing high, her dainty, naked feet cocked up so prettily in the stirrups.

All night we rode, not stopping to rest until daybreak. Then we slept the day in another thick forest, had something to eat and rode westward through another night. I was afraid to head north to Rosewood as it was possible that we were being pursued in that direction.

It took us two days of travelling in this manner before we found refuge at this farmhouse. We were fortunate. Two years ago, this area suffered the same blight that the region of Stonehurst is now undergoing, and the people we're staying with have a daughter who was wrongfully accused, just as Tarin has been. They're sympathetic to Tarin's plight, and they've told us that we can stay hidden here as long as we need to.

As much as I appreciate the hospitality of these good folk, we're leaving tomorrow, this time heading north for a day and then turning eastward toward Rosewood. If fate is with us, we should arrive at the academy in less than a week, just about the time you receive this letter.

At this point, I'm not sure what Tarin's future holds. However, I know that I want to keep her by my side for as long as possible. Needless to say, we've become quite close in more ways than one during this journey, and I wish to keep the girl as my servant and lover. She feels the same.

If fate is with me, I shall see you soon.

Hastily and Sincerely,

Derek H.

———

These letters were found within the walls of Rosewood Academy for Girls. At the time of their discovery, the academy had been abandoned for over 50 years. Somewhere around 1850, it was learned that Rosewood had become a den of flagellation with almost no academic standards. There were even rumors that it was being used as a brothel of sorts, a brothel where young girls were made available for the abusive sexual practices of wealthy fetishists. Researchers agree that these rumors were too numerous not to contain at least some truth. In 1851, the academy was condemned from use, its halls evacuated. Its iron gates were locked and not reopened until near the end of the 19th century.

PRIVATE

The years left Rosewood's records in readable condition, and from them, several facts of interest have been gleaned. Derek Hunter rose to the position of headmaster of the academy, and in a sealed box there is a record of a Miss Tara Black entering the school in 1832. Researchers agree unanimously that Tarin Blake must have enrolled as a student after her escape from Stonehurst, using an assumed name.

Meteorological records show that the agricultural blight on Stonehurst and its surrounding regions came to an end in 1833, and there is no evidence that the persecution of the young girls of these provinces continued.

Only recently, a volume entitled "Flagellation of The Female Student, a Guide" was unearthed in a private library. Its author was one D. Hunter. Little deductive ability is required to conclude that D. Hunter is the Derek Hunter who authored these letters.

Perhaps the most interesting footnote to these rather bizarre events is a playbill discovered in the archives of a dance historian. The playbill is in English, but the performance it lists was staged in Austria. At the bottom of this bill, there is a line that says simply, "Private Performance Upon Request by Tarin Blake, Dance Erotique." The Tarin referred to in these letters must have found her way into the world of dance and perhaps even made a name for herself performing the nude ballet.

As intriguing as Derek Hunter's accounts of these events might be, we must remember that they reflect the darker recesses of humankind, hidden aspects of the psyche that lurk within all of us.

Now for the opening of next months title,
"THE BROTHERHOOD" by *Falconer Bridges*.

ONE

THE OLD SCHOOL

Duke stirred, roused from his slumber by the impact of Lolli's bottom as she dropped on to the pillow beside his head. He smelt the animal muskiness of her sex and felt the smooth flesh of her haunches brush against his cheek. Sleepily lifting one arm in order to fondle the creamy expanse of thigh above her blue stocking tops, the back of his hand brushed against the nakedness of her vulva, the grasping lips of her labia clamping themselves moistly to his flesh. He instantly exploded into full awareness.

"I'm not wearing any," she whispered, as if he needed any confirmation of her lack of underwear.

In one quick movement he rolled between the arched vee of her legs, coming to rest beneath her knees, flat on his stomach with his nose buried between her labia and his eager lips pressing urgently at the entrance to her vagina. It was all that he had imagined as his tongue delved into the tunnel, the exquisite flavour of her juices impacting not upon his brain, but signalling direct to his manhood and precipitating an instantaneous straining erection that was so granite solid it hurt. He pushed his tongue deeper into her, rubbing her unsheathing clitoris with the nub of his nose and then withdrawing to lap at her sex like a cat savouring a saucer of milk.

Looping both arms around her backside he clasped his

hands together and tugged her vagina even closer to his face, and with his mouth squashed tightly against her pudenda he sucked and licked her into a state of squirming fervour.

"Now, now! Fuck me now" she gasped.

He was thunderstruck, totally unprepared for this turn of events. He'd been working on her ceaselessly for the last couple of years, ever since she turned sixteen in fact, with absolutely no success whatsoever. She had remained completely unmoved by his attentions, even though he was Head Boy and lusted after by ninety nine per cent of female contingent of the school. And suddenly here she was, sitting on his face and demanding to be fucked. He didn't waste any time deliberating that conundrum, if she wanted his dick she was going to get it. And fast; the whys and wherefores could wait until later.

He shifted his position and pulled her down the bed, legs wide apart on either side of his hips. Digging his fists into the mattress he lifted himself up and ran his lips over her downy young belly, her ribs and her nubile but wonderfully full breasts, before pulling himself up over her body until his throbbing penis rested at the portal to Heaven and his mouth lay over her own. Pressing a tender but urgent kiss onto her lips, he transferred the lingering drops of her sexual juices to her own taste buds and then, unable to deny himself any longer he lunged his overpowering erection at her pleading womanhood.

Only it wasn't as easy as that. Much a she desired it, her sex seemed reluctant to admit his pulsating member. He inserted a finger, then two and then more, widening her channel and stimulating her clitoris. A caressing palm rolled over her glorious cleavage, his fingers plucking, pulling and teasing at her inflamed nuggets. Easing his helmet between her labia, he confronted her protesting hymen and after an heroic struggle broke through the barrier, gaining a limited entrance into the tightness beyond. A slight retreat, another push, and he was further in. Stronger and stronger, deeper and deeper, his thrusts bored their way further into her virgin tunnel, stoking the fire in her loins into solar heat, floods of her juices lubricating and easing his entry into her welcoming but as yet unpenetrated sex. Moaning with passion, her breath came in short sharp gasps as they ground at each other, his ever swelling penis mercilessly reaming up and down the entire length of her now fully accommodating vagina. Sensations unknown raged through both their bodies until reaching a shattering peak of fulfilment, the oceans of semen boiling in his testes erupted into an overwhelming ejaculation. Wave after wave of seed surged deep into her womb, as her body jerked and thrashed uncontrollably through an endless series of multiple orgasmic climaxes.

Thoroughly sated they remained locked together, drawing deep draughts of calming air into their lungs as their overloaded senses gradually subsided into some kind of normalcy. But something was wrong. What was happening?

"Duke . . Duke . . Wake up!"

A hand was urgently shaking his shoulder, while an authoritative voice thundered in his ear.

"Wake up damn you, we're here!"

Duke struggled to pull himself together, the vision slowly fading from behind his closed eyelids as his senses returned.

It had been a dream. All that was seven years ago now he

235

realised, and he had never got within striking distance of Lolli. It was coming back to the school that had triggered the memories of unrequited teenage passion that had dogged his last years of study at this venerable institution. He'd never got a look in, she was always hanging around outside the Housemaster's study, so much so that Duke reckoned she'd got 'a thing' about him. Him! The most universally feared amongst a faculty of feared tutors.

It had always appeared to Duke that he had been singled out for particularly harsh treatment by the schoolmaster, being given extra tasks and a much more demanding academic workload than any of the other pupils, except that was, for his three compatriots, Connie, Molly and Ham. In his own case, he had fleetingly considered that perhaps the reason was because he presented a challenge for the attentions of Lolli and it was some sort of punishment. Common sense had won out in the end. Don't be an ass, he'd told himself, the old boy's practically a pensioner, which unknown to him was still the greatest mistake he'd ever made in his life.

But, as an eighteen year old he had resigned himself to a life without Lolli on the end of his dick, finding consolation in the thought that as heir to one of the greatest fortunes in the world, he'd be able to shag anything that walked on two legs. After all money could buy whatever he desired, including love. So as much as he was able, he had dismissed Lolli from his mind. Until now. And now it seemed he was again about to meet his once imagined rival in love, except that now he was the Headmaster of the school, having been appointed to that position about the time Duke and Lolli had departed from its hallowed portals.

It was no wonder Duke had fallen asleep though. For some unexplained reason, his father had ordered his chauffeur to remain in London and was driving himself. There was no conversation and the glass privacy partition was closed, so that all alone on the leathered expanse of the back seat of the Bentley and with nothing to relieve the soporific tedium of the journey from town, he'd simply closed his eyes and drifted away. But now here they were, parked right outside the main entrance to the school. Being in the middle of the summer holidays there were no noisy hordes of students milling around the quad and everything seemed dignified and peaceful, his now more experienced eye appreciating the splendid architectural qualities of the old buildings.

He got out of the car and walked towards the magnificent doors that opened straight on to the Great Hall. He'd never given them a second look before; "schoolboys really must walk around with their eyes closed," he said wonderingly to himself. But he still had no idea why he had been taken there.

"Father, what's this all about?" he asked.

To be continued..............

The cover photograph for this book and many others are available as limited edition prints.
Write to:-

Viewfinders Photography
PO Box 200,
Reepham
Norfolk
NR10 4SY

for details, or see,

www.viewfinders.org.uk

TITLES IN PRINT

Silver Mink

ISBN 1-897809-22-0   The Captive *Amber Jameson*
ISBN 1-897809-24-7   Dear Master *Terry Smith*
ISBN 1-897809-26-3   Sisters in Servitude *Nicole Dere*
ISBN 1-897809-28-X   Cradle of Pain *Krys Antarakis*
ISBN 1-897809-32-8   The Contract *Sarah Fisher*
ISBN 1-897809-33-6   Virgin for Sale *Nicole Dere*
ISBN 1-897809-39-5   Training Jenny *Rosetta Stone*
ISBN 1-897898-45-X   Dominating Obsession *Terry Smith*
ISBN 1-897809-49-2   The Penitent *Charles Arnold**
ISBN 1-897809-56-5   Please Save Me! *Dr. Gerald Rochelle**
ISBN 1-897809-58-1   Private Tuition *Jay Merson**
ISBN 1-897809-61-1   Little One *Rachel Hurst**
ISBN 1-897809-63-8   Naked Truth II *Nicole Dere**
ISBN 1-897809-67-0   Tales from the Lodge *Bridges/O'Kane**
ISBN 1-897809-68-9   Your Obedient Servant Charlotte *Anna Grant**
ISBN 1-897809-70-0   Bush Slave II *Lia Anderssen**
ISBN 1-897809-74-3   Further Private Tuition *Jay Merson**
ISBN 1-897809-75-1   The Connoisseur *Francine Whittaker**
ISBN 1-897809-77-8   Slave to her Desires *Samantha Austen**
ISBN 1-897809-79-4   The Girlspell *William Avon**

UK £4.99 except *£5.99 --USA $8.95 except *$9.95

All titles, both in print and out of print, are
available as electronic downloads at:

http://www.adultbookshops.com

e-mail submissions to:
Editor@electronicbookshops.com

TITLES IN PRINT

Silver Moon

ISBN 1-897809-16-6 Rorigs Dawn *Ray Arneson*
ISBN 1-897809-17-4 Bikers Girl on the Run *Lia Anderssen*
ISBN 1-897809-23-9 Slave to the System *Rosetta Stone*
ISBN 1-897809-25-5 Barbary Revenge *Allan Aldiss*
ISBN 1-897809-27-1 White Slavers *Jack Norman*
ISBN 1-897809-31-X Slave to the State *Rosetta Stone*
ISBN 1-897809-36-0 Island of Slavegirls *Mark Slade*
ISBN 1-897809-37-9 Bush Slave *Lia Anderssen*
ISBN 1-897809-38-7 Desert Discipline *Mark Stewart*
ISBN 1-897809-40-9 Voyage of Shame *Nicole Dere*
ISBN 1-897809-41-7 Plantation Punishment *Rick Adams*
ISBN 1-897809-42-5 Naked Plunder *J.T. Pearce*
ISBN 1-897809-43-3 Selling Stephanie *Rosetta Stone*
ISBN 1-897809-44-1 SM Double value (Olivia/Lucy) *Graham/Slade**
ISBN 1-897809-46-8 Eliska *von Metchingen*
ISBN 1-897809-47-6 Hacienda, *Allan Aldiss*
ISBN 1-897809-48-4 Angel of Lust, *Lia Anderssen**
ISBN 1-897809-50-6 Naked Truth, *Nicole Dere**
ISBN 1-897809-51-4 I Confess!, *Dr Gerald Rochelle**
ISBN 1-897809-52-2 Barbary Slavedriver, *Allan Aldiss**
ISBN 1-897809-53-0 A Toy for Jay, *J.T. Pearce**
ISBN 1-897809-54-9 The Confessions of Amy Mansfield, *R. Hurst**
ISBN 1-897809-55-7 Gentleman's Club, *John Angus**
ISBN 1-897809-57-3 Sinfinder General *Johnathan Tate**
ISBN 1-897809-59-X Slaves for the Sheik *Allan Aldiss**
ISBN 1-897809-60-3 Church of Chains *Sean O'Kane**
ISBN 1-897809-62-X Slavegirl from Suburbia *Mark Slade**
ISBN 1-897809-64-6 Submission of a Clan Girl *Mark Stewart**
ISBN 1-897809-65-4 Taming the Brat *Sean O'Kane**
ISBN 1-897809-66-2 Slave for Sale *J.T. Pearce**
ISBN 1-897809-69-7 Caged! *Dr. Gerald Rochelle**
ISBN 1-897809-71-9 Rachel in servitude *J.L. Jones**
ISBN 1-897809-72-2 Beaucastel *Caroline Swift**
ISBN 1-897809-73-5 Slaveworld *Steven Douglas**
ISBN 1-897809-76-X Sisters in Slavery *Charles Graham**
ISBN 1-897809-78-6 Eve in Eden *Stephen Rawlings**
ISBN 1-897809-80-8 Inside the Fortress *John Sternes**

*UK £4.99 except *£5.99 --USA $8.95 except *$9.95*